NO LIFE FOR A LADY

Ladies of the Order - Book 5

ADELE CLEE

No Life for a Lady
Copyright © 2022 Adele Clee
All rights reserved.
ISBN-13: 978-1-915354-12-9

Cover by Dar Albert at Wicked Smart Designs

CHAPTER 1

Hart Street, Covent Garden
Office of the Order

LIGHT SPILLED FROM THE LOWER WINDOW OF THE townhouse owned by Lucius Daventry, a place he used as his business premises.

Olivia had received her employer's abrupt note not an hour ago, but one did not dally when summoned by the master of the Order. Not when she feared she would find herself at the Servants' Registry tomorrow, in search of a new position.

She seized the brass knocker and rapped loudly, her heart hammering with equal force.

Mrs Gunning answered. "Miss Trimble! The master said to expect you this evening." The housekeeper's warm smile settled Olivia's nerves, if only for a moment. "Bless you, dear. Come in out of the cold."

Olivia glanced left and right along the dimly lit street. A

habit formed after years spent imagining the worst. As a woman of thirty, one would think she had outgrown her fear of monsters. But she knew they were real. Knew they were found in plain sight, not hiding beneath the bed or in the armoire.

"Thank you, Mrs Gunning." Olivia scanned the darkness once more and stepped over the threshold for what would undoubtedly be the last time.

Mrs Gunning gave a soft chuckle. "There's no fear of footpads on this street. The crooks avoid this house like they do the watchman."

Yes, anyone would feel safe visiting the headquarters of the most skilled enquiry agents in London. Except Olivia wasn't scouring the shadows for footpads, but for wicked men who thought nothing of murdering a lady. As someone who had once been dragged from a lane in broad daylight, beaten and left for dead, every scenario posed a danger.

"Let me take your bonnet and pelisse, then I shall fetch the tea tray." Mrs Gunning ushered Olivia farther into the hall and promptly closed the door. "Unless you'd like something stronger, dear. Something to bring the blood back to your cheeks. Mr Daventry has sherry in his study."

"How kind. I will have a small sherry." When one's hands trembled, it was better to grip a glass than have the teacup rattling on the saucer.

Mrs Gunning hung Olivia's outdoor apparel in the understairs cupboard, then rapped lightly on the study door and waited for Mr Daventry to bid her enter. "Miss Trimble is here, sir. Are you ready to receive her now?"

"Indeed. Show her in, Mrs Gunning." Mr Daventry's amiable tone came as a surprise. As a man who strived to punish all wrongdoers, he was usually quite brusque and to the point.

"May I pour her a glass of sherry, sir? It's awful cold out."

"By all means."

Olivia straightened her shoulders and hid behind the confident facade that had served her so well. She entered the room and faced the man seated behind the imposing desk. "Good evening, sir."

Mr Daventry stood and brushed a hand through his coal-black hair. "Miss Trimble," was all he said, yet he bowed as if he knew her secret.

Olivia forced a smile and took the proffered seat.

Mr Daventry watched her intently, no doubt noticing every hitch in her breath. "I'm sure you're keen to know why I called you here tonight."

Olivia smiled at Mrs Gunning and accepted the glass of sherry from the tray. "All your female agents are married now, sir." Indeed, the house she managed was lifeless, her days long and endless. She had never felt so alone, although it was her own fault for forging friendships. "I presume you no longer have a use for me and mean to give me notice."

Mr Daventry dismissed his housekeeper and waited until the door clicked shut before speaking. "Never presume to know the workings of my mind, Miss Trimble," he said in a fatherly tone, which was ironic considering they were of a similar age. "When solving crimes and saving lives, a man must be shrewd. A master manipulator."

"I do not sit here as a client, sir, but as a paid chaperone who finds herself redundant. I'm told you have no intention of hiring more female agents, not at present. Therefore, it was a fair assumption."

Mr Daventry relaxed back in his seat and steepled his fingers. "People come to this office because they have been treated unfairly, been accused of crimes they did not commit. They seek an agent to help tackle the injustice."

"Yes," she said, confused as to why it was relevant. "You have saved many a neck from the noose."

"And yet many more suffer in silence."

Good Lord! Was he referring to her?

Despite all efforts to maintain a facade, heat raced to her cheeks like a disobedient child. "I challenge you to show me a person who has not suffered." Some in the most despicable ways. "But what has that to do with my work in Howland Street?"

A tense silence ensued.

She sipped her sherry. Every muscle stiffened, for she did not like the way he looked at her, with a mix of curiosity and pity. "Sir?"

"May I call you Rebecca?" he said.

"Rebecca? Why? That is not my name."

Had he taken too much port, taken leave of his senses?

The master of the Order laughed. "Neither is Trimble, yet you've used it for the year you've worked for me. My friend Wycliffe has known you for five years, and you were using it then."

Like the clang of a church bell, alarm rang in her head. She tried to swallow past the lump in her throat, tried to maintain her composure.

"You're living a lie," her employer pressed, keen to find the chink in her armour. "I know who you are. I believe you have suffered a terrible injustice. Consequently, I have taken it upon myself to help solve your problem."

I know who you are!

He couldn't possibly know.

Olivia Durrant was dead, found hanged in the King's Wood.

She pushed out of the chair, tossed back her sherry, and placed the glass on his desk. "Thank you for providing every comfort, for giving me a purpose this last year." She touched her hand to her heart. "With your help, many women have fought against their oppressors. But you do not need to

4

concern yourself with me. I came to tell you I am leaving London. Tonight."

Now! Without her bonnet and pelisse if necessary.

She would rather battle the cold than confront her past.

She had been a fool to stay in town for so long. And yet she had found true friendship with the ladies of the Order. After years spent living out of a valise, constantly peering over her shoulder, it had been so good to call somewhere home.

Still, the urge to flee, to put some distance between herself and the truth, had her crossing the room. She reached the door, but Mr Daventry spoke the words she had been dreading.

"Lady Olivia! You cannot hide forever."

She froze, and could barely catch her breath. It was as though the thug's hands were still squeezing her windpipe, squeezing the last breath from her lungs.

"Tell me why you faked your own death," he said.

The pure ignorance of his statement forced her to swing around. "Who is making presumptions now? Do you think I live this life by choice?" Tears welled when there should have been no more left to shed. "Do you think I enjoy a solitary existence? Worrying about getting close to people? Fearing they will discover who I am? A life without love or hope or trust?"

She had said too much!

Sheer panic made her take to her feet.

She was at the front door when Mr Daventry appeared behind her and touched her gently on the shoulder. The act of compassion was too much to bear.

"Let me help you. Let me right the injustice. I have a plan, though it will take a considerable sacrifice. Trust me, and you will never have to hide again."

Olivia closed her eyes.

It was a tempting offer.

"You might help me in return," he added, appealing to her kind nature. "I need an enquiry agent, and you're the only person with the necessary credentials. I have a client who needs your help. Someone else with a mystery to solve."

More confused than ever, she turned to face her employer. "Sir, you are not making sense. I lack the wherewithal to investigate crimes." It was enough to keep to the shadows, to avoid seeing anyone she knew.

"You're educated, logical. You have avoided detection these last seven years. That takes skill and mastery. You're living in London, the home of the *ton*, yet only one person has recognised you."

Her heart lurched. "Who?"

"Lord Deville. That's why you feigned illness and missed Honora's wedding. You're sister to the Earl of Mersham. His seat is but twenty miles from Highcliffe, Lord Deville's home. It took Deville a while to make the connection because he believed you were dead."

Olivia felt the life drain from her body.

She had to leave London, leave England.

She had enough money to flee to France.

"Forgive me. I lack the fortitude needed to help you."

Mr Daventry stepped closer. "You need only play yourself."

"Miss Trimble?"

He shook his head. "Lady Olivia Durrant."

Merciful Mary!

"Sir, you ask the impossible." A mocking laugh escaped her, but then her curious mind took to wondering who wanted to hire Olivia Durrant when the world knew she was dead. "Who is this client? Who else knows I am alive?"

There was no point denying it now. The number had doubled in a matter of a minute. Soon all of London would take to whispering the news. Then her devil of a brother would exact another plan to murder her in the woods.

Did Mr Daventry know the enemy was a peer of the realm? Not a fictitious husband she had mentioned once to hide the truth?

"Alexander Grayson," he said.

"Alexander Grayson?" The name rolled off her tongue like sweet music, though she could not recall ever meeting the man. "And he approached you and asked to hire me?"

Suspicion flared.

Had her brother laid a trap?

"No. I told him who you were because it's to your mutual benefit." Mr Daventry motioned for her to return to the study. "Grayson is a close friend. He is attempting to discover how his brother, the Earl of Sturrock, died. He suspects your brother is involved, though it's complicated, and he will want to see you before agreeing to tell you anything."

Olivia remained rooted to the spot. Having kept abreast of the *ton*'s affairs, she noted the glaring discrepancy in the story.

"Lord Sturrock was an only child. His cousin inherited."

Mr Daventry smiled, no doubt pleased she was showing an interest. "Grayson is the illegitimate son. Like me, he inherited much of his father's wealth, which caused great animosity. Meet him. Hear his tale. Decide for yourself."

Olivia fell silent.

Habit said she should ignore all enticements. Instinct said she could not go on like this, always running from her troubles. Hiding in a cupboard like a marionette, letting her fear of her family control the strings.

"Grayson is strong and dependable," Mr Daventry said, filling the silence. "I have never met a man so fearless. He will protect you. It may be your only chance to punish those who hurt you. But you must be honest and tell us your story."

How did one speak of a secret kept for seven years?

How did one dig for buried memories?

"Have I ever failed an agent?" Mr Daventry was determined in his bid to secure her services. "Are the ladies who came to live in Howland Street, plagued by nightmares of the past, not happy beyond measure?"

Yes, the man was like Midas, turning everyone's life into gold.

"I am not looking for love, just a moment's peace."

"Trust Grayson, and you need never hide again."

Mr Daventry was such a skilled negotiator, something inside her shifted while listening to his rousing pleas. Distress gave way to regret and shame. She should have gathered evidence. She should have punished her blackguard of a brother, not fled like a frightened doe.

What if this was her only chance to seek justice?

What if this was her only chance to reclaim her life?

"Very well," she said weakly, remembering how she had been discarded in the woods like rubbish for the bonfire, how close she came to dying. "I will hear what Mr Grayson has to say. Arrange the meeting. Send a note informing me of the time and place."

She would likely change her mind once back in Howland Street, perhaps flee under cover of darkness. How could she bare her soul when she had an utter distrust of men?

"The meeting is arranged." Mr Daventry pulled his gold watch from his pocket and studied the face in the muted light. "Grayson is expecting us within the hour. My carriage is waiting."

MR GRAYSON LIVED IN THE FASHIONABLE NEW CRESCENT IN Portland Place, a row of elegant stuccoed terrace houses designed by John Nash. Doubtless, it was home to a few prominent members of the *ton*. Hence why Olivia kept her head bowed to avoid meeting the gazes of a couple who passed by on the pavement.

Mr Daventry hammered the lion-head knocker against the brass plate and waited for the butler to answer. He presented his calling card to Pickins, a man of ageing years with a wrinkled face and doddery gait.

"The master is expecting you." Pickins took their hats and gloves—she refused to relinquish her pelisse—and shuffled forward at a snail's pace. "Kindly follow me."

The grand hall consisted of a polished marble floor and stark white walls. Olivia prayed the decoration was not a reflection of Mr Grayson's character. Men who lacked depth were often opinionated. Shallow. They made poor listeners and were quick to judge. Not at all the sort who would understand her plight.

Indeed, it was a relief to find herself in a candlelit study filled with books and paintings of ships. It was untidy, the papers on the desk in disarray. The smell of amber and cedarwood cologne wafted through the air. A stimulating scent that teased her senses and stirred her soul awake.

Her attackers had reeked of sweat and the grime that marked them as hired thugs. Men willing to trade a conscience for a quart of ale.

Olivia's gaze moved to the man sitting open-legged in the leather wing chair. A man who defied the need for conformity. His light brown hair was unfashionably long and tied back with black ribbon. His shoulders were double the width of any normal mortal. Despite expecting female company, he was without a coat. One glance at the muscular arms filling his shirtsleeves made her wonder if he had one that fit.

"It seems I owe you a bottle of brandy, Daventry." Mr Grayson's voice was as deep as his chest was broad. He stood, and it took effort not to gasp at the sheer size of him. "How the devil did you persuade her to agree?"

Olivia decided to be equally candid. "I am in the room, Mr Grayson. You may address me directly."

He swept a graceful bow, a feat for a man of his brawn. "Forgive me, madam. Daventry rarely makes mistakes. Yet despite his protestations, I am not certain you are the Lady Olivia Durrant. I leave it to you to convince me."

"Convince you?" Olivia drew back. "I was under the impression you needed me, Mr Grayson. Therefore, it is you who must do the convincing. Why should I risk my neck for your cause?"

Mr Daventry cleared his throat. "Perhaps we should sit."

But Mr Grayson prowled towards her, his movements remarkably sleek for someone his size. He stood so close his presence raised her pulse a notch. "Lady Olivia was said to have natural grace and beauty. You certainly satisfy on that score."

She stiffened, but refused to let him intimidate her. "The fact you stand before a lady in a state of dishabille suggests a disregard for propriety. Is that a true testament to your character, or do you wield your illegitimacy like a weapon?"

The devil smiled like he knew the sight would make her heart flutter. His intense green eyes scanned her face as if he were an artist hired to sketch her likeness from memory.

"We do not stand on ceremony here, madam. It is one benefit of being born a bastard." He perused her form with blatant regard. "You will become accustomed to my habits, as I must become accustomed to yours. We are both old enough to understand the need for compromise."

So, he meant to hire her as his agent.

The man must be desperate.

Olivia raised her chin. "I was born Olivia Allegra Durrant, named after my paternal grandmother, who died in childbirth." She decided to convince him she was the person he needed in the hope he might return to his seat. "Few fathers value their daughters more than their sons, but my father named me heir to his fortune and unentailed properties."

And she had almost paid for his generosity with her life.

"That explains why your brother uses the moniker Leviathan," Mr Grayson said, studying her brown hair like a sultan inspecting the new addition to his harem.

"Leviathan? No one refers to him by that name. Granted, I cannot attest to the fact, as I have not laid eyes on him in seven years." She would likely drive a blade into Hamilton Durrant's black heart if she saw him again.

Mr Daventry motioned to the chairs and urged them to sit. "Perhaps you should explain why you seek an alliance with Lady Olivia, so she might understand the point of this meeting."

Seek an alliance, not hire an agent?

What an odd choice of words.

She supposed Mr Daventry meant they were to help one another, though she would be on the next ship to France if the terms were disagreeable.

Mr Grayson offered her the comfortable wing chair near the fire while he fetched a mahogany chair and positioned it a mere foot away. The wood creaked beneath the weight of his powerful frame.

"What do you know of the Seven Devils?" Mr Grayson looked her keenly in the eye, while she avoided glancing at his broad thighs.

Olivia shrugged at the odd question. "Do you speak of a biblical reference to the seven demons exorcised from Mary Magdalene? Or perhaps a scholarly work relating to the classification of the Princes of Hell?"

Seemingly impressed, Mr Grayson offered another dazzling smile. "In his work, the scholar Binsfeld classified each of the seven demons based on the seven deadly sins. Consequently, Leviathan represents envy. It is the name Hamilton Durrant adopted when he joined the Knights of the Seven Devils."

The Knights of the Seven Devils!

Aristocratic men liked their silly clubs.

Olivia sat back in the chair, still warm from the heat of Mr Grayson's body, and tried to make sense of the information. "And you believe my brother calls himself by this moniker because envy rules his heart?"

"Evidence suggests you are the cause of his discontent."

"Me?" She knew as much. It was quite pathetic considering Hamilton had inherited an earldom. There had been more than enough wealth to share.

"Seven men at Cambridge formed the club," Mr Daventry said, reminding her he was still in the room. "They meet quarterly at a place hidden within the warrens around Seven Dials."

"For what purpose?"

"To prance around in costumes and prove why they deserve a place in hell." Mr Grayson muttered a curse beneath his breath. "My brother took the name Satan purely because wrath was the best description of his feelings towards me."

She was not surprised.

Legitimate heirs often despised their half-brothers.

"Did his anger stem from you inheriting much of your father's wealth?" she said, for this was a most intriguing conversation. In some ways, Mr Grayson's story bore similarities to her own. "Or because your father took a mistress?"

Mr Grayson's green eyes darkened. "You have been misinformed, madam. I am the Earl of Sturrock's firstborn son. My father married after my mother's death. But yes, my brother hated that I was given the lion's share when I am considered inferior."

Inferior was not a word she would associate with this impressive figure of a man. From her perspective, she could find nothing lacking in his countenance.

"I see. Our brothers could have swapped monikers as both despised their siblings." Unlike her, Mr Grayson had not felt the tip of a blade pierce his skin or been punched unconscious in a dark wood. "I am aware your brother died three years ago, but know nothing of the tragic circumstances."

Mr Grayson inhaled deeply before continuing. "Blake Gray, Earl of Sturrock, was found drowned in a private bathhouse in Bishopsgate. The attendant said he was the only person there that night."

An earl found dead in a bathhouse in Bishopsgate?

With her inquisitive mind, she might have asked many questions. One being why it mattered now, after so many years. "On the journey here, Mr Daventry said you suspect your brother was murdered."

Mr Grayson reached into his waistcoat pocket and handed her a folded note, the paper foxed and ragged at the edges. "This was in Blake's coat pocket, though the magistrate thought it irrelevant. Based on the cut to my brother's head and the fact he was found face-down in the water, the coroner reached a verdict of death by accidental drowning."

Olivia peeled back the folds and realised it was a page torn from a book. She studied the black and white drawing of a sea monster and read the inscription.

"But this is a drawing of Leviathan." Understanding the implication, Olivia put her hand to her throat. Hamilton was not averse to hiring cutthroats to murder his kin. He could kill a man and make it look like an accident. "So, you think my brother was responsible?"

"One might easily jump to the wrong conclusion," Mr Daventry interjected in a voice brimming with wisdom. "Rarely does a man leave his calling card on his victim. But one must follow the obvious clues to find the answer."

Mr Daventry was right. They should proceed with caution.

"Mr Grayson, what evidence do you have to suggest my brother was part of this Seven Devils club? Envy rules the heart of many men. What proof is there Hamilton took the name of this sea serpent?"

Mr Grayson brushed his hands down his thighs and stood. He unlocked the drawer in his desk and returned with a small leather-bound notebook.

"Because I found this hidden in Blake's bedchamber." He handed Olivia the book, carelessly brushing his fingers against hers as if it were some sort of test. "It clearly states the names of all the men and their demon counterparts."

Mr Grayson remained standing, looming over her to such a degree she could barely concentrate on the faded words written inside. Hopefully, this meeting would soon be at an end, for he radiated an energy she found wholly distracting.

"But what has this to do with me, sir?" Instinct said she would not like the answer. "Why would you need to hire me when you have evidence of your theory right here?" She returned the little book.

"Hire you?" Mr Grayson's brows knitted together. He faced Mr Daventry. "You didn't tell her? I presumed she knew."

"Tell me what, sir?"

Mr Daventry shrugged. "A lady should not hear it second hand."

"Hear what?" Olivia sprang to her feet. Was Mr Grayson hoping to use her to lure Leviathan into a trap? The plan must be dangerous because the tension in the air proved stifling. "Mr Grayson? Explain yourself."

The gentleman straightened and met her gaze. "I do not wish to hire you, madam. I mean to marry you. Tomorrow. If you agree."

CHAPTER 2

"Marry me!"

Grayson watched the lady's blue eyes widen. Her lips parted on a pant. For the umpteenth time this evening, he imagined closing his mouth over hers and tasting the woman he presumed had already agreed to be his wife.

"There must be some mistake." She clutched the high collar of her green pelisse and faced Lucius Daventry as if he held the noose. "Tell me I misheard. Tell me you have not lured me here under false pretences."

Daventry stood. "Your welfare is my only concern. Grayson will protect you, provide for you, give you the freedom an independent woman craves."

"But only if I help prove my brother is a murdering snake." Anger and fear infused every word. "I swore I would never be beholden to a man. Never!"

"'Tis I who would be beholden to you, my lady," Grayson said. The need to solve the mystery of his brother's death left him restless. Partly because he wanted to prove he was a better man than his kin. "Daventry is correct. As your

16

husband, I will be duty-bound to protect you. No man nor devil will ever hurt you again."

Her anxious gaze scanned the breadth of his shoulders. "Sir, I am in no doubt you have Hercules' fortitude. But you're asking me to trade my soul for a modicum of peace."

Trade her soul?

Did she have a lover?

"Is your heart engaged elsewhere?" Unease settled in his chest. He would not take a wife who yearned for another man. He would not make love to a woman who wished he were someone else.

"My heart is my own, sir. I avoid male company at all costs." She shuddered as if all men posed a threat. "Marriage is a sacred union. I meant I would be betraying myself if I married a man I did not love."

He was surprised a woman of good breeding, one who had assumed a false identity, had such a romantic view of the world.

"Marriage may be deemed sacred. Love is not." His parents had loved one another deeply. Such sentiment was as rare as a moon at midday among the *ton*. "Love is open to bribery and manipulation. It can fade as quickly as stars amid the morning sun." It could be ripped away in a heartbeat. "Is a union based on kindness, trust and loyalty not preferable to one based on something so fickle?"

Silence descended.

The wait for her reply tugged at his patience.

Daventry excused himself on the pretence of needing to speak to his coachman. He left them alone, which only sought to add to the tension.

"Ask me anything, my lady, and I shall give a truthful answer."

She stared in disbelief, as if all men sought to weave complex deceptions. "Is *your* heart engaged elsewhere, Mr

Grayson? Is that what my employer meant when he said this plan required a great sacrifice?"

"No. I am free to form an attachment."

"This would be your first marriage?"

"My first and my last."

"Have you ever loved a woman?"

"Only my mother. She died when I was five." He barely remembered her now. How strange that such a distant memory still made him guarded. "I have cared for no one since."

Her gaze journeyed down his form as if he were a prize bull at the fair. "But you have had r-relations, shared intimacies with women?"

"I'm a bachelor, not the pontiff." He slapped his hand to his chest, ready to swear an oath. "You have my word. I shall not entertain another woman once we are wed. Not in thought nor deed."

"Your need must be great if you're willing to forgo affection."

"I need a woman's arousing touch like any other man."

Recognition flashed in her beguiling blue eyes when she realised he wanted her hand caressing his cock. "Good heavens! Surely you don't expect me to warm your bed!"

"I had not planned on taking a vow of celibacy." Nor would he bed a woman who didn't want him. Their situation would undoubtedly prove troublesome.

She covered her mouth with her hand.

"Rest assured, I shall not chain you to the bedpost, my lady. But at some point, we will need to consummate the union for it to be legally binding." He gestured to the wing chair. "Sit before your legs buckle at the thought of taking me between your sweet thighs." *Damn*. She'd likely think him a coarse brute. "Perhaps we're both in need of a drink. Will you have port?"

She managed a curt nod.

Moving to the small table, he pulled the stopper from a crystal decanter and poured two glasses of fortified wine. He turned to find she stood like a sentry guard, straight and stiff and staring at nothing.

He offered her the glass. "This might help relax you."

"You mean it might rid me of the need to run." She forced a smile, though he suspected she rarely found pleasure in anything.

He didn't like what that thought did to him. How it roused a desire to play the errant knight and rescue her from her foes. How, in mere minutes, her happiness had become as important as his own. In truth, he should be the one to run— as far as his legs could carry him.

He clinked his glass against hers to lighten the mood. "To all the reasons why we should wed." Then he tossed back the contents, though it did little to ease his concerns. "Begin by naming your objections. Other than the fact we are not in love, and you have no wish to bed me."

She gulped her port, and he wondered why she had given Pickins her bonnet but not the high-collared pelisse.

"At almost thirty-one, am I not too old to be your wife?"

"On the contrary. Given an option, you're exactly what I'd choose."

"Exactly?"

"I want a woman, not a girl. I want a partner with life experience, not one who knows nothing but the many ways to describe the colour yellow." Someone bold and passionate, not timid and teary.

Lady Olivia's lips twitched in amusement, and he suddenly wished he had been born a court jester. "Then what you really seek is a woman who is damaged. I fit the criteria in more ways than one."

So, the tide had turned.

Now, she seemed keen to persuade him of her merits.

"If you marry me, you will bear the stain of my illegitima-cy." It was only right she understood he was considered more damaged than most. "Is that not a compelling reason to refuse?"

"All the decent men are illegitimate," she said, no doubt referring to her generous employer. "If you were the Earl of Sturrock, I would be halfway to Dover by now."

It was his turn to smile. Yes, Olivia Durrant was precisely the sort of woman he needed. Her response brought to mind the obvious question. "Do you want children, madam?"

She almost choked on her port. "I beg your pardon?"

"Do you desire children?"

"Children!" She swayed and took an unsteady step back.

He clasped her elbow firmly, fearing she might swoon. "Did I say something untoward? Is there a problem of which I am unaware?"

Hell! Was she barren?

"No!" Tears swam in her eyes. She struggled to catch her breath. "It's just that I never expected to marry. I had convinced myself it was too late. Had come to terms with the fact I would never be a mother."

"I must be honest. My circumstances leave me indiffer-ent." He had not thought to find himself in this predicament. Had not thought to discuss siring offspring. He had assumed she would agree to the match based on her need for vengeance. Yet she seemed reluctant to reveal her story. "But I am a man of honour. A man who rises to every challenge."

Still stunned, the lady sought the safety of the chair.

He poured them both another drink.

Downed his in one swift gulp.

"Perhaps we should get to the reasons why we should marry." He dropped into the chair beside her. "Daventry said you faked your death. That you're running away from something. After what you've told me tonight, I suspect it has to do with your father leaving you his fortune. But if I am to protect you, you must tell me every detail. Leave nothing out."

She swirled the ruby liquid in her glass.

"My lady?" he said, fearing Daventry would return soon.

Their gazes met, the pain in her eyes stabbing at his heart.

She broke her silence with a heavy sigh. "I'm not sure I can say the words. I'm not sure I want to dig up the past and examine the evidence of my brother's treachery."

He understood her reservations. "I disliked my brother, but after all my father has given me, I owe it to him to find the person who severed his bloodline. Your father provided for you financially instead of forcing you to wed a wealthy peer. Did you fake your death because your brother threatened to kill you and claim your legacy?"

It was the only logical explanation.

"I did not fake my death, Mr Grayson."

He frowned. "But they found your body hanging in the King's Wood near Godmersham. They say the crows pecked out your eyes and marred your face. They identified you by your gown and the ruby ring that once belonged to your mother."

He'd assumed she'd paid someone to dig up a corpse. One look at the elegant woman sitting in his chair said she would never disrespect the dead. No matter how desperate she was to survive.

That left one other possibility.

"Then, your brother forced you to flee. He arranged your death so he could claim your inheritance." Hell. He would throttle the earl with his bare hands for being so disloyal. "The devil tricked the coroner into believing—"

"Please! Stop!" She put her hand to her neck as if struggling to breathe. "Give me a moment to gather my wits, and I will tell you."

"Forgive me. I did not mean to be insensitive." He was so absorbed by the mystery surrounding her staged death, he had forgotten she had suffered terribly. "No doubt I sound like one of Daventry's enquiry agents."

Her shoulders sagged. "I've not mentioned the harrowing event to another living soul. The mere thought rouses a pain so unbearable I can scarcely speak. But it is too late to keep the secret."

Silent seconds passed.

Each one punctuated by the ticking of the mantel clock.

"On that fateful day, I went to the village to take a basket to Mrs Walker. She had sprained her ankle and struggled to get about." She stared at her port, not at him. "During the walk home, I noticed two men following behind. They doffed their caps and bid me good afternoon, so I saw no need to be afraid."

Anger simmered. He'd heard the tremble in her voice, felt the icy chill of fear invade the air. "Why the devil didn't you take a maid?"

"My maid took ill on the journey and returned home. It was just a short trip along the lane, and I had lived in Godmersham all my life." She closed her eyes briefly as if disturbed by the memory. "Don't make me repeat every gory detail. Just know the men lost their tempers and hit me many times. They meant to kill me and dispose of my body."

Fury twisted inside him. It took a saint's fortitude to remain calm. "How did you escape?"

With a shaky hand, she placed her glass on the side table. "While out picking wild herbs, two women stumbled upon the scene and screamed for help. The men fled."

"But they came back?"

"At some point. When I failed to return home they

must have presumed I was dead. Marring my face wasn't part of their plan, hence why they found another victim, why they removed my clothes, locket and my mother's ring."

"The items the coroner used to identify you?"

"The items used to suggest I had taken my own life. By all accounts, I left a letter in my bedchamber stating as much." Tears slipped down her cheeks. She dashed them away while releasing a huff of frustration. "I don't know who they hanged from the bough of that tree, dressed in my clothes, but I pray she was already dead."

She must have cried a river over the years. The thought left him floundering. Would he have the strength to pull her from the deep depths of despair, or would they both drown beneath the weight of her misery?

"I'm sorry you had to suffer. Sorry you've had to live a lie for so long."

"It is not your fault, Mr Grayson."

Still, his throat was tight. "And you're convinced Hamilton Durrant paid these men to kill you? Do you have proof?"

An empty smile touched her lips. "Hamilton suggested I visit Mrs Walker. Someone left the note in my chamber. My father was on his deathbed, yet he changed his will. Hamilton inherited everything. It cannot be a coincidence."

Cutthroats would have sold her ring and locket. No, they were paid to plant evidence and ensure everyone thought Lady Olivia had taken her own life. "And so you survived and have been hiding ever since."

She found the courage to look at him, and her brow furrowed. "You think I should have confronted my brother and visited the magistrate. I heard the censure in your voice, the hint of disapproval."

Perhaps he should have lied, but if they were to marry, there had to be a degree of honesty between them. "Yes.

You're the victim yet serve a life sentence. Fighting for the truth is a worthy cause."

"What a noble statement, Mr Grayson. Although when you heave what might be your last breath, the desire to live outweighs the need for vengeance."

"But that is not true anymore." What had prompted her to visit his home tonight? It wasn't to gain his protection because Daventry hadn't mentioned marriage. "You're tired of running. You seek peace, not retribution."

"Peace?" Her mouth twisted into a bitter line. "Peace is like a pot of gold at the end of a rainbow. It doesn't exist."

"Maybe you've been looking in the wrong places."

She held his gaze. Against the candlelight, her eyes dazzled like polished sapphires. "Tell me, Mr Grayson. Can we not lure my brother into a trap without making a great sacrifice? Why do you need to marry me?"

The answer was simple.

Yet after meeting her, matters seemed a damn sight more complicated.

"Because we will visit your brother's estate in Godmersham for a few days. Search the house for proof he killed my brother. I doubt the lord will permit us to stay under his roof if we're not wed. Whether he is innocent or guilty of the crime against you, he will have no choice but to welcome you with open arms."

Lady Olivia gasped. "You want me to return to Mersham Hall? To dine with him when he will probably poison my soup? To sleep yards from the man who tried to kill me?"

A vision entered Grayson's head. Him sprawled in a large tester bed, a knife beneath his pillow, his wife naked and pliant in his arms. "We will use the opportunity to investigate the crime against you. Make no mistake. I shall have my eyes on you day and night."

Her breath quickened. "And that is the only reason you

seek an alliance? To gain access to my brother's private rooms?"

Grayson shuffled uncomfortably in the seat.

A point noted by his astute companion.

"You hesitate, sir. That tells me you do have another reason for marrying. Have the courage of your convictions and name it. I'll not marry a coward."

Never had a woman spoken to him so boldly.

Lady Olivia Durrant would make for an interesting partner, in and out of bed. The thought had him shifting in the damn chair again.

"There are two other reasons," he said, deciding honesty was the first step to gaining her trust. "Perhaps three now we've met."

Intrigued, she sat forward and waited for him to continue.

"I applaud Daventry for having the courage to challenge the *ton*," he said. "They take the moral high ground while wallowing in hypocrisy. As someone who has suffered, I have an overwhelming desire to help you seek justice."

"How noble." Her brittle tone said she doubted him.

She would come to learn he was a man of his word. "The other reasons are far from noble, but I shall reveal them all the same."

"Let me guess. Your father's dying wish was that you marry a blue-blooded lady," she said, stealing the words from his lips.

"Something like that." And his step-mother had said no daughter of the ton would want him. "Seeing as you're so intuitive, perhaps you might like to guess the third reason."

"And miss an opportunity to see you squirm?"

"I fear you will be the one blushing, madam." He watched her intently, eager to note her reaction. "You're a beautiful woman. Interesting. Desirable. The air changed the moment

25

you walked into the room. In short, I feel drawn to you in a way I cannot explain."

The surge of lust had taken him by surprise.

As expected, the lady's cheeks flamed.

Was it possible she was still a virgin? It mattered only in that he would need to proceed with caution. Convince her there was much pleasure to be found between the matrimonial sheets.

"I must be frank, sir, and say the feeling is not mutual."

So why did she struggle to hold his gaze? Why did her lips part when she glanced at his thighs? Why in Lucifer's name was she even considering his proposal?

"Hopefully, your feelings will change over time." Something prompted him to offer an inducement. "You will want for nothing."

"Except love."

"Love is overrated." He pushed aside all doubts regarding the problems they would invariably face. "But I will please you in bed. Be a true and loyal friend. Strive to bring you the peace you deserve."

He may have offered further enticements, but Daventry returned.

"I trust I have given you time to iron out your differences. Trust you have given Grayson's proposal your full consideration, my lady."

She pushed to her feet. "Mr Grayson has agreed to treat me as his equal," the minx said. "He agreed that once we have finished being of use to each other, I may go abroad for an extended period."

Grayson considered her demands. The last clause in their agreement meant they both had a means of escaping if life proved unbearable. But he had one point that was not open to negotiation.

"Unless you are with child, my lady. Then I must insist we

live together in England. It should pose no problem. We are both mature enough to work through any issues."

She placed her hand on her abdomen.

The action made him feel oddly possessive.

"I doubt that will be the case, sir, but I agree. A child's needs must come before our own."

Grayson inhaled sharply. "You agree to marry me?"

She hesitated for a second, no more. "Yes, Mr Grayson. A life with you has to be better than a life on the road. And there's no telling what my brother will do when he discovers I am alive. I should deal with his treachery once and for all."

"It's settled, then." Daventry clapped his hands and grinned like the cat who'd found the cream. "The wedding is arranged for ten o'clock tomorrow morning. You're to marry at St George's, Hanover Square."

Lady Olivia blinked rapidly. "St George's! Can we not marry somewhere quiet, more discreet? I assume you've procured a licence." She gasped and pressed her fingers to her temples. "We cannot marry, not legally. The coroner declared me dead."

The decision would be overturned. Peel was to arrange for His Majesty's coroner to exhume the body and hold another inquest.

Daventry cleared his throat. "Hence why we are meeting with the archbishop in an hour. I have already explained the situation and your need to marry quickly. After giving the Reverend Hudson a sizeable donation for the repairs to the church roof, he found time in his schedule tomorrow."

She looked horrified. "The reverend and the archbishop know I am alive? They might have told dozens of people by now."

"That's not the sort of word they mean to spread. Godly men seek to build others up, not tear them down. But you must convince the archbishop you are not an imposter before he will issue the licence."

Grayson offered a reassuring smile. "There's nothing to fear. Come tomorrow, all of London will know Lady Olivia Durrant did not perish in the woods."

CHAPTER 3

St George's Church
Hanover Square

OLIVIA SMOOTHED HER HAND DOWN HER PALE BLUE DRESS and tightened the bow at her waist. Sybil Daventry offered her a small bouquet of sweet-smelling hyacinths. Early blooms picked from her garden.

"Don't be nervous." Sybil touched Olivia gently on the arm. "Lucius assures me Mr Grayson is the best of men. I am certain he will be a loyal and dutiful husband."

Olivia glanced at the church's vast Corinthian columns. Within the hour, she would stand with a man she barely knew and make promises before God. She couldn't help but think it was all a strange dream, and Miss Trimble was asleep aboard a ship somewhere, sailing to safe horizons.

"What if I am making the biggest mistake of my life?" There was more than her own future at stake. She was in danger of making Mr Grayson's days equally miserable. "What if we don't suit?"

The fact that she had lied to him did not bode well. In truth, she rather liked the illegitimate son of Godwin Gray, though she had no choice but to show her indifference. It would be wrong to give the man false hope. And he had made his views on love perfectly clear.

Mr Daventry appeared from the church, wearing a smart blue tailcoat and a satisfied grin. He descended St George's stone steps and came to greet them. "Grayson is waiting inside, my lady, as are your friends."

Her friends? She had presumed the Daventrys would be the only witnesses. How had he invited guests to a wedding arranged mere hours ago?

"All the ladies of the Order are present with their husbands," he said, showing no sign he was embarrassed for orchestrating the event without her knowledge. "As are the gentlemen agents and their wives. All have come to wish you well."

Mr Daventry's confidence knew no bounds. He must have known she would agree to his plan. He must have written to her friends days ago.

The thought roused her ire.

"You've been busy, sir." She hoped he noted the mild resentment in her tone. Yet, unlike her brother, Mr Daventry's actions were never self-serving. "And if I may say, rather presumptuous."

"You must trust I have your best interests at heart. Four of our friends hold titles. Eight if we include their wives. We may need them to bear witness should your brother accuse you of being an imposter."

Hamilton would use any tactic necessary to discredit her story.

"To rally their support so quickly, you must have been sure I would marry Mr Grayson."

"I hoped you had grown tired of running and could see this plan has merit." He glanced at his wife, his dark eyes softening. "Nonetheless, Sybil thinks I should make running appear more attractive. She believes I gave you no option in choosing Grayson."

Sybil smiled. "Olivia, if you would rather leave England, my husband will give you a considerable sum to secure decent lodgings while you look for work. And so he asks you one last time. Are you certain you wish to marry Mr Grayson?"

A considerable sum? He might have made the offer before she consented to Mr Grayson's proposal! And yet it would not have made a blind bit of difference.

Hearing her real name spoken aloud last night had fanned the flames of vengeance. She could no longer play the intrepid Miss Trimble, not when she needed answers. The poor girl discarded in the woods had a family. After seven years spent in the wrong tomb, was it not time to let her rest in peace?

"Thank you for your kind offer, but you have forced me to face the truth. It's too late to run. Too many people know I am alive." Indeed, Mr Grayson said there was to be another inquest to identify the victim. The wheels were already in motion. It was only a matter of days before Hamilton learnt the news.

Her employer inclined his head. "If it is any consolation, I believe this path will reap greater rewards."

"I pray you are right."

As it happened, Mr Daventry was not the only one to question Olivia's logic before she exchanged vows. Mr Grayson, who looked remarkably handsome in a black tail-coat and gold waistcoat, sought to ensure she still wished to proceed.

"You do not have to marry me," he whispered against her ear while they stood at the altar and their guests looked on. "Perhaps you would prefer to wait and marry a peer. A gentleman who is not considered second-rate."

Second-rate? Mr Grayson was far from mediocre.

"You must decide now, Olivia."

Her name slipped smoothly from his lips. The sweet sound had her heart thumping against her ribcage. His hot breath against her skin did strange things to her insides.

She met his gaze. "I don't want to marry a gentleman." Having spent seven years without her family's protection, she was considered tarnished goods. "I want a man. A man who says what he means and means what he says."

A smile touched his lips. "Then you have found him."

"I believe you found me, sir."

Mild panic fluttered in her throat when his gaze dipped to the blue silk ribbon tied around her neck. It hid the small scar where the blade had pierced her skin. And though it was easily covered with ointment and powder, the mere sight reminded her of those painful seconds as she waited to die.

The rector gave a discreet cough.

Olivia asked he give them a minute, for she felt the need to offer her own assurances. "Come, Mr Grayson, let us proceed. Whatever fate awaits us, know I shall strive to be a good wife."

Mr Grayson smiled. "You've survived worse things." He clasped her hand with his long, inelegant fingers and pressed a kiss to her gloved knuckles. "I swear you will not regret your decision."

The outward sign of affection robbed Olivia of breath. Never had a man looked at her so tenderly. Never had a man's touch roused such conflicting emotions.

But it was all an act.

They were both playing roles.

Doubts surfaced once the service began, but she recited the words from the Book of Common Prayer when prompted. When Mr Grayson did the same, Olivia thought she might cry. It was all so cold and formal. Her heart was bursting with fear, not love. Happiness would surely elude them both.

Damn Mr Daventry and his meddling!

But then Mr Grayson plucked a ring from the book and looked at her. "This belonged to my mother, but you do not need to wear it, not if it displeases you. It's the only thing I have of hers, and you may prefer something grander."

Olivia's breath caught at the sight of the pretty gold ring. It composed a small turquoise stone set amid a cluster of tiny pearls. It was delicate and dainty, precisely what she would pick for herself.

"Why would you give it to me?" she whispered.

He lowered his head, his mouth a mere inch from her ear again. "It's the only thing I possess that means something to me. Perhaps one day it will mean something to you."

She met his gaze. "Will it fit?"

"Fate decrees so." His face was so close, his breath breezed over her lips. "It is not an heirloom passed down through the centuries, but a ring worn by a woman who sacrificed everything for love. As in all things, the choice is yours, Olivia."

How could she not take the ring given by her husband?

Did it not mean he hoped they had a bright future?

She nodded. "I shall wear your mother's ring if it fits."

It did fit. Perfectly. Nothing prepared her for how it felt to see it sitting on her finger. As if it had been made for her. As if this had always been her destiny.

When the rector declared them husband and wife, the tears did fall. Not because she dreaded a life with Mr

Grayson, but because they were forever joined in spirit, bound together in the eyes of the Lord.

The knowledge enveloped her like a shield wall. She was no longer alone. This man would protect her until he drew his last breath. Never had a thought proved so comforting.

Her friends surrounded them as they exited St George's, congratulations ringing like the peal of the church bells. Their beaming faces were the only evidence this was a joyous occasion. Olivia scanned the other onlookers gathered near the steps, anticipating seeing Hamilton's face and hearing the loud crack of pistol fire.

But like a proud father, Mr Daventry ushered them to his carriage and instructed the guests to meet them at Mr Grayson's home in Portland Place. Amid the whirlwind, it occurred to her that she lived at the prestigious address, too.

"Did Mr Bower collect my belongings from Howland Street?" she said while squashed next to Mr Grayson on the carriage seat.

"Indeed."

Mr Grayson turned to her. "I told my housekeeper not to unpack your valise. I suspect you're protective of your possessions and want to tend to them yourself."

She stifled a gasp of relief. "Thank you, Mr Grayson." Mrs Foston's letters were for her eyes only. Servants were known to spread gossip faster than rats did the plague. And she needed to protect the person who mattered most. "Privacy is important to me."

"Call me Grayson," he said softly, drawing her eyes to his. "There should be no formalities between us, Olivia."

"No, of course." And yet she had married a stranger.

Unable to look at Lucius and Sybil Daventry, she gazed out of the window. The couple were deeply in love. Love thrummed in the air. Love was there in every touch, every stolen glance. It only made her realise what she had sacrificed for this spurious marriage.

The wedding breakfast served as a much-needed distraction. Thankfully, in light of it being her special day, the guests only touched on her need to hide her identity. The hours spent eating and drinking and laughing with friends were perhaps the happiest of her life.

Nerves pushed to the fore as evening approached and she anticipated being alone with her husband. The guests must have sensed her disquiet because it was almost eight o'clock when they departed.

Mr Daventry was the last to leave. "Instead of your usual coachman, take Bower with you to Kent tomorrow," he said, keen to speak of the investigation. "I would prefer you had someone capable to offer support when you visit Mersham Hall."

Grayson nodded. "I'm told Bower's help was crucial in solving Lord Deville's case." He cast her a sidelong glance as if waiting for her approval. "We will take him if you're in agreement, Olivia."

"We need all the help we can get. Mr Bower is used to dealing with devious servants. Someone at Mersham Hall must have known about my brother's wicked plan."

And yet no one had tried to warn her. Had Frances been paid to feign illness? Had her maid conspired against her?

Mr Daventry took it upon himself to remind them what was at stake. "The road ahead is fraught with danger. You're fighting two battles, not one. The Knights of the Seven Devils will close ranks and may seek to silence you both. And if Hamilton Durrant is innocent of the crime against you, my lady, then the real perpetrator will go to great lengths to keep his identity secret."

Mr Daventry's warning chilled her to the bone. The suggestion that Hamilton might be blameless came as a shock. But it was his mistake in assuming she would retain her title that forced her to correct him.

"Sir, I have not used my title these last seven years. Out of respect for the man who has sacrificed much to marry me, I have decided to take the name *Mrs* Olivia Grayson."

While Mr Daventry grinned, her husband gasped. Perhaps a man who had suffered for his illegitimacy might want a lady for a wife. Then she faced Grayson and saw nothing but appreciation in his compelling green eyes.

Mr Daventry must have sensed it was time to depart. He reminded them to call at the Hart Street office upon their return to London, said Mr Bower would arrive at the mews promptly at ten, then left to join his wife in the waiting carriage.

As soon as Pickins closed the front door, Grayson cupped her elbow and drew her closer. "Your brother stole your inheritance. I'll not take what's left of your legacy. I understand if you wish to continue using your title. I have the fortitude to bear it socially, should that be your concern."

Olivia smiled. She didn't tell him she had been touched by the offer of his mother's ring. Or that this was a way to repay the kindness he had shown her.

"We do not stand on ceremony here," she said, reminding him of the words he had spoken only last night. "In the name of vengeance, you have married someone you do not love. The coming weeks will be difficult, but we must remain united. And so, I have no desire to be known as anything other than your wife."

He studied her silently amid the candlelight. "I see why your father wished to leave you his fortune. You're a remarkable woman, Olivia."

Heat rose to her cheeks. Grayson knew how to make a lady's heart swell, how to rouse hope in her chest. He might easily seduce her into believing this was a proper marriage. Seduce her into believing in love.

But only a fool believed in fairytales.

"I'm tired, Grayson, and must rest if we're to travel to Kent tomorrow." And she needed a moment alone to gather her wits and guard her heart. It was as if she had been caught in a wild tempest, whipped about to such a degree she had lost her bearings. "Might you point me in the direction of my bedchamber?"

"I can do better than that. I shall escort you there myself, and we shall both retire." He must have heard her sudden intake of breath. "To rest. I do not expect to share anything other than polite conversation." He lowered his voice to a whisper. "And we must sleep in the same bed tonight, Olivia, else the servants will talk."

The same bed! Her pulse beat a fast rhythm in her throat. She should raise an objection, but did their situation not demand they play the game?

"There must be other options."

"None that spring to mind."

Lord have mercy. How would she sleep?

"You will wear a nightshirt? Pray tell me you possess one."

He raised a roguish brow. "It's impossible to find one that fits. Besides, we must become accustomed to each other's habits. Is it not better to begin now? You've surely seen a man naked."

She blinked against a host of explicit images. "Only in a book my brother made me open when I was sixteen." When there had been no talk of inheritance, no animosity between them. "I get the sense nothing will prepare me for the sight of you." When it came to gazing upon his fine form, she would struggle to show her indifference.

His grin spoke of masculine pride. "You may avert your

gaze for now. Soon I pray you'll want to stare at every hard muscle."

He had confessed to being but a few years her senior, yet he made her feel like a naive debutante who knew ochre and jonquil were shades of yellow.

"There's no need. I shall simply snuff out the lamps," she said, trying to be brazen. An intelligent woman, who had seen the worst of men, did not need to cower behind her embarrassment. "Equally, I am quite used to dealing with disappointment."

Her husband laughed, and dimples appeared in his cheeks. They softened his features, made him appear youthful and somewhat mischievous. She had been holding her breath since exchanging vows, waiting for his mask to slip. Yet she couldn't help but feel she had married a genuine man, one with no need to hide behind a facade.

He raised his hands in mock surrender. "For fear of you calling me a braggart, I shall refrain from making comment. Let us continue this conversation in our private chamber."

"Our chamber?" she said as he drew her towards the grand staircase. "Do we not have adjoining rooms?"

"Of course. But the forced proximity will help banish any awkwardness. I suggest we share a room for the foreseeable future."

Did the thought not leave him tense?

Did he face every challenge with unwavering confidence?

"It occurs to me that we should delay our trip to Kent," she quickly said as they mounted the stairs. It was better to discuss the case than imagine her husband stripping off his clothes.

"I see no reason to delay. We must face your brother sooner rather than later." Grayson stopped before an oak door on the landing. "If we're to find evidence of his duplicity, we must spend a few days at Mersham Hall."

He opened the door and gestured for her to enter.

Her heart missed a beat as she stepped over the threshold.

So this was where she would spend her wedding night. In a masculine room that smelled of leather and wood and cedar. In a large bed that dominated the space like the man she had married. Absently, she stroked the red counterpane, aware Grayson's alluring scent clung to every fibre.

She raised her hand to her nose and inhaled deeply.

Sweet heaven!

Sleep would definitely elude her tonight.

"Let us assume Hamilton is guilty of your brother's murder," she said, seeking a distraction. "When he learns we are married, he might attempt to cover his tracks." Talking helped stem her nerves. It helped her forget they would sleep inches apart, that every breath filling her lungs carried his potent essence. "Should we not visit the bathhouse and question the attendant? Should we not examine the scene? Seek to find flaws in the coroner's verdict?"

"I have questioned the attendant twice." Grayson closed the door, and the room seemed suddenly smaller. He seemed infinitely larger. "I held a knife to his throat and demanded he tell the damn truth. He insists he knows nothing, saw nothing, heard nothing."

The mere mention of a knife had Olivia blinking away a vision of her own attacker. "He is lying. Why would an earl bathe with other men when he has adequate facilities at home?" A few reasons sprang to mind. Reasons too lewd for a lady to repeat. "Who owns the establishment?"

Grayson faced her and began untying his cravat. "Mrs Swithin. Despite visiting at various times of the day, the bathhouse is always closed."

"In three years, you have never gained entrance?" She kept her eyes locked with his, didn't dare glance at the open neck of his shirt or the way his fingers moved deftly over his waist-coat buttons.

"Once. The day after Blake died. It was empty but for the attendant and the coroner. I called again last week and encountered him as he left for home in the early hours, but his story remains the same."

How strange. One would think a private bathhouse would have an influx of male visitors.

"Of course, it might not be a bathhouse." She was reluctant to speak of men and their vices while her husband stood in a state of dishabille. "But that still fails to explain why it is always closed."

Grayson threw his waistcoat on the chair, then dragged his shirt over his head to reveal a chest of Herculean proportion. "Perhaps you're right. We should attempt to learn why the place is shrouded in mystery."

Olivia stared in awe, gawping like a woman starved of love and affection. She could not tear her gaze away from the magnificent man she had married. His skin was a beautiful bronze stretched taut over bulging muscle. He looked strong, robust, sculpted like a statue paying homage to the gods.

The devil ran his hand over his pectoral muscle and massaged his own shoulder. "Daventry would have us journey to Kent this evening. But a lady should not spend her wedding night in a carriage."

"In a carriage, we could have kept our clothes on."

"In a carriage, you would have been forced to sleep in my arms." He grinned as he dropped into the chair and removed his shoes, a wicked grin that said he found the situation vastly entertaining. Then, with a rakehell's confidence, he unbuttoned his trousers.

"On the contrary, I doubt I would have slept at all." Olivia turned away and focused on examining every fleck in the wallpaper. Like the parable of Lot's wife, she longed to glance over her shoulder at the sinful scene behind.

She heard him pour water into the washbowl and tend to his ablutions.

The temptation proved too great, and she caught a glimpse of her husband's firm buttocks as he strode towards the bed.

He slipped between the sheets and sat propped against the pillows, his hands clasped behind his head. "Perhaps we should visit Bishopsgate before leaving for Kent."

Olivia stood rooted to the spot, too scared to move. "During the journey, you may explain what prompted you to conduct an investigation three years after your brother's death. And I will need to examine Lord Sturrock's notebook."

Grayson smiled. "There is much to do tomorrow. But for now, I suggest you tug the bell pull and summon a maid. Unless you want your husband to strip you out of your gown and undergarments."

The devil enjoyed teasing her.

"Move one muscle, and I shall sleep in the chair tonight. I've not had a maid undress me in seven years and am remarkably self-sufficient."

"Excellent. I'm keen to watch you perform the task."

Nerves abound, she strode to the washstand, dipped the linen square into the water and pressed it to her face. It might have been a moment to breathe easily again, but she knew Grayson studied her with a scoundrel's intensity.

He observed her pulling the pins from her hair and brushing out her curls. He sat up straight when she removed her shoes, inhaled sharply when she turned away to remove her garters and stockings.

Lacking the confidence to strip off her clothes, she made a swift decision. "One's wedding day is over far too quickly. I believe I shall sleep in my gown tonight." It was something old she had found in the armoire, a dress worn to Eliza's wedding. She padded across the room, doused the candles and climbed into bed. "Good night, Grayson."

"Breathe and you're liable to fall out," he said when she turned her back to him and teetered on the edge.

She didn't dare tell him she was a restless sleeper, a fidgeter who would likely wake with her gown bunched to her waist, her legs entwined with his.

A woman who would likely face a lifetime of regrets.

CHAPTER 4

GRAYSON HAD INSTRUCTED BOWER TO PARK THE CARRIAGE on Old Bethlem, a narrow street running between the snuff makers and the popular White Hart tavern.

Being midday, the three-mile journey across town had taken a little more than an hour. A couple so recently wed might have lowered the blinds and ravished each other senseless. Sadly, Olivia wished to talk about the weather and Pickins' retirement plan, anything other than their embarrassing encounter this morning.

Indeed, he had woken with an erection as hard as a blacksmith's hammer. A situation made worse because Olivia's bare legs were wrapped around his, her limp arm draped around his waist. Within seconds of opening her eyes, she had shot out of bed as if the mattress were ablaze.

Grayson smiled at the memory.

He had no intention of abandoning his wife once the investigation was over. And so he would make time to woo her. Show her she could trust him. Seduce her into wanting to cling to him every night in bed. He could live without love, but not the physical aspects of an exclusive relationship.

He flung open the carriage door, vaulted to the pavement, and handed Olivia down. She wore the green pelisse with the high collar, a means to hide her porcelain skin from his hungry gaze.

"We'll walk to Widegate Street," he informed Bower—Daventry's hulk of a man sitting atop the box. "Should we fail to return in thirty minutes, come and find us on foot."

Bower nodded. "I trust you have a weapon, sir."

"Indeed. I have a knife in my boot, two mallets for fists, and a wife with a tongue as sharp as a sabre. Mrs Grayson can cut a man to shreds with one word."

Olivia rolled her gaze heavenward. "Perhaps you should save your witticisms for the attendant." Then she marched ahead to avoid holding his arm.

Grayson caught up with her as she turned onto Bishops-gate Street.

"Tonight, we should sleep with a wall of pillows between us," he said, alluding to the apparent cause of her discontent. "Lest your legs seek mine in the darkness."

Her tut was like a prod to the ribs. "It is impossible to keep to my side when you occupy more than half of the bed. I have a better suggestion. Tonight, you can sleep on the floor."

"And have your brother think we married for the purpose of proving he's a murderer? When we reach Mersham Hall, everyone must believe we're desperately in love."

She came to an abrupt halt and tilted her proud chin. "I hardly know you. Everyone will see through the facade."

"I don't see how. You played Miss Trimble for years and even convinced Daventry you were a spinster." Seven years was a long time to lose sight of oneself. The strain must have taken its toll. Indeed, his wife's character posed many contra-dictions. She was formidable and fragile, self-assured and shy. "It shouldn't be difficult to play the part of Mrs Grayson."

She fixed him with a challenging stare. "Playing chaperone

to a group of young ladies is hardly the same as playing a devoted wife."

"I'm not sure a devoted wife is what's needed. More one who can barely keep her hands off her husband." He fought to suppress a chuckle. "You had no problem last night. I woke to find your fingers a mere inch from my—"

"Mr Grayson!"

"My hip, madam." He raised his hands in mock surrender. "What the devil did you think I meant?"

"That is the point, sir. I cannot think. It's impossible to tell whether you're teasing me or speaking in earnest. Either way, you enjoy provoking a reaction."

"I enjoy a little light-hearted raillery." A means to help his wife relax, to distract her mind from the arduous task ahead. "But the last thing I want is to make you feel uncomfortable. No more talk of this morning," he conceded. "I swear it."

"Thank you."

"But Hamilton must believe we are besotted." He gestured for her to continue walking and moments later pointed to the pressing reason they had delayed their departure to Kent. "That's the bathhouse, there on the corner."

Olivia stared at the narrow house with bricked-up windows, the only means of entry being a paint-chipped green door. "There are no plaques or signs to suggest it's a business premises," she said. "Although private bathhouses survive mainly on recommendation."

They observed the building for a few minutes.

No one approached the entrance.

"Are you certain it's a bathing house, not a bawdy house?" Olivia suddenly said while engaged in their task. "I'm more inclined to believe your brother sought a female companion than somewhere distasteful to wash."

"I saw no evidence to suggest otherwise." Though would not surprise him to learn the establishment catered to men's vices. "As I said, it was empty the day I gained entrance."

A curious hum escaped her lips. "Mr Daventry said you've only recently taken up the gauntlet again and are determined to learn what happened to your brother. May I ask what prompted your renewed interest?"

There was no better way to say, "The death of Lucifer."

"Lucifer?"

"Mr George Kane was accidentally shot and killed in a duel. His name is written next to Lucifer in Blake's book. Pride was his deadly sin. I planned to explain all during the long drive to Kent."

Neat furrows appeared between her brows. "Is there evidence to suggest his death was not an accident? Maybe his opponent meant to kill him."

"Kane died a year ago. I've recently discovered that they found a drawing of Leviathan in his coat pocket."

Olivia inhaled sharply. "Leviathan!"

"Bromley—Kane's opponent and subsequent killer—fled to France, but not before insisting he had aimed high and missed. He swears the fatal shot was fired from somewhere amidst the trees." Yet the witnesses had not been so sure.

"Did the duel take place in London?"

"No." Grayson hesitated, knowing the news would cause her distress. "In the King's Wood. The men had been visiting Mersham Hall." Daventry had made him aware of the details a month ago and, at that point, had no knowledge of Miss Trimble's true identity. "Bromley was at Cambridge with your brother. Hearing about Daventry's reputation for uncovering the truth, Bromley wrote to him and begged him to prove his innocence."

She fell silent and stared at nothing.

"Olivia?" he muttered a few times until she replied.

"Yes."

"What is it you find disturbing?" He knew the reason for her disquiet, but it was better to talk than let feelings fester. "If we're to find answers, there can be no secrets between us."

It took her a moment to find her voice. "The mere mention of the King's Wood reminds me of that dreadful day. And in a distant corner of my heart, I prayed I had made a mistake in blaming Hamilton."

Grayson touched her gently on the upper arm. "But the more evidence we find against him, the more you have no choice but to believe in his guilt."

"Something like that." She shrugged, then visibly shook herself. "Come. If the private bathhouse is a brothel, those working in the White Hart tavern will surely know of its existence. Ask inside. Play the desperate rake looking for a bit of afternoon sport."

"Pretend I would rather bed a harlot than my wife? Most people would see through my facade." He grinned, hoping humour might drag her from the doldrums. "But in the name of necessity, I shall do my best to act like a rakehell."

Refusing to let Olivia wait alone near the bathhouse, Grayson insisted she return to Old Bethlem so Bower could keep her in his sights. Then he entered the White Hart's yard and spotted a stable hand busy shovelling excrement.

"Boy! Would you care to earn a sovereign?" Ignoring the stench of hard work and horse shit, he spoke in the voice of a lazy ne'er-do-well. "I'm to meet with a golden-haired beauty at the *bathhouse* on Widegate Street." He gave a sly wink. "But I'm so damn sotted, I must be knocking on the wrong door." He stumbled and hiccuped for effect.

The boy tugged down the dirty rag covering his nose and mouth. With beady eyes, he scanned the yard before whispering, "A sovereign, you say? Let's see the blunt, guv'nor. Happen you're so fuddled you ain't got a penny."

Grayson delved into his coat pocket and removed a gold

coin. "It's yours if you tell me how the devil I get into the brothel."

"I don't know anything about no brothel," he said before lowering his voice to a whisper. "A lad with a loose tongue might find himself bobbing about in the Thames. I'll need two of them shinies if I'm to squeal." He held out his grubby hand. "Be quick about it. If old Mr Cabot sees, I'll be out on me ear."

Grayson dropped two coins into the boy's hand and listened to the mumbled instructions. Then he was told to clear off before Cabot strung them both from the upper gallery.

"Well? Is it a house of ill-repute?" Olivia said when Grayson rejoined her. "Or have we had a wasted journey?"

"When I told the stable hand I was to meet a golden-haired beauty at the bathhouse, he raised no objection and confirmed it is a brothel. One catering to those from the upper echelons."

Olivia narrowed her gaze. "You said you were meeting a golden-haired beauty? Is that your preference, Mr Grayson? It must be. Why else would you have said so?"

His confident wife sounded a little insecure.

"I have no preference, nor do I bed whores."

She arched a brow. "Never?"

"Never." He sensed she wanted to ask about his past. There was not much to tell. And he couldn't explain why he was so captivated by this particular woman.

"But you have kept a mistress?"

"I'm thirty-four. I've had several."

"Were they married?"

"No. The only married woman I intend to bed is my wife." He took advantage of the opportunity to ask his own questions. "What of you, Olivia? Are you chaste? Have you ever known a man's touch?"

She swallowed deeply and glanced along the street. "It occurs to me that we cannot simply walk into a brothel. You will have to enter under the guise of hiring a harlot."

Grayson laughed at her attempt at deflection. "We'll devise a plan once you've answered my questions as honestly as I did yours. Shall I repeat them?"

"No! There's no need." She huffed and tutted. "I don't know why it's so important."

"We should be able to speak freely."

She grumbled beneath her breath. "Then I am, as one might say, intact. May we go now?"

"Has a man ever touched you intimately?" Pressing her for answers was about more than satisfying his curiosity. She had to know she could tell him anything. "Has a man ever made you moan with pleasure?"

"No." Her look was firm, the word but a whisper. She pressed the backs of her fingers to her cheek. No doubt it was warm from the flush of embarrassment. "I have led a rather lonely existence. I couldn't risk anyone discovering my identity."

His heart softened upon hearing her confession. He had spent an inordinate amount of time alone, too. "Now you have a husband to keep you warm at night. Now you can be yourself."

She gave a weak smile but said nothing.

He might have prompted her to reply, but one glance along the street suddenly reaped rewards. Indeed, he could hardly believe their luck.

"We were right to come here. Fortune favours the bold, it seems." He pointed to the man in the ill-fitting coat and no hat, meandering through the crowd. "That's the attendant. Quickly. Let's follow him."

Without asking permission, he reached for Olivia's hand and drew her along the street. Despite keeping his gaze fixed on their quarry, his thoughts turned to the dainty fingers trapped in his meaty paw. His own insecurities surfaced. They were mismatched. He was often coarse, blunt, a bastard in expensive clothes. She was refined and elegant, a paragon of virtue posing as a woman of the world.

Why the hell had he presumed they would suit?

His pulse raced, though it had nothing to do with chasing after a devious devil. What if he was too uncultured for her tastes? What if she struggled with the sheer size of him in bed? What if this damn marriage would forever be a sham?

"The attendant has stopped outside the bathhouse," Olivia said. She clutched her bonnet to her head and kept his pace, made no attempt to tug free from his grasp. "What's the plan?"

"We wait until he opens the door, then barge inside." The attendant was busy fumbling about in his coat pocket, surely searching for the key. "Unless you would rather avoid a confrontation. After the violent incident in the woods, perhaps you—"

"Only a fool would attack you. And I would rather you wrestle with the attendant than entertain a harlot."

There was no time to consider an alternative.

Grayson whipped the knife from his boot. He crept behind the attendant, who had turned the key and opened the door wide enough to slip inside the shabby building.

"Make a sound, and I shall drive this blade deep into your back." Grayson forced the man into the dim hall and prodded him with the knife's sharp tip. "I've no qualms killing a man. You'll likely bleed to death right here. It will be days before anyone finds your body."

The attendant raised his hands aloft and whimpered. "The house is empty. There ain't nothing of value here. I've but a few pence in my coin purse."

"I don't want your damn money." He called to his partner

in crime. "Lock the door, madam, and remove the key. We'll not have the rogue escaping."

Olivia secured the door and dropped the key into her pocket.

"We want to see the bathhouse." He forced the blackguard to take the tinderbox from the crude table near the door and light the lantern. Then he gripped the attendant by the scruff of his coat and thrust him towards the cellar. "You will tell us everything we want to know. Else it will be your lifeless body sprawled face-down in the water."

The attendant gasped, evidently recalling their brief meeting last week. That was before Grayson had a letter from Peel permitting him to conduct his own investigation.

"Mr Grayson, sir!" The attendant strained to glance over his shoulder, his wide eyes pleading innocence. "I've told you. I know nothing of what happened that night."

"Then I may as well kill you. You were the last person to see my brother alive. Perhaps you hit him with a Roman urn, held his head beneath the water while he lay unconscious, robbed his pockets."

"No, sir! I swear he was dead when I found him."

"Take us to the bathhouse," Olivia said with Miss Trimble's determination. "The killer has struck again. There is evidence to link both crimes. Come tomorrow, this place will be overrun with men seeking answers. You will tell us what we want to know, or Mr Grayson will take you into custody."

Unsure what to believe, the attendant hesitated. Another dig in the back saw him open the cellar door and lead them down the flight of stairs. They descended into what was an ordinary basement but for the large hole in the floor and the set of wooden steps disappearing into the bowels of hell.

Grayson insisted the attendant climb down into the subterranean chamber and followed closely behind.

"Have a care," he told Olivia. "The floor is wet."

She navigated the rickety steps and came to stand in the vast stone chamber illuminated by candles in the wall sconces. "Goodness! It's like stepping into a bygone era."

"It's part of an old Roman bathhouse." The rows of Doric columns supporting the roof made it look like a temple from biblical times. One would expect it to smell damp, but it carried the soothing aroma of sweet-scented oils. "A few have been unearthed beneath the city, one recently in Billingsgate. While this is privately owned, I imagine the Crown might seek to claim it for its historical value."

Olivia pointed to the rectangular plunge pool occupying half of the chamber. "Is that where they found Lord Sturrock's body?"

"Yes." Grayson gripped the attendant's arm lest the fellow be inclined to flee. He had questions of his own. Who had lit the candles? How did one access the brothel? "They found Blake a few feet from the steps, floating in the water."

"Where were his clothes?"

"Folded neatly on the stone seat in one of the alcoves."

"So one would assume he had come to bathe."

Bathe. Meet a lover. Partake in an orgy. Who knew?

"There were two towels hanging from the iron rings on the wall." When he'd questioned the attendant, he'd learnt Blake visited often and always demanded two. "Though that doesn't mean he bathed with a friend."

"I can see why someone would pay to come here," Olivia said, leaning over the pool and staring into the inky depths. "The setting is rather romantic."

"Until your lover smashes your head against the steps," he mocked. But when she turned her head sharply, her blue eyes full of apology, he added, "But yes, making love here would fulfil most people's fantasies."

Forced to banish an image of his wife slipping out of a sheer white toga, Grayson turned on the attendant. "Was my brother here with a woman that night?" He fixed the man with a menacing glare. "Tell me! Else I will drag you through the mews to the rear of the house three doors down. That is how one gains access to the brothel."

The attendant paled. "I'm paid to keep the place clean, hand out the towels, keep the house locked."

"Who lit the candles?" Olivia asked, their thoughts aligned.

"Someone from the brothel," Grayson guessed. The bathhouse was the perfect place to hold illicit parties. There had to be a door leading to the other house. "Perhaps we should wait and see who arrives. Give their names to the local magistrate."

The attendant gasped. "No! They'll think I blabbed and brought you down here." He thrust his hands through hair as black as his fingernails. "I'll lose more than my position."

"My brother was not bathing alone," Grayson stated. "He did not slip on the wet floor and hit his head. You saw someone else down here. You lied to the coroner."

Beneath the weight of relentless probing, the attendant crumbled. "Yes! Yes! I saw his lordship with Claudette. He paid to use the bathhouse for an hour. I left them alone, went upstairs, and returned to find him arguing with a man. So I made myself scarce."

Grayson inhaled sharply. A heady mix of anger and relief swept over him. For three damn years, he had sat on his arse while the blackguard roamed free. Now, he was one step closer to learning the truth. One step closer to capturing the devil.

"Describe the man," Olivia demanded, obviously keen to learn if he bore any resemblance to Hamilton Durrant, Earl of Mersham.

"It was dark. I never saw his face. He was almost as tall as the earl but not as broad." The attendant winced and wrung his hands. "When I came back downstairs, I saw the fellow rummaging through his lordship's coat pockets."

Olivia frowned. "Where was his lordship?"

Ashamed, the attendant looked at his feet. "I didn't see him at first, but he was already dead in the water. The fellow left through the door leading to Mrs Swithin's place. I reported the matter to her, and she told me to call the watchman."

"You craven bastard!" Grayson clenched his fists at his sides, resisting every urge to punch the scrawny coward. "Had you not hid in the shadows, you may have saved my brother's life."

"Or I might be dead too!"

Olivia stepped into the fray, preventing Grayson from battering the buffoon. "Were you told to lie about what happened?"

"Mrs Swithin don't want everyone knowing about her business. And after what happened to Claudette, I knew to keep my mouth shut."

"Why? What happened to Claudette?" Olivia's confident tone faltered.

The attendant glanced surreptitiously behind. "Some say she died by another's hand. Some say she took her own life."

Olivia paled. "Why would they think that?"

"Because they found Claudette hanged in the North Wood, an upturned stool beneath her feet."

CHAPTER 5

AFTER CALLING AT HART STREET TO LEAVE A NOTE FOR MR
Daventry, asking him to investigate the brothel in their
absence, they set out for Kent. They had been travelling on
the country road for an hour, and Grayson had barely spoken.

The tension in the air was palpable.

Olivia considered the man staring absently out of the
window, suspecting guilt was the basis of his quietude. It was
clear he felt conflicted. He could not visit Mersham Hall *and*
spy on the house of ill-repute. But the disturbing news about
Claudette being found dead in the woods surely meant all
lines of enquiry led back to Hamilton.

"Perhaps we should spend the night at a coaching inn,"
she said to break the silence. "We've another six hours before
we reach Godmersham." Then she realised the beds were
considerably smaller than Grayson's bed at home, and she
would likely awake atop him in the morning.

Grayson glanced at her as if he had forgotten she was
there. "Is it not better to arrive at a late hour and catch
Hamilton unawares? There's less chance of him turning us
away."

It was better not to arrive at all.

Nausea roiled in her stomach at the thought of seeing her brother again. The need to run had her itching to leave when they next stopped to change the horses. The need to put a thousand miles between her and Hamilton had her plotting how she might steal away with her valise. And yet the invisible rope binding her to Alexander Grayson made her dismiss the notion as folly.

Change was meant to be uncomfortable. Breaking old habits was supposed to be hard. What was the alternative? Spend her days festering in a wealth of self-pity?

"You're right," she said in a brighter tone. "Hopefully, Hamilton will be embarrassed when he's forced to greet us in a silk nightshirt and banyan."

"The devil sleeps in silk?" Grayson's lips curled in disdain as if only real men slept naked. "No doubt he wears a jaunty nightcap with a long tassel he whips about when annoyed. Hardly what one expects from a powerful sea serpent on a mission to wreak havoc and destruction."

Talk of men and their sleeping habits conjured an image of Grayson's toned physique. She had done more than witness the strength in his solid thighs. She had wrapped her legs around those hard muscles. Muscles that could easily bear the weight of a woman's woes.

"It's perhaps hypocritical of me to say, but we must remain objective when dealing with my brother." Anger made a man irrational. They would need their wits to uncover evidence. "I fear your temper is like a beast you're struggling to keep caged."

His broad grin said he liked being thought of as savage. And though he spoke with the well-rounded vowels of an aristocrat, a dangerous man lurked beneath his fine coat. Not that he would ever hurt her. She suspected Alexander Grayson would fight to the death to protect his own.

"We both believe Hamilton is guilty of murder," he said resolutely. "I would prefer to wring his damn neck and force a confession. Still, Daventry assures me things are never what they seem. So, we must play the doting couple if we're to prove his duplicity."

"Why doting? We might have married for convenience." Nothing about this arrangement was convenient. Every scenario brought a flurry of conflicting emotions.

"People in love are fools." Grayson laughed like he was the only sane man amid a horde of imbeciles. "We want Hamilton to think we're idiots, noticing nothing but how the sun glints in each other's eyes. We want him to think we're so drunk with desire, we can barely rouse a coherent thought."

She would have to touch him.

Lovers were often tactile, even in polite company.

"Surely the fact I failed to return home proves I suspect him of attempted murder. He will be on his guard. Suspicious."

Grayson relaxed back in the seat and rubbed his firm jaw. "Then we'll tell him you were attacked but have suffered amnesia. That you've recently regained your memory and remembered who you are."

So now she would be playing two roles.

Both while her nerves were in shreds.

And yet she could see the logic in his suggestion. "Then how did we meet?" It was a story often repeated by fools in love, fools who gorged on giddy emotions. "Where have I been for the last seven years?"

Grayson gave her a speculative look. "We'll keep to the truth where possible. You were managing a house for women down on their luck. The charitable owner found you injured on the roadside and brought you to London, where you have lived ever since."

Yes. That would be easy to remember.

"Though we will not mention Mr Daventry or the nature of his business." Aware of the tremendous task ahead, she thought it better to settle into her role immediately. "When did I first lay eyes upon you, my love?"

Grayson jerked his head at the endearment, but then a slow smile formed. "At a charity ball hosted by your employer. It was love at first sight. I couldn't take my eyes off you." He played the part well because his voice dropped low and husky. "I'm a man obsessed. We make love morning and night, in the bathtub and hay barn, any damn place we can find. Though we shan't tell your brother that. I merely mean to paint a picture."

And he did—rich and vivid, like an erotic Renaissance.

Heat rose to her cheeks.

The lack of air in the carriage made it hard to breathe.

What would it be like to be loved so passionately?

"Someone recognised me," she said, keen to banish all thoughts of making love to Mr Grayson. "That's when fragments of my memory returned. Visiting Mersham Hall is the last piece in the puzzle."

"Yet you still have little to no recollection of what happened on that fateful day seven years ago."

Oh, it all sounded so easy when alone with a man as confident as Grayson. How would she fare when interrogated by her brother and consumed by every negative emotion?

"But I perceive a problem," her husband added. "You're too nervous around me. You'll likely flinch when I touch you. I should be the one person you feel safe with, and so we will use the time we have at our disposal to correct the issue."

Panic flared. "What are you suggesting?"

He patted the seat beside him. "Come here. Let us work on fostering a certain intimacy that might easily be mistaken for love."

Every part of her sought to resist, but she had come too

far on this precarious road to turn back now. "I trust you will ask permission before doing anything untoward, Mr Grayson."

A wicked smile played on his lips. "So now I am Mr Grayson, not your love? If we're to solve our problems and put the past behind us, you must lower the barricade and welcome me in."

She had built the barricade brick by brick, stone by stone. It had been her only protection. If he wished to gain entrance, he would need to chisel away the mortar. Though she suspected Grayson would prefer to use a sledgehammer, reduce it to rubble and leave her exposed.

"Come here," he repeated in a velvet-edged voice.

Swallowing past every reservation, she crossed the carriage and sat beside him. "What would you have me do?"

"Everything. But I must remind myself patience is a virtue. For now, you must become accustomed to me touching you." He breathed deeply as his gaze journeyed over her hair. One would think she had pulled out the pins provocatively, let the curls fall around bare shoulders.

"I shall try my best to please you." Why did she feel so nervous?

Why was her stomach a tangle of knots?

She was a mature woman, not a chit making her debut.

"You please me without trying." He captured a stray tendril and marvelled at the texture. "Your hair is so soft it slips like silk through my fingers. It smells divine, almost exotic."

She met his gaze, her heart racing. "A man in Covent Garden sells oils and soaps from the Far East. Moringa and Frankincense is my preferred blend."

"It's so captivating it kept me awake last night."

She didn't want to think about him watching her sleep, him studying her without her knowledge. "He makes shaving

balms. I shall purchase one for you when we return home."
Home was Portland Place now, though at any moment she
might wake and realise this was all an absurd dream.

"What husband wouldn't want a special gift from his
wife?" Lightly, he caressed her cheek with the backs of his
fingers. "Is every part of you as smooth, love? Would your lips
part in much the same manner if I stroked you elsewhere?
Would you sigh and whisper my name?"

A flutter of panic caught her unawares. She wasn't afraid
of this man, more afraid she might fall under his hypnotic
spell.

"Perhaps one day you may find out," she said boldly.

"Then I find myself counting the hours." His breath came
a little quicker, not as quick as hers. "Might I touch your
lips?"

"For what purpose?"

"For no purpose other than to feel the coil of intimacy
wind tighter. For no purpose other than to revel in their soft-
ness, too."

He didn't need to wind the coil. It was so tight it would
likely snap. Still, she nodded and held her breath.

Slowly—building an anticipation beyond anything she had
felt before—Grayson traced the outline of her mouth. But he
didn't stop there. He ran his finger along the seam of her lips
and slipped inside to where the flesh was plump and wet. Just
as wet as the flesh between her thighs.

"Hmm." His sweet moan sent her pulse skittering.

She pulled away. "That's enough."

"Because you like it, Olivia?" he teased. "Because you
don't want me to stop, and that's what you find frightening?"

"Because it is apparent we have no problem feigning
desire."

Grayson smiled. "And yet it felt so real."

She didn't know what was real anymore. The thought had

her scooting across the carriage, keen to put some distance between them. Danger didn't just lurk beneath his expensive coat. It was there in every word, every look, every tempting touch.

He sat back in a languid fashion. "Now we know each other a little better, it will be easier to fool your brother."

"Yes." She would likely start panting if he touched her again.

Besides, she wasn't supposed to like him. She wasn't supposed to trust him. She was meant to keep up the pretence that she preferred a lonely life to being shackled to the illegitimate son of Godwin Gray.

"Do you have Lord Sturrock's book?"

Her husband nodded. "It's in my valise. I shall retrieve it when we stop to take refreshment and change the horses."

"Excellent. I must read it before we reach Mersham Hall." It would divert her attention from the man sitting opposite, and it might give her insight into Hamilton's role in the Seven Devils club.

Although how did one even begin to understand a man who thought of himself as a monster? How did one come to know the workings of a murderer's mind?

* * *

It was late, approaching midnight, when their carriage rattled along the tree-lined drive leading to Mersham Hall. Grayson had insisted they stop for supper at a quaint coaching inn with an ornate bridge and a babbling brook.

Stressing a need for them to stretch their legs, he had captured her hand and led her to the dark wood at the rear of the property.

"You have nothing to fear," he'd reassured her as they

approached the thicket of trees. "As God is my witness, I'll not let anyone hurt you again."

"Then why am I shaking to my toes?"

"Because your mind recalls all the terrible things that happened to you and means to protect you like I do."

She had struggled to breathe as they ambled along the winding path. Every noise had her jumping like a scared hare. Then Grayson spoke of how he loved walking in the country-side, beneath hills and majestic mountains, described beautiful starlit skies and stunning sunsets.

Slowly, her fears melted away. By the time they returned to the carriage, she wasn't afraid of what lurked in the shadows. She wasn't afraid to hold his hand.

"Are you ready to play a role, Olivia?" Grayson's smooth voice dragged her from her reverie. "Remember, defer to your husband if you're unsure what to say. Hamilton will not think it odd that you look to me for advice."

"I have no issue seeking your counsel. For the most part, we think alike and are both driven by the same goals." Except Grayson would bed her tonight were she so inclined. "Should you be at a loss at any point, you may defer to your wife. All wise men do."

His smile seemed to light the dim confines of the carriage. "That's the first time I've heard genuine amusement in your voice. A man might find he defers to his wife often if it brings her pleasure."

The last word slipped from his lips like honey from a spoon, slow and smooth and strangely seductive. Yet she wondered if that was his intention. Not to offer every temptation. To distract her from thinking about the place where she had almost died.

"I see what you're doing," she said, keen to let him know she wasn't a fool and understood his motives. "This is a game of diversions."

Grayson sat forward, his gaze serious, intense. "It's not a game. Not when we're alone together. We married for the wrong reasons, but do we not owe it to ourselves to make it right?"

"Yes," was all she said, but felt more confused than ever.

One could not force oneself to love someone.

One could not convince oneself they were happy.

She glanced out of the carriage window. The shock of seeing Mersham Hall's imposing facade, of the sudden flood of memories, stole her breath.

Filled with dread, she turned to Grayson. "Miss Trimble is strong and forthright. An experienced woman who has survived the worst atrocity. I have lived as her for seven years, yet I find myself floundering now, unsure what to say or do."

Grayson's eyes softened. "The woman Daventry brought to see me was strong and forthright. She challenged me, demanded answers, used logic to inform her decisions. That woman was you, Olivia, not Miss Trimble." He opened the carriage door, vaulted to the ground, and offered his hand.

She moved to accept his assistance, but he settled his hands on her waist and lifted her to the ground. He held her there, close to him, the heat of his palms penetrating the layers of fabric.

"You have been dishonoured. Abused. You need to ignite the fire in your belly, draw strength from its flames." He pressed a chaste kiss to her forehead. "Vengeance will be yours, but you must feel its power raging within."

His words would rouse men into battle, yet he had kissed her as if she were a timid child. In that moment, for no sensible reason, she might have preferred being ravished.

But there was no time to think of what it meant.

Bickford opened the door and came to stand on the stone steps. The butler held his lantern aloft and peered at them in the gloom. "May I help you?" His hoarse voice was so familiar

—an echo of a lost life—it almost made her cry. "This is Mersham Hall. Have you taken the wrong turn?"

"Introduce yourself," Grayson whispered, releasing her.

She swallowed past the lump in her throat, straightened her shoulders and stepped forward. "Good evening, Bickford."

The ageing servant shuffled closer and angled the light to examine her face. "Who are you, madam?"

"Is that how you welcome me home? With indifference and an absent stare? Do you not recognise the girl who used to tug on your coattails as you served dinner?"

Bickford lowered the lamp, his shaky hand lacking the strength to keep it raised. "Lady O-Olivia?" He clutched his heart as if it had suddenly stopped beating. Then he stumbled back in horror. "Begone, ghost! Begone, I say! Leave this place. Christian men live here."

Had the years affected the man's sense and reason?

She supposed it was a logical conclusion. She was, after all, dead and buried in the family tomb. "Would a ghost ride in a carriage? Would gravel crunch beneath a ghost's feet? Be assured, I am Lady Olivia Durrant." There was no point in confusing matters and giving her married name. "I am alive and well and have returned home."

In a desperate bid to retreat, Bickford almost tripped over his shiny shoes. "Impossible! The devil doth torment the weak!" Then he hurried over the threshold and slammed the front door shut.

"That went well," Grayson mocked.

Olivia swung around to face him, resisting the urge to climb into the carriage and return home. Although nowhere felt like home at present. "He is old, and it is late. The moon is full and lends itself to dark omens. We should have arrived by the light of day. Then he would not have been so scared."

"Perhaps Bickford has every reason to fear you," he countered, as calm and as rational as always. "Perhaps he was complicit in your brother's wicked plan."

"Bickford? He has served my family since he was a boy of twelve." An orphan caught scrumping in the orchard. "He's been loyal to a fault for over fifty years."

Grayson shrugged. "He may think your father failed to do his duty in naming you heir to all that was unentailed. His loyalty may rest with the law that states the firstborn son should inherit."

She braced her hands on her hips, determined to argue, yet she had no defence. He was right. She did not know who to trust. Mersham Hall was no longer her beloved home but a nest of scheming vipers.

With renewed determination, she climbed the steps, aware Grayson followed languidly behind. She seized the brass knocker and hammered loudly, only stopping when she heard a commotion in the hall.

"Who is it, Bickford?" came a smooth voice she recognised—that of a traitor, a Judas. "Why are you standing against the door?"

"No good comes of venturing outside during the midnight hour, my lord. Might I suggest you return to the study? I pray the devil will grow tired, and the noise will soon cease."

"Bickford, you're talking in riddles."

Olivia knocked again. "Hamilton!"

"Open the door!" her brother shouted.

"My lord, you must not look upon her likeness."

"Good grief, man, are you ill? Have you a fever? Stand aside. I shall deal with the matter myself."

The clip of booted footsteps on the tiled floor preceded Hamilton yanking open the door.

Their gazes collided.

It took no more than a second for her brother to recognise her. Stunned, his blue eyes bulged, and his chin almost hit his polished Hessians. The rogue blinked more times than she could count before whispering, "Olivia?"

She took an unsteady step back and would have turned and fled had Grayson not placed a reassuring hand on her back.

"Olivia?" Hamilton said, astounded. "By Jove, is it you?"

Shock held her in a vice-like grip. Not because she had finally found the courage to face her brother. But because she did not feel hatred twisting in her gut. Nor did she feel the bubble of anger she had kept simmering all these years. The warmth of familiarity, of blood ties, of the history they had shared infused every part of her being.

Words escaped her.

Grayson stepped forward, a confident presence she would not be without. "Forgive my wife. It has taken immense courage for her to come here tonight. After all she has suffered, she is at a loss to know what to say."

Every word spoken rang true.

Hamilton looked dazed. He dragged a trembling hand down his pale face and shook his head. "How can this be?"

And then he dropped to his knees and sobbed.

CHAPTER 6

GRAYSON WATCHED THE IGNOBLE EARL OF MERSHAM crumple to the floor like a newborn foal. Tears trickled down the fiend's face. He couldn't catch his breath, couldn't look his sister in the eye.

"H-how can this be?" the earl cried.

Oh, this was a performance better than any seen in Covent Garden. Grayson would have given a mocking round of applause had there been no need to play roles and keep secrets.

"Might I suggest we go inside?" Grayson kept his tone calm and even, though he wanted to throttle the peer, grab him by his floppy cravat and string him up in the King's Wood. "My wife is cold and in shock and needs to sit before the strain becomes too much."

Olivia stood statue-like, stiff and silent.

Bickford stepped forward, offering his master a handkerchief. "I beg your pardon for my rudeness, milady, but you're the last person I expected to knock on the door this moonlit night."

Olivia barely raised a smile.

She made no attempt to ease the servant's conscience.

Grayson slipped his arm around her waist, fearing she might be next to collapse to her knees. "Please. My wife is suffering from shock. We must get her inside." The panic in his voice was not part of their act.

What if her sanity had been hanging by a thread?

What if seeing her brother was the impetus to make it snap?

Hamilton scrambled to his feet, unable to contain his elation. "Olivia! You're alive! Praise be!" He hurried forward and tried to grasp her hands, but she shrank back.

"Can you not see she is distressed?" Grayson cried, though his anger dissipated when she slipped her arms around his waist and hugged him tightly. "Please!" It was unlike him to beg. "She needs rest. Seeing you has roused a host of horrid memories."

Hamilton's brow furrowed. "Quickly. Bring her inside. We are all in need of a stiff brandy, including you, Bickford."

They were ushered to the drawing room, but Olivia came to a crashing halt in the hall. "Y-you once chased me with a croquet mallet," she said, her voice distant, weak. "You swung and hit Mama's ormolu clock. Smashed it into a hundred pieces."

Hamilton stared at her. "Yes, you took the blame."

"I would have done anything for you."

Hamilton seemed confused. "We were always close."

So close he had let his sister wander the lanes alone. Hired thugs to remove his rival. Indeed, it took Samson's strength for Grayson to hold his tongue and curb his temper.

"Do you recall my favourite painting?" She spoke in a whisper they had to strain to hear. "Of a black stallion galloping across verdant fields? The one promised to me?"

"Yes, it's hanging in the study. Why do you ask?"

Olivia shrugged. "For no reason other than to prove I am

your sister, not an imposter or a figment of your wild imagination."

Hamilton approached her again. "I would know those blue eyes anywhere. Come. My mind is awhirl with questions." His tone was a mix of excitement and burning curiosity. "Where have you been, Olivia? Who is buried in the family tomb? Why was she wearing Mother's ring?" Then the devil blinked as if he had suddenly woken from a confounding dream. He turned to Grayson, shaking his head. "Did I hear correctly? Did you refer to Olivia as your wife?"

"We were married yesterday." Grayson relished the look of disappointment on the fool's face.

"Surely you know my husband." Olivia placed her hand on his chest the way a woman in love might, unaware he felt an odd stirring whenever she touched him. "Grayson is the son of Godwin Gray, Earl of Sturrock."

"I believe you were at Cambridge with my brother," Grayson said, watching this villain like a hawk. "Blake died tragically three years ago."

And he had your damn calling card in his coat pocket.

A muscle in Hamilton's cheek twitched. "I knew him well. You're the illegitimate son," he said, looking like he had eaten something sour. "You went to Oxford. Inherited more than half of your father's fortune." The earl's tone was full of accusation. "Yet you were not a close family and barely spoke to your brother."

He was not to blame for their estrangement.

"Blake took issue with many things, though in light of your sister's sudden return from the grave, I hardly think it relevant."

Perhaps the swift change in her brother's countenance was the reason Olivia raised a limp hand to her brow and said, "Hamilton, can the questions not wait until tomorrow? We can sit together during breakfast, and I shall relay the story from the beginning." She hesitated. "Assuming you will permit us to stay tonight."

"Permit you to stay?" Hamilton gave an incredulous snort. "This is still your home, Olivia. Bickford will send a maid to your bedchamber to light the lamps and remove the dust sheets."

She swallowed deeply. "My bedchamber?"

"But for the maid's monthly clean, your room has remained untouched for seven years."

Olivia gripped Grayson's arm. "You kept my clothes, books, Mama's silver hairbrush?"

"Indeed."

"Then you will not mind if I say goodnight?" She was breathless, full of impatience. "Do not trouble the maids. Grayson can help me make the room serviceable, and I know my way."

Something flashed in Hamilton's eyes, perhaps fear or suspicion or blinding panic. "Where did you marry? I would have known had the banns been read."

"We married by licence at St George's, Hanover Square," Grayson informed him. "The Lords Roxburgh, Deville and Devereaux were in attendance. The announcement should be in today's *Times*."

The earl shifted uncomfortably. "Then everyone within fifty miles of the Thames will know."

"Presumably, though now is hardly the time to concern yourself with the *ton*. We've been travelling for most of the day, and my wife is exhausted."

Hamilton's glare might be considered hostile. Indeed, the chill between them was enough to make a man reach for his greatcoat. "Then we shall save the mountain of questions until the morning. I doubt I shall sleep and will probably rise with the larks. Pray join me at your earliest convenience."

Damnation. He had hoped the fool would lie in bed until noon, give him an opportunity to search the study.

"Doubtless we shall suffer a sleepless night, too." Grayson reluctantly bowed to their host before taking Olivia's hand and mounting the broad oak staircase.

Hamilton remained in the hall, watching them intently, his penetrating gaze burning into Grayson's back.

Once upstairs, Olivia drew him along the dim corridor to the east wing. She stopped to peer at portraits in the dark but said nothing. She came to a halt at a door and stared at the wooden panels before inhaling deeply and finding the courage to enter.

The room was as cold as a crypt, dark but for slithers of moonlight seeping through a gap in the curtains. Furniture shrouded in white sheets filled the space like a family of spectres. The smell of dust and desertion hung in the air. He had no time to consider the eerie silence, for it was suddenly broken by his wife's uncontrollable sob.

Grayson closed the door quickly and gathered her into his arms. "We knew you would find the reunion traumatic," he muttered against her hair as she drenched his waistcoat with tears. "It is better to cry than let emotions rage within."

He wasn't sure how long he stood there, holding her, stroking her back in gentle circles. Long enough for him to feel a tightening in his chest. A sensation he quickly dismissed as compassion or pity.

When her last sob subsided, she pushed out of his embrace. "Forgive me. You need a wife who is in control of her emotions, not one who's a blubbering wreck."

"I need a wife with life experience." She did not recoil when he dashed a tear from her cheek. "A wife who is not afraid to show me every aspect of her character."

She managed a smile. "Now you've seen me at my worst."

"And I look forward to seeing you at your best."

He held her gaze and was surprised when she touched him under the guise of brushing her tears from his waistcoat. "I've ruined this. You should undress and hang it over the chair to dry."

"And force you to stare at every hard muscle?"

"I shall busy myself with folding the dust sheets." She moved to open the curtains and let the moonlight illuminate the room. "There seems little point lighting the lamps."

As she stood bathed in the moon's iridescent sheen, he took a moment to appreciate the woman he had married. With her graceful bearing, delicate chin and beguiling blue eyes, she was perhaps the most beautiful woman to make his acquaintance. Yet it was what the eye could not see—her courage and wit and unwavering loyalty—that roused a sense of pride in his chest.

"We should retire," he said before he started drooling like a love-sick buffoon. "Attempt to get some sleep. Tomorrow will be just as taxing." Especially when they visited the King's Wood and he asked probing questions. But it was necessary. Not for the case. Olivia needed to face her past if they were to find lasting peace.

With a heavy sigh, she dragged the sheet off the tester bed. "Might we remove them all? I would rather see the room as I remember it, not as a mausoleum for a woman who isn't dead."

They spent a few minutes folding the sheets and placing them in a pile on the floor. Then Olivia reminisced about her old life. She opened drawers, looked at trinkets, showed him the white gloves in a box she should have worn to her come-out ball.

"You were twenty-three when you were abducted. Why are the gloves still tucked at the back of the drawer?"

"My mother wanted me to wait until I was eighteen to make my debut. Then she took ill, and so I missed my first season." Her gaze skimmed the breadth of his shoulders. "Perhaps we would have passed each other in a crowded ballroom. You might have asked me to dance."

He cleared his throat. "The only balls I have ever attended are those hosted by the demi-monde. Our paths would never have crossed had it not been for Daventry's intervention. You would have married someone of your own ilk, not a man like me."

The thought left him oddly bereft.

She averted her gaze to the pristine white gloves. "Then for the first time in seven years, I'm grateful to the rogues who dragged me from the lane."

The veiled compliment was a cue to touch her, perhaps kiss her. Had theirs been a marriage by usual standards, the kiss would lead to a night of passionate lovemaking. But they were taking small steps on a journey that would last a lifetime.

"My mother's death affected me deeply." She returned the box to the back of the dusty drawer as if that's where dreams belonged. "I spent the next two years in mourning instead of the required *one*. Then my father took ill, and life seemed like a perpetual cycle of sickness and sadness."

Yes, he might boast of suffering from the same conditions.

"When this is over, we shall host a ball in celebration. Invite people we like, not just those bearing titles. We might pretend it is your come out, and mine shall be the first name on your dance card."

Her eyes brightened. "Based on my distinct distrust of men, yours will be the only name," came another compliment he did not rightly deserve.

"I would happily dance every waltz with you. To hell with the scandal." He gestured to the red leather book hidden amongst her kid gloves. "You kept a journal?"

"Yes, but it's full of silly nonsense. The ideals of a young woman who knew nothing of the real world." She removed the book and tried to hand it to him. "You may read it if you like."

He waved his objection. "I would not presume to read a person's private thoughts. There's a reason you hid it from plain sight."

She laughed. "I'm not that person anymore. It was written by a woman I no longer know." She crossed to the window and flicked through the pages. "Would you care to hear of my hopes and aspirations?"

He would rather not face the fact she had settled for less than she deserved. Still, he could not deny her a moment's happiness.

"By all means, regale me with your wisdom."

"Well, it seems I longed for a dress of scarlet silk, but my mother said a lady needed the confidence to wear such a gown."

Grayson smiled. "When you charge your new wardrobe to my account, be sure to order two gowns in scarlet. To marry the scandalous son of an earl, one must possess a certain *je ne sais quoi*."

"Yes, one must," she said proudly, angling the book to better read her notes. "Though you're only scandalous when you insist on strolling about the room naked."

"Then I am scandalous most days."

Her gaze roamed over him. "Doubtless it is something I shall get used to." She flicked past a few pages. "Oh, and I wished to visit Brighton in the summer."

"We shall add it to our list of adventures."

She fell silent, engrossed in reading the words on the page. Then her smile died, and she quickly slammed the book shut. "That's enough for tonight. As I said, it's just silly talk that has no bearing on real life."

He wondered what she had read to prompt her reaction. Probably a young woman's aspirations of love. "No doubt you dreamed of a love match, not marrying a stranger out for vengeance."

Olivia hugged the book to her chest. "It's of no consequence now. We are married and must make the best of it." Raising her chin, she added, "I'll not disappoint you again, Grayson. Tomorrow, I shall rise with Miss Trimble's fortitude."

Evidently, she had forgotten the part where he praised her for being herself. He would have to appeal to her romantic nature if he hoped to find the real woman, not the one who relied on Miss Trimble's fake resolve.

"We should retire before we freeze to death, although you cannot sleep in your clothes tonight." Lovers were supposed to crave closeness, crave the touch of bare skin, not hide beneath a mountain of layers. "We cannot risk a maid seeing us and gossiping to your brother."

"No," she said, resigned to the fact.

"Amid the emotional reunion, we forgot to tell Bower to unload our luggage. Doubtless he will attend to the matter himself when he realises we're staying. But we must expect Bickford to knock on the door at any moment."

Her eyes widened. "Then I shall sleep in my chemise. I shall disrobe behind the screen while you undress and climb into bed."

He smiled to himself when she took sanctuary behind the partition. The lady clearly knew nothing of what men found arousing. He slipped out of his coat, his mind running amok as he listened to the rustling of material, to her little pants and groans.

As expected, she draped her discarded dress over the screen, leaving him to skip past a vision of her petticoat and imagine soft round breasts bursting out of her stays. The thought left him near bursting out of his breeches.

"Have you ever seen a man in a state of arousal?" he said when she added her stockings and petticoat to the growing pile.

Silence, not a sigh or a groan.

"Have you?" he repeated, dragging his shirt over his head.

"No, Mr Grayson. Have I not admitted to being intact? Where would I have seen such a sight?"

He was always Mr Grayson when she was embarrassed or angry. "Were you not a governess in Vienna for a time? Did a randy footman not flash at you from an alcove? Did a licentious lord not try his luck?"

"No! It was a respectable household. I rarely saw my employers and spent all my time with the children." She huffed. "Why do you ask?"

"I thought you might like to look upon your husband. Decide if we might suit." He meant fit, but didn't want to alarm her.

Silence, but for a sudden pant.

He removed the last of his clothes and palmed his erection. "Don't you want to see what you do to me, Olivia? How the mere thought of you undressing fires lust through my veins?"

He expected her to object profusely and almost staggered back in shock when she came out from behind the screen wearing nothing but a thin chemise.

Standing ten feet away, she inhaled sharply as her gaze dipped to his jutting manhood. "I—I have a confession to make."

"Yes." His interest was more than piqued.

"When I woke this morning, I may have inadvertently touched you. When you stirred and opened your eyes, I feigned sleep because I didn't want you thinking I had done so intentionally."

"I see. And you're telling me because ..."

"I need you to hold me tonight." She wrapped her arms around her chest, hugging herself tightly. "Because I don't want to lie alone on the edge of the bed thinking about the last night I spent in this room. And because I am a woman of thirty, not a green girl plucked from her mother's breast and forced into bed with a beast."

He couldn't help but smile.

"And because you're warm and, dare I say, familiar."

"Familiar? We married only yesterday." Yet it felt as if he had known her for more than a lifetime.

"If one counts the hours, I have spent more time with you than anyone else these last seven years." She glanced at his throbbing manhood with a mix of intrigue and trepidation. "I mean for us to comfort each other, Mr Grayson, not partake in something salacious."

It was a vast improvement from her sleeping in her dress and treating him like a leper. Indeed, he looked forward to what tomorrow would bring.

"Then I shall climb into bed and think of how I despise your brother." Anger sent blood surging to a man's fists. Anger was the antidote to lust. And, by God, he needed something to distract him from his wife's curvaceous silhouette. "That will most definitely dampen my ardour."

Olivia nodded. She waited until he was settled in bed before venturing to her dressing table, removing the pins and brushing her hair. When she finally padded towards him, a tempting vision of loveliness, he pulled back the coverlet.

She slipped in beside him. "You don't need to hold me all night, just until I'm asleep."

"You speak as if it's a hardship." He gathered her close so

she could rest her head on his shoulder, though he inhaled sharply when her cold feet brushed against his shins.

"I tend to fidget and sometimes act out my nightmares."

He might have reassured her and soothed her fears, but he had never held a woman in bed, had never experienced a profound burst of tenderness in his chest. And so he chose to lighten the mood.

"With your wandering hands, let's pray you're not aboard a sinking ship and need to grab hold of something sturdy."

CHAPTER 7

Olivia woke to find her leg draped over her husband's thigh, her palm pressed to his chest. His body was as hot as a furnace. She might have inhaled the earthy scent of his skin—had she not glanced up and met his amused gaze.

"Good morning," he said, offering a broad grin.

Slowly, she slid her leg from his and shuffled to a respectable distance. "Good morning. Have you been awake long?"

"Since dawn." He blinked against the sunlight streaming in through the window. "We forgot to close the curtains last night. And I found myself waiting with bated breath, hoping you might inadvertently touch me again."

Olivia chuckled to herself. She usually woke distressed from a bad dream, only to realise life was more frightening than any nightmare. Never did she experience a flutter of amusement in the morning.

"The maid entered half an hour ago and left our luggage." He stretched his arms and yawned. "Thankfully, you were clinging to me like ivy to a tree trunk."

She sat up. "Perhaps because you're so sturdy."

Their gazes locked for a few heartbeats.

"You seem different this morning. Much brighter." He glanced to where her chemise had slipped down to reveal her bare shoulder. A sensual hum rumbled in his throat, but he looked away swiftly. "There's clean water in the pitcher. The maid said Hamilton went riding at sunrise. Perhaps Bower will know where the devil he went."

The mention of her brother tightened her chest.

Had he gone to meet the men who had beaten her? To berate them for lying and not doing a proper job?

She swallowed against the bitter taste in her mouth. "For a moment, I had forgotten why we are here." Vengeance seemed like a foolish plan now that she had something to lose. "But I must focus on the task ahead, give the case my undivided attention."

"And you must try to keep a tight rein on your emotions. Think of the poor girl buried in your family's tomb."

"Think about her? Grayson, she's the focus of my thoughts most days." And the nights when she woke cold and alone in the darkness.

Grayson touched her gently on the arm. "We will do our utmost to ensure those who've lost their lives rest in peace." He threw back the coverlet and climbed out of bed. Naked, he strode to the window and gazed out across the meadow. "We must play the game. Advance with caution."

Olivia perused her husband's fine form. Confidence radiated from every toned muscle. A vulnerable woman might come to depend on him, might find the quality highly arousing. Was that why heat pooled between her thighs? Why her breasts ached? Why she lacked the strength to look away?

"Know this," he said, his tone carrying a serious edge. "I will kill the next man who attempts to mark your skin."

Mark her skin!

She clutched her throat and vaguely recalled untying the

silk ribbon last night. "You speak of my scar? It's small and hardly noticeable." Though it reminded her someone had wanted to cleave her in two.

"Yet you cannot bear to look upon it."

"Yes." Had she spoken in her sleep, whispered the words while deep in slumber? "Though I do not recall saying as much."

"I know what it's like when your body reminds you of your limitations. My blood is tainted. During those difficult years at school, it felt like poison flowing through my veins."

As children, the illegitimate were often tormented by the sons of lofty lords. Hamilton had spoken of the terrible things he had witnessed at Cambridge and Eton. Had her brother formed the Seven Devils as a means of protection or to intimidate his prey?

"But you don't feel that way now?"

"No. You come to realise your imperfections make you stronger. You observe your peers and know you're the better man." He pushed away from the window, unperturbed by his nakedness. "What I'm trying to say is you don't need to hide your scar from me."

"I wasn't hiding my scar from you." She took a moment to appreciate the man who appeared perfect in the cold light of day. "Seeing it reminds me of what a fool I was to trust my brother."

"But you're a fool no more." He moved to pour water into the washbowl. "Let's venture downstairs and move our pawn into place. Let's begin playing the game so we might finally uncover the truth."

It was her cue to get dressed. Although with a newfound appreciation for a man's buttocks, it took her no end of time to crawl out of bed.

Hamilton was back from his ride and sitting at the head of the table when Olivia entered the dining room with

Grayson. She pasted a smile, hoping to fool the man who had so cruelly deceived her.

"Good morning, Hamilton."

She noticed the dark shadows beneath his eyes.

Hamilton threw down his napkin and pushed unsteadily out of the chair. "It is indeed a glorious day. I've spent a sleep-less night fearing your return was nothing but a fanciful dream. Yet here you stand, Olivia, alive and as beautiful as ever."

Far too vividly, she recalled peering into Mrs Foston's looking glass, seeing her face bruised and bloodied after the attack. She had learnt a hard lesson that day. Beauty was as fleeting as Hamilton's loyalty.

"You must forgive me." Her voice was somewhat shaky, too. "My memory is a little vague. It's seven years since we last laid eyes on each other. Yet it feels like a lifetime ago."

Hamilton pressed his hand to his heart. "Pray put me out of my misery. Tell me what happened to you, Olivia. You left for the village and failed to return. I thought you had taken your own—" He choked on the last word, then grabbed his napkin and dabbed his eyes.

No doubt her smile faltered. "May we sit?"

"Of course." He composed himself. "Please, help your-selves to breakfast. Will you take coffee?" He didn't wait for a reply, but gestured for the footman to draw out the chairs and pour the beverage.

"I shall plate your breakfast while you speak to your brother," Grayson said, taking on the footman's role and helping her into the chair.

She smiled at him when he touched her gently on the shoulder. It was the only genuine expression she had formed in minutes. "You're too good to me." She meant that, too.

Hamilton watched Grayson beneath lowered lids. Despite being a trickster, he was struggling to hide his contempt. He barely gave her time to sip her coffee before discussing the day she almost died.

"Mrs Walker confirmed you arrived at her cottage with the basket. She said you were perfectly well when you left her. That you gave no indication you were in a fragile mental state."

She steeled herself. Imagined putting on the cloak of an enquiry agent, ready to relay the evidence with cold indifference. "Two men attacked me on the lane and dragged me into the woods."

"Attacked you!" Hamilton looked ready to chase the blighters and wring their rotten necks. "Who in Lucifer's name were they? Footpads? Outlaws? Vagrants out to steal your coin?"

"They were hired men." She was convinced of it.

Behind them, Grayson dropped the silver lid of the serving dish, causing a loud clatter. He found it hard to master his temper, but he turned and apologised for the mishap.

Hamilton threw daggers of disdain at her husband's back, forcing her to defend her only ally. "I am here because Grayson encouraged me to come. He knows how the memories terrify me and is my most trusted confidant."

Hamilton grumbled beneath his breath. "How did you meet?"

She told the tale they had rehearsed, though her brother seemed shocked she had attended a social function in London. More so that no one from the nobility remarked upon her likeness to an earl's dead sister.

"It was not an event for the upper echelons," Grayson said, placing a plate of ham and eggs before her and then taking his seat, "but for those on the fringes of society, like myself."

"I've had a deep-rooted fear of men for years." She met

her husband's gaze across the table and wondered why she was not afraid of him. "Grayson is helping me to realise not all men are mean and vengeful."

"Then he has my utmost gratitude." Hamilton watched Grayson over the rim of his coffee cup. "I cannot bear the thought of you being alone all these years without a man's protection."

"One learns the art of self-sufficiency quite quickly." Truth be told, she was rather proud of her achievements. Not so proud of letting this villain escape punishment for his crime. "I have worked in Paris and Vienna. Spent six months touring Egypt as Mrs Montague's paid companion." She declined to mention her dreadful sojourn to Chesterfield.

Hamilton gave a dismissive wave. "For heaven's sake, don't mention you worked for a living. Needs must and all, but it will only make others think less of you. And you must tell no one those men hurt you." His eyes widened. "Good Lord. Pray tell me there isn't a child."

Anger flared. She noticed Grayson laying down his cutlery and so swiftly said, "How dare you! How dare you presume to advise me on how to live my life."

Hamilton looked confused.

"The men beat me and left me for dead," she said, pain and shame and anger imbuing her tone. "They meant to hang me from the bough of a tree, but someone came and foiled their plan. And all you care about is what people might say."

"Olivia, I—"

"And if me bearing illegitimate offspring is what you fear most, know they did not force themselves upon me. There is no child because I am still intact."

Grayson coughed into his fist. "You were, my love."

"Yes, I meant I was until two days ago."

Hamilton raised his hands. "Forgive me, Olivia. I did not mean to cause you distress. It's clear you've had to fight for survival. It was wrong of me to judge. My comments reflect nothing but a need to protect you."

"That responsibility is mine now," Grayson said sharply.

The men stared at each other.

A duel with gazes, soon to be knives.

Silence ensued.

They ate their breakfast.

"But you left a letter," Hamilton eventually said when he could no longer hold his tongue. "Frances found it on your nightstand. It was addressed to me."

"I did not write a letter."

"Then who did?"

"I have no notion, but it had to be someone who had access to my bedchamber." His accomplice, or the traitorous maid. "May I ask what it said?"

Hamilton swallowed like he had a piece of ham stuck in his throat. "That you were sorry. You wanted to be with Mother and couldn't bear to watch Father die, too."

The words were familiar. They were words she had written in her journal when consumed with grief. Someone had read the book, composed the letter and left it in her room.

But who?

Or maybe her brother was a lying scoundrel.

And there was no letter at all.

"Do you still have it? I'd like to examine the penmanship."

"No."

"No?"

Hamilton frowned. "Frances mentioned your letter during her interview with the coroner. I had no choice but to submit it as evidence. Equally, having read the contents, I couldn't watch an innocent man hang for your murder. The magistrate would have been under pressure to find someone to blame."

"It wasn't my letter. But it must have been written in what appeared to be my hand."

"It looked convincing enough. When they brought your body home, I—"

"Not my body," she interjected, though it pained her to think someone else had suffered in the name of greed. "You have buried another poor soul in the family tomb." She drew on Miss Trimble's boldness and mother wit. "She must be a local woman. Someone of a similar height and build and hair colour. The men acted quickly. They fled the woods, returned to find me missing, and so had to improvise."

Grayson cleared his throat.

She was supposed to have a poor memory.

Instead, she had a moment of clarity, saw pieces of the puzzle she had been too afraid to remember. She had fought for her life, taken a few thumps to the face. They could not have hanged her and made it look like suicide.

"The men knew the area and must live within a ten-mile radius," she said bluntly. "Perhaps they're farm labourers"— judging by their strength and brawn—"with a penchant for theft. Though I suspect their criminal activity amounts to poaching, rustling and stealing from hay barns." She recalled their argument about the ruby ring. They had said her brother needed proof she was dead. If she told Grayson that, Hamilton would be the one swinging from the gallows. "They coveted Mother's ring."

She caught Grayson's gaze, and he raised a brow.

"I doubt they would have remained in the area," Hamilton said, though his concerned tone was likely an act. "And you were missing for a week before they found your body." He shifted uneasily in the seat. "You said someone arrived to disturb them. Do you recall who?"

Who!

Heavens! She would rather die than reveal their names.

Mrs Foston and her cook were the only witnesses to the crime. They had been clever enough not to show themselves, but made enough noise to scare the blighters away. They were the reason she could still draw breath.

"My memory is rather—"

But she was saved by the sudden appearance of a woman she knew. Of course, she had read that her brother had married while mourning his beloved sister. While his father lay broken-hearted on his deathbed. And he had the effrontery to lecture her on keeping appearances.

Miss Anna Stowe was now the Countess of Mersham.

And Olivia's mother was likely turning in her grave.

The golden-haired beauty came to a crashing halt. "Olivia! It is true! I can scarce believe it." The lady clutched her breast—to draw attention to her impressive cleavage, not convey her immense relief. "Hamilton woke me last night, but I'd convinced myself it was a dream until Frances spoke of the news this morning."

Frances—the turncoat.

Olivia stood, as had the men. "It is good to see you again, Anna," she said to the lady who had stolen her maid and her position in the household.

"After breakfast, we will go for a stroll in the garden, and you must tell me where you've been. Tell me every scandalous snippet." Anna's gaze drifted to Grayson. From the quirk of her brow, one could tell she found his countenance appealing. Who wouldn't? "And you must be Mr Grayson."

Grayson offered an elegant bow. "It is a pleasure to make your acquaintance, Lady Mersham."

Jealousy bubbled like acid in Olivia's throat. Had Grayson lied? Did he have a penchant for golden-haired nymphs? Nymphs with large breasts and a come hither twinkle in their eye?

"Likewise, sir. I knew your brother well. Lord Sturrock

was a regular visitor here at Mersham Hall. Please accept my condolences on his passing." Anna gave no indication she was affected by Grayson's illegitimacy. A fact that must have pleased the man no end.

"Thank you, my lady."

Aware that he had neglected to offer his sympathies, Hamilton said, "The circumstances of his death must have affected you quite profoundly. I know what it's like when one's mind is plagued with unanswered questions."

Grayson inclined his head but said nothing.

She didn't like not knowing his thoughts.

Old fears surfaced. Would those who lived in this hive of deceivers seek to destroy her marriage? Hamilton clearly disliked her husband. Anna looked like she wanted to tear off Grayson's breeches and bounce on his lap. And how well had she known his brother Blake? Well enough for Hamilton to kill him in a jealous rage?

Feeling the need to escape and protect the only good thing in her life, Olivia did not sit down when prompted. "Forgive me. I wish to give Grayson a tour of the village. We will leave you to enjoy a private breakfast. Later, I wonder if I might meet my nephew."

Hamilton jerked his head. "But you can't leave. We have much to discuss. Why did you not come home? Why the devil did you run? And why would anyone want to hurt you?"

Why indeed?

The motive had to be money.

She forced a smile. "Talk of the tragic event unsettles me. I would rather take some air and resume our conversation this afternoon. We will be but a few hours."

Though disgruntled, her brother gave a curt nod. "I wasn't sure you knew about Tobias. I should have mentioned him sooner, but he's staying with his grandparents for a few days. They dote on the boy."

The last comment carried a hint of malice.

Which explained why Anna quickly added, "Having never had a son of his own, my father tends to spoil Tobias. It is a point of contention. But I shall send a note to Crundale Manor and ask my parents to come visit tomorrow."

Despite Hamilton's desperate efforts to persuade them to stay, they left the stuffy confines of the dining room and dressed in their outdoor apparel.

Olivia waited until they were marching along the gravel drive before asking, "Did I say too much? It would have seemed odd had I not attempted to describe my attackers."

"It's not what you said that made me nervous," Grayson replied, his voice warm and reassuring. "I sensed your anger and feared it might get the better of you. I had visions of you springing from your seat and calling the devil out."

"So you do think Hamilton is responsible." Tears had trickled like raindrops down her brother's face. But the guilty often cried with remorse when forced to face their victims.

"The evidence suggests so, but Daventry warned against making assumptions." Grayson cast her a sidelong glance. "Perhaps you *should* walk in the gardens with Lady Mersham and probe her for information. She appeared quite free with her opinions."

Anna appeared free with more than her opinions.

But then some women knew how to capture a man's attention.

"Perhaps *you* should walk with her," she teased but felt nauseous at the thought. "Is that not your preference? To bed a golden-haired beauty who speaks her mind?"

Grayson came to an abrupt halt. He faced her, slipped his hand around her nape, and dropped his voice to a whisper. "I want to walk with *you*, Olivia. I want to bed *you*. I want to lay you down and pleasure you until you forget every horrid memory."

Sweet heaven!

Her throat worked tirelessly just to say, "Why?"

A slow grin formed. "Because I suddenly find myself looking for you when you're not in the room. Because you arouse me with nothing but a smile. Because your comment means you feel a stirring of desire for me, too."

Perhaps a little more than a stirring.

"Lust is a powerful emotion." Would it wane? Would they tire of each other quickly? When this was over, would they be desperate to part ways? "What if marriage proves a disappointment?"

"What if it doesn't?"

"I don't know how to please a man." She was a grown woman, soon to be thirty-one. She had journeyed to faraway shores yet was unable to navigate these waters.

"If you like me, it will come naturally." Grayson's gaze dipped to her lips. "Perhaps avoiding the issue is not the answer. Might I at least give my wife a chaste kiss?"

Her heart raced, but she nodded. "We must start somewhere."

Grayson lowered his head.

She expected the first brush of his mouth to feel foreign. For her insides to cramp, her distrust of men and their motives to make her jerk away. Thought he would crush his lips to hers. Feared even pleasurable acts left bruises.

But a man who could seduce a woman with a teasing grin and a kind gesture knew better than to frighten her.

Indeed, his mouth was soft and pliant and moved over hers with a husband's reverence. He did not attempt to control or claim her as men were wont to do. He opened his mouth a mere fraction, lulling her to do the same until their lips melded together and moved with ease.

Just as she got used to the enticing taste of coffee and the earthy essence of virile male, Grayson broke contact.

A little bereft, she frowned and stared at his lips.

"You seem surprised it was over so quickly," he said, his voice carrying a hint of amusement. "I did say a chaste kiss. If you want something hot and wild, Olivia, simply say so."

Hot and wild!

Lord, it sounded divine.

Should she lie or tell him she liked kissing him?

Should she say she craved the closeness?

"You have a way of making everything sound appealing. Perhaps anything more is best tackled in a private place, away from prying eyes."

He glanced at the row of lime trees lining the drive, then he captured her hand and pulled her behind a broad trunk. "No one will see us here. Now tell me. Do you want me to kiss you again?"

She hesitated.

He straightened and was about to step away.

Brazenly, she gripped his lapels. "Yes."

He moistened his lips. "Is it to be a chaste kiss, love, or something to heat the blood?"

She pulled him closer and looked into the emerald pools that made her knees weak. "Something wild and wicked." Something that made her forget everything but how it felt to be with this man. "A kiss without a gentleman's restraint."

"With hands, too, or just mouths?"

Based on the fact her body tingled whenever he touched her, and they were outdoors, after all, she decided to take small steps on this voyage of discovery.

"Just mouths this time."

"Push me away if you want me to stop."

She nodded, then gasped as her husband pinned her to the tree trunk and claimed her mouth in a searing kiss.

He wasted no time coaxing her lips apart, slipping through the opening, drugging her with every sensual sweep of his tongue. It wasn't an assault but a deep exploration. He was on a crusade to learn her taste, steal the breath from her lungs, ignite a fire in her blood.

He kept his word and braced his strong hands above her head, gripping the trunk though his body moved against hers in an erotic rhythm.

"Grayson!" she gasped when he moved to kiss her neck.

"Do you ache, love?"

Ache? Her insides clenched, seeking the adventurer who had plundered her mouth. "Tell me. Is making love as pleasurable as kissing?" Did it leave a woman drunk with need? Did it leave her lost in a hazy mist of arousal?

Grayson put his mouth to her ear, sending a shiver down her spine. "One day soon, you shall find out."

CHAPTER 8

FEW THINGS UNNERVED GRAYSON.

But kissing his wife had left him unsettled.

Two hours had passed since he'd locked lips with Olivia, yet her jasmine perfume still teased his senses. He could still taste her, could still feel his blood thrumming wildly in his veins.

Despite kissing plenty of women, none had left a lasting impression. None made him count the minutes until they might kiss again.

It would pass.

Else how the devil would he concentrate on the case?

"Must we stay here tonight?" the object of his desire said as they returned through Mersham Hall's impressive iron gates. "I doubt we'll find anything useful. My brother is a virtuoso when it comes to playing roles. Could we not return to London and investigate the remaining Knights of the Seven Devils?"

The kiss had affected her, too.

She hugged his arm as if pinned to his coat, had wrapped her hand around his bicep as if guessing its girth. That said, they had spent an hour exploring the King's Wood, and she had not left his side for a second. Tensions had run high when she refused to reveal the identity of the person who had come to her aid.

"We'll search Hamilton's study tonight once the house is abed. I'll attempt to access his bedchamber during dinner." While they should concentrate on questioning Mrs Swithin and Hamilton's pompous friends, gaining access to her brother's private rooms was the main reason they had wed. "Are you happy for us to decide then?"

Olivia squeezed his arm affectionately. "Of course. And I must speak to Frances about that dreadful day, though it will take every effort not to accuse her of lying."

"Play on the fact your memory is vague, and ask her to fill in the missing pieces. It won't look odd when you bombard her with questions."

As they continued along the drive, she glanced at the tree where they had awakened their passion. He was about to suggest they stop and experiment further, but Lady Mersham came striding across the lawn in her red pelisse, heading in their direction.

"There you are. I was on my way to the gatehouse to look for you." The lady stopped and rubbed her lower back. Like the whores selling their wares at the docks, the action was a means of drawing attention to her breasts. "I would avoid the house if I were you. At least until Hamilton's temper has cooled."

"What has him so vexed?" Olivia said.

No doubt he disliked the fact his sister had married a bastard. Or that he was no longer the man she turned to in a crisis. Or the person he needed rid of most had reappeared on a moonlit night.

Not that it mattered. They were about to discover the

reason for his ire. Lady Mersham's tongue was as loose as a harlot's pantaloons.

"My parents arrived a moment ago." The lady spoke as if a band of brigands had taken over the drawing room. "Hamilton is furious."

"Your parents?" Grayson wondered at the coincidence. "But you've barely had time to send a note."

"Mr and Mrs Stowe own the neighbouring estate," Olivia explained. "It's but a fifteen-minute ride on horseback. Perhaps Hamilton is annoyed because they have arrived unannounced."

"No, he's enraged because they left Tobias at Crundale Manor in the charge of his nursemaid." The lady attempted to persuade them she was a rose between two thorns. "Hamilton blames me, of course. But I specifically said you wanted to meet your nephew, yet they have shown a blatant disregard for my wishes."

Grayson cast Olivia a sidelong glance. She looked as bewildered as Lady Mersham. Yet when a man bore the stain of illegitimacy, he was used to being treated like a leper.

"Let's return to the house," Olivia said. "An element of calm is needed. I'm sure there's a reasonable explanation."

"Indeed." Lady Mersham glanced back at the house as if being asked to scale Skiddaw. "Might I take your arm, Mr Grayson? This entire business has left me so dreadfully out of breath."

Unable to refuse without offending their hostess, he inclined his head. "Certainly. I shall try not to charge ahead." He felt like sprinting to the front door.

"Thankfully, it's but a short walk." Olivia gripped his other arm, and he touched her hand as a gesture of reassurance.

"Do you fence, sir, or is pugilism your sport of choice?" Lady Mersham's fingers were like creeping vines, searching every nook and cranny, latching on, staking a claim. "I have never known a man with arms so muscular. Well, except for your brother."

His brother?

"You knew Lord Sturrock well?" he asked, keen to prolong the walk and interrogate this strumpet. How well? That was the burning question.

"Blake came to stay for a month the Christmas before he died." Her voice broke on the last word. Unlike everything else about her, her distress seemed genuine. "We miss him dreadfully."

So, while Blake spent Christmas in the company of friends, Grayson had spent it alone.

"And the earl permitted you to use his given name?" Olivia said, though he knew what she was insinuating.

Lady Mersham's laugh sounded hollow. "Hamilton's Cambridge friends often come to stay. The men are as close as brothers. So close, I believe they made a blood pact and swore an oath beneath the light of a full moon."

Anger and resentment festered. Blake had refused all attempts to reconcile but had played brother to a man who wasn't his kin.

"Although poor George died in a duel with Mr Bromley last year. Despite numerous invitations, no one has deigned to visit since."

Probably because the remaining knights feared Hamilton was out to murder his brethren. Particularly since Bromley swore that a mystery devil had fired the fatal shot.

Odd that the lady professed to be on friendly terms with all her husband's *chums* yet had used Bromley's prefix. Perhaps she enjoyed taunting her husband. A man who loved this jade might be spurred to kill in the name of jealousy.

When they reached the front door, Lady Mersham failed to release him. Such was her reluctance to let go, he had to peel her fingers from his coat sleeve and offer a fake smile. "Perhaps you might inform your parents we have returned."

The lady leaned closer in her overly friendly manner and whispered, "Be warned. My father can be a condescending prig. Despite Hamilton being the heir to an earldom, my father initially refused his suit."

It was hard to know whether this woman, who clearly had wool for brains, spoke earnestly. The only way to know for sure was to keep prompting her for information.

"Did he take much persuading?"

"To marry while in mourning, my brother must have been besotted," Olivia interjected, her tone caustic. "Evidently, he won your father over in the end."

The lady tittered and tapped her finger to her lips. "My father had no choice but to agree. Our little plan to see me compromised worked a treat." Then she flounced into the house and called for them to follow.

"So, Lord and Lady Mersham are a devious pair," he whispered to Olivia. "You will hate me for saying this, but you must spend more time with your sister-in-law. The lady has no shame and cannot hold her own water. With luck, we will solve both mysteries before the day is out."

Olivia patted his arm playfully. "And I shall suffer her company gladly, for I have no desire to don widow's weeds."

"Widow's weeds?"

"Based on Anna's voracious appetites, she will likely devour every inch of you and leave nothing but bones."

He bent his head. "Yours is the only mouth I want ravaging my flesh."

Her cheeks turned a pretty shade of pink, but she managed a smile. "Good, I mean to nip you when your gaze wanders."

"It won't. I am blind to all but you."

She shook her head. "It's a good thing I know you're

teasing me, Mr Grayson. Else one might think you're growing attached to your wife."

He should have offered a witty retort, but he suspected there was an element of truth to her quip. In his effort to forge a friendship and nurture romantic tendencies, he felt connected to her in ways that proved confounding.

Lady Mersham appeared in the hall and beckoned them inside. "Father suspects you're an imposter, Olivia," she whispered, holding on to Grayson's arm as if he were a crutch for the faint-hearted. "Be prepared for a barrage of blunt questions."

Unable to curb his tongue, Grayson shook free of the lady's grasp. "Be prepared. I may well call him out for his effrontery. No one insults my wife. I suggest you do everything in your power to prevent him from signing his own death warrant."

Lady Mersham's eyes widened. He noticed lust's twinkle in those sludgy green pools. "What can I do, Mr Grayson? I have been browbeaten all my life and must look to you for support."

This lady wanted a damn sight more than support.

"I suggest you grow a backbone, Anna," Olivia snapped. "Are you not tired of having your opinion disregarded?" She cast him a sidelong glance. "Grayson despises feeble women. Is that not so, my love?"

"Indeed."

As if struck by a bolt of courage, Lady Mersham steeled herself. "Then come. Let us display a united front against my father." She led them into the drawing room and cleared her throat. "Papa. Mama. May I present Mr and Mrs Grayson? Your concerns are unfounded. You only need cast your gazes over Olivia to realise there has been no mistake."

"I shall be the judge of that." A portly man sitting in the fireside chair tried to push to his feet. Such was the weight of his paunch, it took him three attempts to stand. He straightened his brown velvet coat, pulled a monocle from his pocket and stepped closer. "Let's have a good look at her, then."

"Sit down, Henry," said the woman in a dull dress sitting next to Hamilton on the settee. "Put that thing away. Anyone with an ounce of sense can see she bears more than a likeness to Lady Olivia." The woman shook her head. "Welcome home, my dear."

"Thank you, Mrs Stowe." Olivia smiled, ignoring the slobbering oaf eager to make an inspection. "Are you well?"

"I fear I shall die of embarrassment if my husband persists with his unwarranted observations."

"When a man is challenged by the laws of logic, what can he do but make a thorough study?" Stowe held his monocle in place with his saggy eyelids and leant forward. "I recall Lady Olivia had a freckle—"

Grayson placed a firm hand on the man's chest, stopping him mid-stride. "Perhaps Lord Mersham is used to your prodding and poking, Mr Stowe. If you must study someone's face, study mine. Then you may boast of seeing the devil's own fury."

Stowe paled.

Grayson was not of a mind to hit a man twice his age, but he imagined shoving a whole pheasant in this fool's mouth and watching him choke on the bones.

"Maybe Lord Mersham failed to inform you of my scandalous lineage," he continued. "As Lord Sturrock's by-blow, I often forget my manners."

Hamilton cleared his throat. "My father-in-law merely finds Olivia's sudden reappearance unnerving." He fixed Stowe with an exasperated stare. "Still, that does not give you the right to make my guests feel uncomfortable, Henry."

They were hardly guests.

They were not here at the fop's behest.

Stowe inclined his head by way of an apology, though he was clearly not sorry. "One hears stories of imposters, and my memory is vague. It might help if we had a point of reference, but someone stole the only portrait."

Olivia jerked her head. "Stole it?"

"We don't know what happened to your portrait," Hamilton said with some irritation. "One day, it was here. The next, it was gone."

"It seems odd nothing else was taken." Stowe returned to his seat and gave a sigh of relief when he dropped into the chair. "One might think someone had a personal vendetta."

Hamilton bristled. "It sounds like you're accusing me of something, Henry." He turned to Olivia, no doubt keen to reveal what had happened before Stowe twisted the tale. "I had your portrait removed and stored in the attic."

"In the attic? Why?"

Lady Mersham jumped to her husband's defence. "It was a constant reminder of what happened, of how he failed to protect you. Well, what Hamilton thought had happened." She lowered her voice to a whisper. "Clearly, you did not kill yourself in the woods."

Everyone looked at Olivia as if she had deliberately misled them. As if she concocted the story of thugs beating her and stripping off her clothes, and had simply run away of her own volition.

She looked up at him, the pain in her eyes evident, before turning on those one might call family. "You don't believe me. You think I wrote the letter and faked my death." She gasped. "Surely you don't think I hurt that poor girl."

Hamilton sprang from the chair. "Of course not."

"But you think grief affected my faculties."

"Truth be told, I don't know what to think."

Mr Stowe spoke up. "The thought of losing your father proved too painful to bear. Shock can sever the threads of one's sanity. The strain can make a person snap." He clicked his fat fingers. "And your manner at the time might be considered erratic."

"You were most definitely not yourself when your mother died," Mrs Stowe added with some sympathy. "And Hamilton says your memory is still vague. That you barely remember anything of what happened."

Anger flared. Even the kind comments were a veiled means of attack. "My wife did not imagine being beaten in the woods. And I shall call out the next man who suggests she is insane or dares hint she killed a woman in an effort to flee."

Lady Mersham joined the fray. "Yes, I think it's dreadful that you're all blaming Olivia. Why would she invent such a shocking tale? And you must admit, what happened to the painting is extremely odd."

"What is odd about a painting being stored in the attic?" Olivia demanded to know, though her voice carried the strain of the last few days.

Perhaps they should leave this place and search for clues elsewhere.

"Because someone stole the wretched thing," Stowe said.

Mrs Stowe was quick to support her husband's theory. "Did I not say your friends from Cambridge weren't to be trusted? They may have thought to play a prank. Though why anyone would think it amusing to tarnish a dead woman's memory is beyond all comprehension."

So, the painting must have been stolen over a year ago. By Lady Mersham's own confession, no one had visited the property since George Kane was shot dead in the woods.

Hamilton scrubbed his hand down his face. "The portrait is missing, misplaced. We have no proof it was stolen." He gestured to the settee and gave an exasperated sigh. "Why don't we all sit down and take tea? Then we may discuss why my son is at Crundale when I asked he be brought here."

Mrs Stowe's gaze shifted nervously to Olivia. Despite openly disagreeing with her husband, it was clear she had supported his decision to leave the child behind.

"We thought to come ourselves," the woman said in the gentle voice that might be mistaken for timidity. "Once we've gathered the facts, we will know what to tell Tobias."

"Should that not be his father's decision?" Olivia said, defending the man who she believed tried to murder her.

Hamilton raised his hands in the air. "At last, someone who speaks sense. I want my son returned to this house in the morning. These regular visits to Crundale must stop."

Lady Mersham groaned as if the idea of having her son come home was abhorrent. "He means for a month or two, Papa. That is all." She turned to Olivia and whispered, "The boy is rather wild, too headstrong for a lady of my delicate sensibilities."

Hellfire! For the first time in a year, Grayson wondered if Hamilton might be innocent of any crime. A man capable of murder would have done away with his wife and insufferable in-laws.

He glanced at Olivia, thankful he had married a wise woman. A woman with a kind heart and passionate nature.

"I mean indefinitely," Hamilton snapped.

"That's preposterous!" Stowe harrumphed. "You cannot keep the boy from seeing his grandparents! He thinks of us as—"

"You can visit him here."

Stowe's cheeks turned beetroot red. The fool was about ready to combust. Lord knows what he would have said had Bickford not arrived looking flustered.

"What is it, Bickford?" Hamilton was at the end of his tether.

"Might I speak privately, my lord?"

"You may speak in front of present company. My wife will ensure everyone knows come nightfall."

Lady Mersham's eyes widened. "That is grossly unfair."

"Yet true." Hamilton waved for his butler to continue.

"It's Frances, my lord. We've not seen hide nor hair of her since she attended her ladyship this morning. Mrs Wilmslow checked her room and found her belongings missing."

"Missing!" Hamilton looked at Olivia, suspicion marring his brow.

"Missing!" Lady Mersham pulled a lace handkerchief from the sleeve of her day dress and waved it about to signal her distress. "But who will dress my hair? Frances is the only one able to fashion a Psyche knot."

Olivia asked the only logical questions. "Has Frances ever left the house before? Have you spoken to the maids? If not, I suggest we question them individually."

Mrs Stowe chuckled. "Why the fuss? Maids run off all the time."

"Not in my house, madam."

"No. In your house, sisters disappear, and friends are shot. Then you wonder why the poor boy prefers visiting Crundale." Mrs Stowe clasped her hand to her mouth as if the devil had held her hostage and conjured the wicked words.

An argument ensued whereby Hamilton complained about his in-laws' constant interference, and his wife complained about the lack of decent maids. No one considered that Frances' disappearance might be connected to Olivia's return to Mersham Hall.

"Silence!" Grayson bellowed. He waited until he was the focus of all their stunned gazes. "There's less sniping at a cock fight. One would think I was the earl, and you were all base-born ingrates."

Lady Mersham tittered.

"Perhaps you were all pandered babes, and that's why there's not an ounce of sense between you." Grayson turned to Olivia. "Frances must know something about the day you were abducted. Else why would she leave? What would you like to do about the matter?"

She stared at him until all traces of uncertainty vanished. Then she faced her brother. "Summon Mrs Wilmslow. She will accompany me when I interview all the staff and search Frances' room. You may assist me, too, Hamilton. A task shared is a task halved, and this is your house."

Clever.

While she kept the earl and the housekeeper busy, he would rifle through the lord's armoire. Perhaps venture up to the attic. And he would talk to Bower. Maybe he knew something about the maid's disappearance.

"Very well," Hamilton agreed, looking pleased to have something to distract him from his meddling in-laws. "We'll begin at once."

Lady Mersham clapped her hands, her mood much improved. "Excellent, I shall keep you company, Mr Grayson. Do you ride?"

Cursed saints!

Why did he feel the question carried a sexual connotation?

"Of course." Whatever his reply, she would suggest a reason to spend time alone together. That said, he was an excellent horseman and could easily outride her. Although a gentleman would not leave a lady floundering behind.

Grayson smiled to himself.

Thank God he was a bastard.

CHAPTER 9

OLIVIA HAD BARELY HAD A MOMENT TO HERSELF SINCE Bickford's revelation yesterday. The servants knew nothing about Frances' disappearance and had sat gaping at her with a mix of fear and wonder. Hamilton used the opportunity to interrogate her, hence why she had left him in his study and gone in search of Grayson.

She found him in the library, though the door was locked, and he made her answer personal questions before agreeing to let her enter.

"How many reasons did I give for wanting to marry you?" he called from behind his wooden barricade.

She smiled to herself. "Four. Now let me in."

"Name the last reason, and I shall."

She did not have to scour her mind. His words had left an indelible mark on her memory. Since kissing him, she had thought of little else.

"You said you felt drawn to me in a way you couldn't explain."

The thought sent her heart racing. There were things

about their relationship she couldn't explain, either. Why she felt more than at ease in his company. Why every instinct said she could trust a man she hardly knew. Why her body shivered with excitement whenever their eyes met.

"And what was your reply?"

"That the feeling was not mutual." Yet it was the worst lie she had ever told. There had been an instant attraction. And a woman who kissed her husband with unbridled passion surely felt more than indifference.

The key clicked in the lock, and the man she grew more attached to by the hour opened the door and peered into the hall. "Hurry." He pulled her into the room and locked them inside.

A giggle escaped her. "I pray Hamilton doesn't know you're hiding in his library, searching through his things."

His arm circled her waist, and she placed her hands on his chest for stability. "I'm not here on a mission to solve the case. It's more a means of self-preservation."

"Ah. Anna did ask if I had seen you," she teased. Anna was more interested in Grayson than answering questions about her missing maid. "I believe she wants you to join her on a stroll to the village. She said you looked lonely and in need of company."

Was he lonely?

He never spoke about himself.

Her welfare was his only concern.

"I need your company." His breath breezed over her lips in a whisper of a kiss that left her wanting. "I should have agreed to help question the staff and search for Frances. Let Hamilton see to his wife's insatiable needs."

Olivia would have preferred spending the time with Grayson than answering her brother's probing questions. They might have halved the task and dealt with the servants in a matter of hours. But Hamilton was like her shadow, insisting they went everywhere together, stretching the duty over two days.

Did he fear what the servants might reveal in private?

Did they know why Frances was missing?

"In the process, I have learnt a few things about Hamilton's life." He had been reluctant to say anything, so she had bribed him and swapped stories, told him about her benevolent employer. Most of it was true. "He had to marry Anna because she was with child. He held an affection for her when we were young, but my father hoped he would marry someone from a titled family."

"Your father would turn in his grave if he knew you'd married an earl's misbegotten son." His tone was that of amused mockery, yet she suspected the thought pained him.

"Father would have seen beyond the circumstances of your birth. You're more of a gentleman than any man I know. You proved that yesterday, during the argument in the drawing room."

He inhaled as if breathing in the compliment, letting it infuse his entire being. Then a sinful smile formed on his lips. "I'm no gentleman, love. I'm a scoundrel who prays you'll sleep without your nightgown tonight. A man who can barely keep his lust on a leash."

"Be patient with me," she said softly, despite being overwhelmed by this irresistible attraction.

"When it comes to you, I'm a walking monument to patience. All the good things in life are worth waiting for." He pressed his hot mouth to her neck, a sensual kiss above the silk ribbon, a kiss that made her heart flutter and legs tremble. "I am at your beck and call, Olivia. When you want me, you'll need to tell me."

He released her and stepped back to a respectable

distance. She thought about grabbing his cravat and capturing his mouth, but he said, "So, Tobias is six years old yet has no siblings. Has Hamilton sired children elsewhere? With a mistress or lover?"

"Not that I'm aware." That was all she could think to say because her mind invented a story of a married couple making love in a locked library.

"Then Tobias may not be your brother's son," he said quite matter-of-factly. "An earl would want at least an heir and a spare."

Olivia blinked. A little amazed he could continue as if he had not wound the coil of intimacy tightly. "Can a man ever know for certain? As we've not met the boy, it's impossible to tell."

Grayson rubbed his jaw thoughtfully. "Perhaps that's why the Stowes left Tobias at Crundale. They feared we may ask questions."

She shrugged. "Or because they love their grandson and believe his parents are the epitome of everything immoral. I assume Anna propositioned you and won't take no for an answer."

"It's evident she thrives on men's attention, though I'm not sure she wants to indulge in anything more than flirtation. She was quick to say I had my brother's impressive shoulders, though no man wants to be likened to a pompous prig."

"Hamilton said his friends from Cambridge came to my funeral. What if Blake is the boy's father and he refused to accept his responsibilities? What if that's why Hamilton killed him?"

Instinct said her brother lacked the strength to kill a man with his bare hands. Cowards hired thugs to get rid of problems. They hid amid the trees to fire a fatal shot.

"Or George Kane might be the boy's father," she added,

though it was all supposition. It would be impossible to know for sure. An earl was unlikely to cast doubt over his only son's lineage. "Perhaps the servants know something. Hence why Hamilton insisted we interview them together."

They had seemed nervous around her.

Then again, she *had* risen from the grave.

Grayson thought for a moment. "We need to search the study tonight. See if we can find a letter or document, a reason why Hamilton would want to kill my brother."

They had attempted to search the study last night, but they had found Hamilton ensconced inside, hiding from his wife, drunk on brandy. They'd had no choice but to join him and listen to his complaints about the Stowes.

"We should wait until the witching hour before venturing downstairs. Perhaps take it in turns to sleep." It was easier said than done when lying next to a naked man with a body as warm as hell's flames. A man who watched her intently every second of the day.

"Or we could find a reason to stay awake." He offered a wolfish grin. "I could woo you with poetry or something equally stimulating."

She bit back a smile. "I am rather fond of the seventeenth-century poets. Milton could keep us entertained for hours."

Teasing a man with her husband's sharp wit proved futile. "I was thinking more along the lines of Marvell's *His Coy Mistress*. It's a classic poem of seduction."

Olivia braced her hand on her hip. "You mean to tempt me by reminding me that I am getting old? Perhaps if you convinced me I was in the bloom of youth, I might be persuaded to behave recklessly."

"Is it reckless to make love to one's husband?" he pondered aloud.

They both laughed, which was indeed a reckless thing to

do when in enemy territory. Especially when their nemesis prowled the hall and took to rattling the door handle.

"Mr Grayson!" Anna called, attempting to gain access to the room. "Are you in there? The door is locked." She lowered her voice. "Let me in. I'm alone."

"Stone the crows," Grayson whispered, "Quickly. Pull a few strands of hair loose. Let her think I've been ravishing you on the sofa. Let her know we're madly in love, and you're the object of my desire."

Finding the situation annoying and amusing in equal measure, Olivia pulled a few pins from her hair and let the curls tumble down. Still, she was of a mind to scold her sister-in-law for her unsolicited attentions.

"Mr Grayson?" came Anna's concerned call. Then she hammered on the door in frustration. "Why won't you let me in? Are you unwell?"

"What in God's name is all the noise?" Hamilton had joined the fray. "Why are you banging on the library door when you should be at Crundale, discovering why my son has not returned home?"

"I—I heard noises and fear Mr Grayson is inside and has lost the key. Or he might have fallen and hurt his head."

"Grayson!" Hamilton cried impatiently.

"Just a moment!" Grayson assessed her with unnerving scrutiny. "You don't look like a woman who's been ravished by her husband."

"What shall I do to convince them? Yank down my stockings and hike up my skirts?" When he looked to be considering the matter, she added, "I speak in jest."

"You look too composed. Had I ravished you, you'd be near mindless with lust, so drunk with it you'd struggle to stand."

"You certainly know how to create a vivid picture."

"Grayson!" Hamilton did not sound pleased.

"Give me a moment."

"Why don't we just open the door?" she muttered.

"Because he will think we've been snooping and will watch us like a hawk. There's nothing for it. I'm going to kiss you quickly. Say now if you object."

"No, I don't object, but—" was all she managed to say before her husband's mouth was on hers.

It was not a chaste kiss by any standards.

It was not a gentle exploration either.

It was hot and wild and so fast it stole her breath. She had to grip his coat to keep her balance. He was equally unsteady because he moulded his hands to her buttocks and crushed her to his hard body.

Lord have mercy!

The lustful movements of his mouth proved hypnotic. She found herself swept up in the intoxicating rhythm. Her heart pounded in unison with their thrusting tongues—faster, more insistent.

"Mr Grayson! Open the door!"

It took immense effort not to shout "bugger off" but nothing would make her drag her mouth from his now. Despite marrying for the wrong reasons, these intimate moments made everything feel right.

Grayson broke contact but was panting like he had run to the gatehouse and back. "Push me away before I reach under your skirts and take liberties."

"Is touching one's wife taking liberties?" she said, near desperate to ease the ache between her thighs.

"Yes, if you knew of all the ways I want to touch you."

"Yet I don't know what's real or what's part of the game."

He captured her hand and let her feel the solid length straining against his breeches. "This is real. This is how badly I want you."

The feel of him growing against her palm proved a potent

aphrodisiac. More so when she caressed him and saw his handsome features straining in pleasure.

His mouth came crashing down on hers again, a frantic melding that did nothing to satiate the hunger. The maddening pulses of her sex were like the loud beats of a drum—overpowering her thoughts, making her deaf to the inner voice that said this was sheer folly.

Not quite deaf enough.

"Grayson, open the damn door before I take my boot to the thing."

"Hell," Grayson whispered as he tore his mouth from hers. With a playful chuck of her chin, he said, "We shall continue our exploration into the delights of marriage soon." Then he strode to the door and turned the key in the lock.

Hamilton and Anna burst into the room as if expecting to find a scene of pure carnage. They took one look at Olivia and were suddenly drenched in a shower of embarrassment.

Hamilton cursed beneath his breath.

Anna looked practically green with envy.

"Forgive me," Grayson said, though he sounded far from sorry. "I was distracted and couldn't find the impetus needed to reach the door."

Hamilton firmed his jaw. "Next time you seek a diversion, I suggest using your private chamber."

"A couple in love might easily find themselves caught unawares," she dared to say, knowing lust held her and Grayson in its spell.

"Perhaps," her brother mumbled. He glanced at his wife as if love were something unpalatable. "Most men would show a little restraint," he added before capturing his wife's arm and striding from the room.

"I am not most men," Grayson called.

No. Alexander Grayson was unlike any man she had ever met.

"OLIVIA? WAKE UP, LOVE." GRAYSON'S WORDS ECHOED IN her head.

She snuggled closer to him, found she liked the feel of her breasts squashed against his chest.

"Olivia." He brushed her hair from her face and kissed her forehead. "If we're to search the study, we must go now before the maids wake."

The thought of moving tore a groan from her lips.

Grayson chuckled. "Once we've searched the study, we can return home," he said by way of an inducement. "Then, we shall spend all day abed. Then, you won't have to sleep in a nightgown."

The thought dragged her from the soothing arms of half-slumber.

They had grown comfortable with each other while at Mersham Hall. They had kissed again last night while strolling in the garden. Each time, she gave a little more of herself. And though it was evident he wanted to take her to bed, he was always considerate and patient.

A lady might easily come to love a man like that. Yet while they were growing physically close, while he helped her speak about the terrible event in the King's Wood, he rarely spoke about himself.

"Tell me something about you," she said when he climbed out of bed to get dressed in the dark. "What do you do with your time?"

"I spend most days in my study."

"Doing what exactly?"

"Dealing with business matters." He poured water into the washbowl and splashed his face. "I own numerous proper-ties in town. And I'm a partner in a shipping empire that imports goods from Italy and India. I own some of the largest warehouses on the London docks."

"I'd like to learn more about it when we return home."

He nodded.

Most men would have refused to entertain the idea.

Being somewhat used to his nakedness, she slipped out of bed and met him at the washstand. "Are you a White's man or a Boodle's buck?"

"Neither." He dried his face with a towel. "I would rather drink with working men at the Dog and Gun than take brandy with a popinjay and hear him bemoan his new tailor."

There was something attractive about a man who knew his own mind. A man who sneered at conformity. Perhaps that's why she had a sudden urge to touch him.

"Do you have any family, any aunts or cousins?" she said, cupping his upper arm when, in truth, she wished to run her hands all over his hard body.

She felt him stiffen, felt the air turn chilly.

"No, not on my mother's side. My father's family refuse to acknowledge me." His ice-cold tone said their rejection had hurt him deeply, cut to the bone.

It was perhaps unwise to press him further, but this conversation proved more intimate than kissing.

"They take issue with the fact your parents weren't married?"

"They take issue with the fact my mother was married to another man. Her husband was presumed dead and, to this day, has never returned home."

Sensing a shift in his mood, an undercurrent of hostility, she decided to avoid more questions about his mother for now. "What do you do at Christmas?"

He narrowed his gaze as if it were a ridiculous question. "I spend the day alone, as many people do."

She had to swallow past the lump in her throat. Her heart ached to think of him sitting silently, having no one to dine with or join him in a toast. It occurred to her that Mr Daventry excelled at matchmaking. She had spent too much time alone. But the future didn't have to be bleak. What was to stop her having ten children with this man and creating a loving family home?

First, they needed to consummate their union.

Then pray lust turned into something lasting.

"Now you will have to put up with me drinking too much sherry," she said, hoping they were not living in separate houses or continents come Christmas, "and me being appalling at charades."

His mouth curled into a warm smile. "I can't imagine you being appalling at anything, but I look forward to all the ways you might amuse me."

She stared at him, a little lost in his magnificence, a little giddy from the mere thought of what the next few weeks might bring.

"When we return home, I think we should move beyond kissing." Like a wanton, she stroked his bare chest. "We should—"

"Hush, love." He pressed his finger to her lips. "Don't tell me now. Not when I'm naked. Not when I need your soothing touch. Else I might say to hell with our investigation and take full advantage of my wife's sudden eagerness to please."

Heat pooled low in her belly.

But she ignored lust's persistent tug. She did not want to make love in a room tainted by past memories.

He breathed deeply. "Get dressed. Get dressed behind the screen. We shall continue this conversation tonight once we're alone in our bedchamber."

Desire was like a devil in one's head, whispering for her to caress his body, stroke his manhood, feed her addiction. Yet the pressing need to search her brother's study cut through the chaos.

They dressed quickly, lit the lamp and carried it downstairs to Hamilton's study, relieved to find the room empty.

"Shall I search the drawers?" She pushed aside numerous papers and placed the lamp on the desk. "Do you suppose Hamilton owns a book like Blake's?"

"One would presume so." Grayson removed a leather-bound volume from the walnut bookcase and flicked through the pages. "Let's hope we find it, and it contains more than a list of members and their vices."

Olivia recalled what was written in Blake's book. On the page dedicated to Leviathan were notes explaining why her brother might claim envy's crown. He was envious of how close Olivia was to their father, of her intelligence and kind heart. He had called upon Leviathan's strength to help his father see that he was the true heir, not a slip of a girl who knew nothing of the world.

The first drawer contained an accounts ledger and a pile of bills for the farrier, the chandler and Anna's modiste in Mayfair. Another had spare ink and quills, a heraldic seal stamp and sticks of vermillion wax.

The bottom drawer was locked.

She rooted through the other drawers looking for the key, found a silver letter opener, knelt and used it to probe the lock.

"You need a set of skeleton keys," Grayson said, joining her at the desk. "And I doubt a man with wicked secrets would hide the key in here. Hamilton probably wears it around his neck."

"I'm merely examining the opening." Olivia removed two

pins from her hair and started bending them into shape. "Mr Hewson taught me how to use hairpins to trip the mechanism."

Grayson crouched beside her. "Who the devil is Mr Hewson?"

"The gardener at Middlecroft." Who proved to be another traitor in the midst. "Before becoming Mrs Montague's companion, I worked in Chesterfield for six months as a governess to a gentleman's daughter."

After the dreadful business there, she had been glad to leave England and venture to warmer climates. Yet the nightmares always followed her, no matter how far she roamed.

"Why only six months?"

"Because Marina was abducted." She recalled the night with perfect clarity. Woken by a disturbing dream, something had drawn her along the dark corridor to check on her charge. "Her father was without funds, so her uncle paid the ransom."

Grayson breathed deeply. "It must have brought back terrible memories of your abduction. I pray the child was returned unharmed."

"Mr Hewson came to me with an incredulous tale, and we sought to prove his theory, hence why we rummaged through the master's private things." Much like they were doing now.

"Do you mean to keep me in suspense?" he teased. "Though I suspect the father kidnapped his own daughter to extort money from his kin."

"Precisely. He drugged Marina so she wouldn't remember. I went to her uncle with proof, and they found her alone in a house a mere mile away. The family reconciled their differences, and I was dismissed. Mr Hewson denied any culpability and kept his position."

It had been a hard lesson.

A servant was dispensable.

A servant could trust no one.

"They told you it wasn't your place to interfere in family affairs," Grayson said as if he had stood in the stuffy room and witnessed both men tearing her to shreds. "It wasn't your place to judge the morals of your betters."

"Yes. Exactly that."

"I was told a similar thing once."

"By whom?"

"Blake's mother, Lady Sturrock. I said her son was a disgrace to our father's name. An earl should behave with some dignity, not whore about town and fritter away his inheritance. She said I was the only disgrace and threw me out."

Through no fault of their own, they had both been mistreated.

She gathered her hairpins in one hand and cupped his cheek. "There is nothing dishonourable about you, Grayson."

He held her gaze for a few heartbeats, then captured her hand and pressed a lingering kiss to her palm, another to her wrist. "I'm tempted to forget about Blake. Tempted to leave all this behind and focus on making something of our marriage. Yet it must be the honourable streak in me that demands I make someone pay for hurting you."

Miss Trimble would suggest they run and hide. Despite appearing composed and in control, she let fear rule her heart. The innocent Lady Olivia was dead. Mrs Grayson, on the other hand, had gained more than her husband's name. She had gained his confidence.

"We will deal with the past and put it to bed. Then we will never think of it again." She offered a reassuring smile. "The Graysons do not run from their troubles. It's a motto by which we will raise our children should we discover we're compatible."

A sudden click cut through the chill air.

A pistol being cocked.

An icy shudder ran through her veins.

"I'm glad you've decided to stay," Hamilton said from somewhere in the room. "Now tell me what the hell you're doing in my desk."

CHAPTER 10

Hell and damnation!

Grayson clutched Olivia's hand as they both came to their feet. Panic danced like the devil inside. Not because he feared the fool would shoot. Hamilton's hand shook so violently he was liable to drop the pistol. But because he suddenly realised he had something to lose, a reason to live.

"Explain yourselves!" Hamilton snapped. He stood hidden in the shadows, and Grayson cursed himself for not having the foresight to lock the damn door.

"Would you believe I came to look at my favourite painting?" Olivia gestured to the image of a black stallion hanging on the far wall. "That I happened to lose a hairpin, and Grayson agreed to help me find it?"

"No more than you believe I would shoot my own sister."

It was the worst thing he could have said.

Olivia reacted instantly, her mocking snort echoing in the dim room. "That's the problem, Brother. I lost faith in you when your men snatched me from the lane and beat me black and blue."

Mother of all saints!

This was not the time to accuse the man of murder!

"My men?" Hamilton jerked his head as if reeling from a slap. "You think I had something to do with what happened? That I would hurt you, hurt that poor woman?" He stepped closer, the desk being the only barrier to Grayson grabbing the pistol and ramming his fist down his brother-in-law's throat.

"You're no fool," she said, though Grayson begged to differ. "Ask yourself why I never came home. Ask yourself why I am here now."

Grayson faced her. They had no choice now but to hit the buffoon with a list of his offences. "We may as well tell him everything. If he shoots, we'll know he's guilty. If he lays down his weapon, we might at least hear some semblance of the truth." He spoke in the blithe manner of a man who cared for no one. It was perhaps the best performance of his life.

Olivia nodded, then turned to her brother. "You were the only one to benefit from my death. The thugs said you needed the means to identify the body. It's the only reason they ripped our mother's ring from my finger."

The blood drained from Hamilton's face, though he already looked drawn and haggard. He fixed them with a glassy stare before firming his grip on the pistol.

"Don't think you can fire and live to tell the tale," Grayson growled, calculating whether he could vault the desk before Hamilton pulled the trigger. "Before I draw my last breath, I shall make sure you rot in hell."

"Then I shall release the hammer and lay down my weapon." He did exactly that, placing it gently on the table as if it were a sleeping babe likely to cry at the merest sound.

Olivia gave a gasp of relief.

"What you say is true." Hamilton raised his hands in mock surrender. "Father changed his will and left me every-thing. When they came to tell me they had found your body,

I did demand proof. But despite seeing the evidence, I refused to believe I had lost you, too."

Olivia gripped the edge of the desk and leaned forward. "Who else would benefit from my death? Why would someone want to hurt a woman in such a despicable way? It makes no sense."

"Do I look like a man who would murder his sister?" Hamilton threw open his arms by way of a challenge. "Have I ever given you cause to doubt me?"

The earl had walked into a trap of his own making. They had proof he despised his sister. That envy flowed like blood in his veins. That he had joined a stupid club because he had wicked intentions.

Olivia went to speak but hesitated.

"Tell him," Grayson snapped, knowing her loyalty to her husband was the only reason she guarded her tongue. "Tell him we had another motive for coming to Mersham Hall. Tell him how we suspect he is guilty of two other crimes."

"This is ludicrous!" Hamilton braced his hands on the desk and glared at his sister through bloodshot eyes. "I don't know what lies your husband has told you, but it's evident he despises Sturrock's friends. Perhaps he has his own motive for forcing you to come here. Ask him to tell you what he did to Lord Elderton."

The devious bastard!

Grayson clenched his fists, ready to thump the fop. "Elderton deserved more than a broken nose." The lord's devil moniker was Asmodeus. Lust was his sin.

Olivia's head shot in his direction. "But we spoke about Lord Elderton at length during the journey to Kent. You never mentioned an altercation."

"It was an argument over a mistress," the earl was quick to say, icy contempt flashing in his eyes. "It's evident a woman in your position had limited choices, but surely that tells you all you need to know about the rogue you married."

Curse the devil to Hades!

Grayson wasted no time offering an explanation. "Olivia, it was two years ago. Mrs Walker was no longer my mistress but remained a good friend. Elderton forced himself upon her. I would have called the scoundrel out, but Mrs Walker did not want to make an enemy of the *ton*."

Tears welled in her eyes, and she clutched her abdomen. "Then why did you not mention it? Why keep me in the dark?"

"I thought it irrelevant. And I swore an oath never to speak of it again." He was a man of his word. Surely that counted for something.

Without warning, Olivia grabbed the pistol from the desk. She shuffled back and took aim. "It's relevant in that your wife has spent seven years not knowing who to trust."

"You can trust me," Grayson reaffirmed.

Surely she knew that by now.

She shrugged. "Mr Daventry said as much, and he is never wrong. But then one wonders why he was so keen to support this union."

"I don't give a damn about Daventry's motives. Trust me because you know I lack the capacity to be devious. Trust me because you know I would never hurt you."

She pointed the pistol at her brother. "Logic says you're a liar. For years I feared you would find me, yet seeing you has changed everything. You don't look like the black-hearted beast of my nightmares. And now instinct and logic are waging war, and I don't know whose side I am on."

Hamilton clasped his hands together in prayer. "Olivia, I swear on our parents' graves, I had nothing to do with what happened to you in the woods. You must believe me."

"And yet I've read the words written in Blake's book," she

spat. "I know of your silly Seven Devils club, know you were granted the name Leviathan because you were so envious of me."

Hamilton's chin dropped.

"You killed Blake," Grayson said, feeling immense relief at being able to accuse the villain. "They found a picture of Leviathan in his coat pocket. Just like the one the coroner found in George Kane's coat when he attended him in the King's Wood."

Hamilton scrubbed his hand down his face. "Mother Mary! Why would I leave evidence pointing to me as the killer? Someone wants to make it look like I'm guilty."

Daventry had stressed the same point when advising they consider the evidence with an open mind. Grayson wasn't sure why, but like Olivia, seeing the cowardly fop made him suspect someone else was to blame.

"If you're innocent, open this drawer and let us examine the contents. Prove you have nothing to hide."

Without hesitation, Hamilton rounded the desk. "It's locked because I don't want anyone seeing what's inside," he said, pulling a brass key from his waistcoat pocket. "It's locked because my son refuses to do as he's told and a curious mind can be deadly."

With shaky fingers, he unlocked the drawer and yanked it open. Glass bottles clinked against more glass bottles, and Hamilton pulled one out and held it up as if it were Jesus' chalice.

Grayson squinted in the muted light and read the label. "It's laudanum. You have enough in the drawer to kill your entire household."

"Do you know how many times I have sat here and considered consuming every last drop? More than a man can count."

"Why?" Olivia whispered.

Hamilton snorted. "My parents are dead. My sister was found hanged in the King's Wood. Two friends were killed. And my wife is a whore, parading as a lady."

A heavy silence descended.

The mantel clock ticked like a death knell.

"Yes," Olivia said solemnly. "I can see why you would seek to escape this world." She placed the pistol on the desk. "In not coming home, I have added to your burden."

"We could have resolved this matter years ago. Tried to find the real person responsible." Hamilton pulled the stopper from the brown bottle, swigged the liquid and gave a weary sigh. "I couldn't sleep tonight. The Stowes say my son is sick and cannot return home for a week. I would march over there, but my wife has told them of my habit, and that is why they seek to protect Tobias."

Grayson studied the earl and had to acknowledge the man was struggling to keep his wits.

Hamilton returned the bottle to the drawer and removed a letter. "I received this after Sturrock was killed. It may go some way to proving I had nothing to do with his death."

Olivia took the letter and peeled back the folds. She read silently before revealing the contents. "*An eye for an eye is the saying, though Sturrock was the first of many. I mean to make you pay.*" She looked at her brother. "You did not think to go to London and deliver it to the coroner?"

"I thought it a prank."

"And you have no idea who sent it?"

"No."

"What about your brethren from the Seven Devils?" Grayson wondered at past grievances. The men had known each other for years. Did one of them have a secret grudge against Hamilton? "Are you all as close as your wife claims?"

"We've not met since Kane was shot and killed last year."

The comment raised an important question. "Bromley

says he aimed high, that the shot came from the woods. Can you attest to the fact?"

Hamilton glanced briefly at his boots. "I wasn't there. I refused to be party to their petty squabbles. Still, we assumed it was just a means to provoke one another and so stayed abed."

"We?"

"Besides myself, Newell and Featherly remained here."

According to Blake's book, Featherly's sin was sloth, so it came as no surprise he neglected to join the duelling party. Though Newell was not listed as a member of their select little club.

"Robert Newell?" Olivia said with some surprise. Clearly, she knew the gentleman well enough to use his given name. "Robert Newell was at your house party the day Mr Kane died?"

Hamilton shrugged. "Yes, he was here as part of an initiation." He seemed reluctant to say more, but Grayson fixed him with a stare to rival Medusa and so he added, "He wished to take Sturrock's place and join our club, though after the shooting we all decided to disband."

"And you've not met since?" he asked. Daventry spoke of quarterly meetings at a place near Seven Dials. It was unlike him to relay inaccurate information.

"No. I have invited the men here numerous times, but with two members dead, the rest are too nervous to be seen together."

So Lady Mersham had told the truth.

Grayson glanced at Olivia, who seemed lost in thought. "Is there anything I should know about Robert Newell?"

She blinked rapidly. "Not really. After his first visit to Mersham Hall, he wrote me a rather romantic letter. You know the sort. One's eyes twinkle like stars in the night sky. One's lips are like forbidden fruit."

Oh he knew the sort.

Indeed, jealousy possessed him like a demon spirit. A being sent to create havoc with his mind, to torture him with wicked images of his wife loving another man.

"You never mentioned it." Hamilton sounded most displeased. "I would have spoken to him, explained it was inappropriate. Thrown him out had he persisted with his forced attentions."

"Hamilton, our mother had died. Father was not long for this world. Mr Newell's letters brought light relief at a difficult time."

"Letters?" Hamilton said before Grayson found his voice.

"He wrote eight in total." Her derisive laugh did little to calm the beast writhing in Grayson's veins. "Lord Elderton and Lord Kipling both made inappropriate suggestions while visiting. What did you expect? I was a young woman alone in a house full of men."

Hamilton cursed beneath his breath. "I presumed they would have respect for the fact you're my sister. Not treat you like a harlot in a bordello."

"And you did not think to mention this while we were examining Blake's book?" Grayson said, barely able to control his temper. Indeed, he felt like grabbing the pistol and threatening every man and his dog.

"In all honesty, I did not think it relevant."

"It's relevant in that a man consumed with jealousy is capable of the darkest sin." He took a calming breath. "Some men refuse to take no for an answer. Some men would rather kill the object of their desire than see her with another man."

Hamilton raised his arms as if praising the Lord. "Did I not say I was innocent of any wrongdoing? You should be looking at other motives, not trying to conjure evidence against your brother."

Matters had become more complex than expected.

Grayson had come to Mersham Hall to prove the earl was a cold-blooded killer. Now he didn't know what the hell to believe.

"I should have broken Elderton's jaw and his fingers," Grayson complained. He would stalk the rake through the shadows and finish what he started. As for Robert Newell, he would gather more information from his wife before deciding on a fitting punishment.

"I forgive you for breaking his nose," Hamilton added, sounding more relaxed than he had in days. "Believe me when I say I shall strive to prove my innocence. I shall tell you everything I know."

One might think the earl's impassioned speech was a means to mislead them. Hamilton Durrant was still a suspect.

Grayson thought to raise the issue of Tobias' parentage. And the need to ask about the Knights of the Seven Devils, to learn how Blake had slandered him, had been the most prominent thought in his mind until now.

Now he was intent on pursuing one line of enquiry.

How his wife felt about Robert bloody Newell!

"We're leaving for London come sunrise," he said, keen to be away from Mersham Hall so he could think. Olivia was right. No one here could be trusted. "I suggest you focus on finding Frances. Maids flee out of desperation." Mostly when randy masters sought to take advantage.

Hamilton's gaze flitted left and right. He knew something. "I can but question the staff again. Perhaps my wife knows why Frances left and is reluctant to say."

Reluctance was not a word in Lady Mersham's vocabulary.

"No doubt His Majesty's coroner will want answers when he arrives to exhume the body," Olivia said with a subtle dose of spite. After seven years spent blaming her brother, she would find it hard to take him at his word. "You should receive legal documents within the next few days, and a letter explaining how he means to proceed."

Hamilton gulped. "The King is sending his own man?"

"The King wishes the matter dealt with swiftly," she replied. "The coroner will see that all those in Godmersham are questioned."

"Good Lord." The earl glanced at his laudanum drawer as if he might empty the bottles into a barrel and dive in headfirst.

Indeed, after repeating his intention to find Frances and telling them everything he knew, which amounted to nothing damning, the fop ushered them from the room.

"You don't think he means to kill himself with laudanum, do you?" Olivia whispered after closing the study door.

"Not if he's innocent."

Hamilton had asked them to return with news and so meant to drown his sorrows, not consume a lethal dose of the tincture.

"Although it's fair to say someone staying in this house did shoot George Kane," Grayson continued. "While looking inside the book of mythology on Hamilton's shelf, I found something incriminating."

"What?"

"The black and white drawing of Leviathan is missing."

CHAPTER 11

THEY LEFT MERSHAM HALL AT DAWN, BUT NOT BEFORE venturing to the study to check on Hamilton. Olivia had found him asleep on the sofa, snoring loud enough to wake the dead. Thankfully, he'd left an empty decanter on the floor, not a pile of brown bottles.

The instant tug on her heartstrings left her silently cursing. Only a fool would believe he spoke in earnest. Yet she couldn't help but pity the feeble boy who had grown into an equally feeble man.

Although any man would appear weak next to Alexander Grayson. Except when her husband was suffering from a rare bout of melancholy. She had presumed it would pass once they left Mersham Hall. But fifteen minutes into their journey, his countenance had not improved.

Much like the day they journeyed to Kent, he was quiet, pensive. He had been that way since she failed to mention Mr Newell's letters, so it had to be the cause of his disquiet.

"Shall I tell you why I agreed to marry you?" she said, keen to bring an end to the uncomfortable silence.

Grayson looked at her. The flash of torment in his eyes

made her heart clench. "You married me because you were tired of running. And you needed help to find the pot of gold at the end of the rainbow."

He referred to her quest for peace.

But something else had given her the courage to take a risk.

"I married you because you said we were both mature enough to work through any issues. Yet you failed to mention you would sulk for hours before having an honest conversation."

He jerked his head at her bluntness, for she had clearly hit a nerve. "Men do not sulk, they brood."

"Oh! No doubt it's an important distinction. Still, as a mature man, you should have the courage of your convictions and say what is on your mind."

He straightened, gathering his arsenal. "You lied to me."

"Lied?" It was a rogue shot. One she had not anticipated. "I have spoken nothing but the truth. Yes, I might have failed to mention certain things,"—namely Mr Newell's love letters—"but that is not the same as telling a blatant lie."

"You told me your heart was not engaged."

"It isn't." He stole a bit of it every time he kissed her.

"Yet your eyes brightened at the mention of Robert Newell."

She couldn't help but laugh. This was ridiculous.

"From surprise. I care nothing for Mr Newell. He asked me to elope with him, and I respectfully declined." In truth, she found his attentions unnerving. "I never wrote to him. I never encouraged him. Yes, it was flattering at first, but I did not sleep with his letters beneath my pillow. I tossed them into the hearth and watched them burn."

Amid the pregnant silence, they locked gazes.

Her pulse thumped a steady beat in her throat while she waited patiently for his reply.

Having considered his position, Grayson sighed, waved his white flag and surrendered. "I cannot explain these shifts in my mood. Jealousy is a trait I despise, yet I'm likely to throttle the next man who looks at you."

Her breath caught in her throat. Did this glimpse of possessiveness mean something? Was it a beacon of hope on a long, dark road?

"It's to be expected," she said, attempting to access the logical part of her brain, not the part that turned to mush when he showed her the slightest affection. "We hardly know one another. Every day, we learn something new. Every day, we grow a little closer."

Yes, they were bound to have these spats.

Disagreements brought a greater understanding. The best way to approach the situation was to acknowledge his pain.

"Grayson, I can see why you would think the worst when you have spent a lifetime suffering disappointment. But we must be honest about our feelings if we're to avoid any confusion."

His gaze slid over her, and his mouth softened. "You're right. I should have spoken directly instead of making assumptions."

"Doubtless we shall learn these things in time."

He scanned their surroundings. "We should take advantage of our current situation. Use the next six hours to know each other better."

Adept at reading his less than subtle subtext, she smiled. "At one time, our definitions of knowing each other differed. Now I believe our thoughts are aligned." She could no more deny herself the pleasure of his kisses than she could deny her lungs air.

"Are you telling me you seek a pleasurable distraction, Mrs Grayson?" He rubbed his solid thighs as if he found the idea arousing.

"Perhaps." But she would not forgo an opportunity to ask personal questions. "First, tell me about the worst day of your life. You already know mine."

He inhaled sharply, closing the shutters so she could not peer beyond his indifferent facade. "It's too long ago to remember."

Being a master of evasive techniques, she would not let him escape so easily. "Losing your father must have been difficult. He was the only family member who cared for you."

He swallowed, his throat working tirelessly as if to dislodge the lump obstructing his airways. "Now you're suffering from my affliction. Don't make assumptions."

Confused, she frowned. "You didn't love your father?"

Fear raised its head. Did he lack the capacity to love anyone? Lust would not sustain them through the harsh seasons of their lives.

"He did not love me."

She sat dumbfounded, failing to understand how anyone could not appreciate his merits.

"He loved my mother obsessively. There was nothing left for anyone else. Why do you think Blake despised me? He made foolish assumptions, too. Because I inherited a large portion of my father's wealth, he believed I was the favourite son." He sounded angry and bitter, yet they were just ways of dealing with the hurt. "The truth is, he promised my mother he would protect me. The Earl of Sturrock would not dishonour the woman he loved by breaking a vow. Not when he had already ruined her good name."

Now she understood why he thought love was overrated. She couldn't imagine not feeling cherished by her parents. When she tried to picture him as a boy, she realised his life was a blank canvas. Had Lady Sturrock taken him in? Had he grown up with Blake?

"Where did you live as a child?"

He closed his eyes briefly before answering. "At school."

"At school? You did not go home?"

"Hardly ever. I reminded my father of what he'd lost."

Tears welled, but she blinked them away.

The last thing he needed was her pity.

"My housemaster kept me company during the holidays," he added. "It wasn't Eton or Harrow but a place in the wet and windy wilds of North Yorkshire."

"Too far for anyone to visit," she managed to say.

"I spent many summers alone until a new boy came." He spoke a little easier now. "Lucius Daventry was a few years my junior, but we became friends, spurred each other on to be better men than our fathers. He invites me to Bronygarth every Christmas, but I cannot bear to be reminded of those lonely years."

"I'm sorry," she said.

"It is not your fault."

"Still, I wish it had been different for you."

"But then I wouldn't be the man you see today." He glanced at the window as if watching a sad memory play out beyond the glass. "I planned to squander my inheritance. Put paid to my father's dreams and aspirations and punish him the only way I knew how. But Daventry persuaded me to look to the future, not the past."

Mr Daventry was the wisest of men.

Many people owed him a huge debt of gratitude.

"Money alone is not enough to change the world," she said. The kindest people were often penniless. "A person must be strong of heart and mind. Determined. Courageous. You are rich in all ways except one. You need to stop thinking you're unworthy of love. Pretending love is something to be reviled."

Was that why he had married her? Because he trusted Lucius Daventry? Because he feared other women would want more than he could give, whereas she wanted nothing more than vengeance?

"Enough of this morbid topic."

He had revealed more than she'd hoped, but she was equally eager to lighten the mood. "Tell me about the best day of your life."

His gaze raked boldly over her. "It's the day I journeyed to London with my wife. I was desperate to make love to her, but vowed to wait until we were in the comfort of our bed."

The prospect of what tonight might bring had her body tightening with anticipation. "But how is that your best day if you were left unsatisfied?"

The rogue shrugged out of his coat. "While I spent six hours consumed with unsated lust, my wife came twice in a moving carriage."

Olivia touched her hand to her throat to calm her racing pulse, not hide her scar. "And how did you master such a daring feat?"

"I asked her if she wanted to feel my mouth caressing her body. Her blue eyes glazed, and she said—"

"Yes."

The corners of his lips curled into a languid smile. "And so I told her to draw her skirts up to her waist. She obliged, so slowly I was hard in seconds."

"She must have been eager for your touch."

"More than I could have hoped." He fixed her to the seat with his intense green gaze, watched her slowly unbutton her pelisse and slide her skirts up past her lace garters.

"I begged her to part her thighs," he said, his voice warm and so persuasive. "To brace her feet either side of me and bend her knees."

Preferring his erotic tales to his sad stories, she pushed aside all embarrassment and spread her legs.

Grayson hissed a breath as his gaze lingered on her sex.

She was so wet it must be glistening. He rubbed the obvious bulge in his breeches before dropping to his knees. "You do know what I intend to do?"

"Yes. But is it not terribly uncomfortable down there?" A man his size would likely get cramp squashed between the seats.

"I would walk over hot coals to feast on your flesh, to watch you shudder and cry my name."

Despite her sex pulsing at the thought of what he would do, she recalled something Mr Daventry had said. For three hundred years, the Sturrock bastards had carried the name Grayson. Yet this man was undoubtedly unique.

"Who calls you Alexander?" She inhaled sharply as he smoothed his broad hands over her stockings. Then he hooked his arms around her legs and tilted her hips.

"No one." His warm breath breezed across her inner thigh, then he pressed a hot kiss to her bare flesh.

"Then I shall, whenever we're intimate."

"I might need to hear it often," he said before setting his mouth to her sex and licking her.

"Alexander!" She gasped from the shock and the sudden bolt of pleasure. She cried his name again when he flicked his tongue over her aching bud. "Alexander!"

He must have liked the sound of his given name because he gorged on her flesh, devoured every inch, breathed her scent and slipped his tongue into her entrance.

"Sweet mercy!" She thrust her hands into his hair and gripped hard as the pressure within built to a crescendo. She came apart, panting his name, shuddering against his mouth.

But he did not give her time to bathe in the wonderful sensations. He straightened, leant over her and kissed her passionately on the mouth. The moment he pushed his fingers inside her, and his thumb circled her bud, she knew he meant to make her come again.

It was too much!

Too sensitive—yet equally exquisite.

"Do you want more than my fingers, Olivia?"

"You know I do."

"You're so wet, love. I'm in danger of breaking my own vow and taking you here. I can think of nothing but you milking my cock."

He kissed her again, his tongue making love to her mouth, the way his fingers made love to her sex. And yet it wasn't the rampant hunger of a rake she tasted in his desperate kisses. It was the need of a lonely man longing for affection.

"Lord in heaven!" Her legs stiffened, and she came hard, her inner muscles clamping around his fingers, her body shaking violently.

He watched her, looking more than gratified.

She thought to ask if she might pleasure him in return, but a loud crack outside preceded the window opposite shattering into a hundred pieces.

"Take cover!" Mr Bower cried from atop his box as he struggled to control the spooked horses.

Shards of glass littered the carriage seat, but seeing the hole in the panel made her blood run cold. What if Grayson had been sitting there?

"Stay down," she said as the carriage swerved so violently they slid across the leather seat. She held him so tightly to her breast neither of them could breathe. "We're under attack. Someone from Mersham Hall wishes to ensure we never reach London."

Had her brother feigned sleep and rode like the devil to catch them? Had everything he'd said been a dreadful lie?

Another shot rang out, the sound tearing a shriek from her lips.

"That's Bower firing in retaliation." Grayson pulled her down to the floor before their attacker discharged his weapon again. "I swear I shall beat your brother to within an inch of his life."

"We're not going back to Mersham Hall." She doubted she would ever visit again. "We're going home."

Home to Portland Place.

Home to the office of the Order where she would hire Mr Daventry to make sure her husband didn't die.

The carriage came to a crashing halt, though it only added to the rising panic. "What if Mr Bower has been shot?" What if the blackguard was waiting to murder them, too?

"Bower!" Grayson shouted.

"Aye, sir!"

"Are you hurt?"

"No, sir! The blighter rode off into the woods."

Grayson pulled himself up onto the carriage seat. "Remain here. Don't move until I have checked the surrounding area."

"You're not going out there?" Should they not keep moving? Find a coaching inn, stop somewhere safe?

But he opened the door and vaulted to the ground.

Lord have mercy! It was hard enough being scared for one's own life, never mind having to worry about a husband.

Olivia sat on the seat and righted her skirts before joining Grayson and Mr Bower outside on the roadside. "Did you see the assailant?"

"No, ma'am," Mr Bower said while calming the horses. "The rogue knew the area well. He wore a hooded cloak, weaved in and out of the trees so I couldn't fire a decent shot."

"You're sure it was a man?" she said, praying it wasn't her brother. "Might it have been Lady Mersham?" Though why Anna would want to kill them was a complete mystery.

Mr Bower shook his head. "From his height and position in the saddle, I'd lay odds it was a man." He paused before adding, "It would have been easier to shoot me first, ma'am, if he'd been intent on murdering us all. Happen he meant to kill Mr Grayson."

Grayson cursed beneath his breath.

She felt suddenly cold, chilled to the bone. "Then let's be on our way before the devil returns. Keep watch, Mr Bower, while I clear the glass off the seat."

"Aye, ma'am."

"I shall clean the seat," Grayson said, striding ahead.

Perhaps it was a good thing he had shrugged out of his coat and knelt between her legs because most of the glass had landed on the garment.

Grayson chuckled as he carried his coat to the roadside and shook the shards onto the grass verge.

"Pray tell me what you find so amusing," she said when he returned. "It is hardly a laughing matter. You might have been killed."

He winked and shot her a wicked grin. "When you parted your legs, I thought I'd die if I didn't taste you. Who knew I would come to mean it literally?"

CHAPTER 12

Hart Street, London
Office of the Order

DECIDING TO CONSULT MR DAVENTRY BEFORE RETURNING home to Portland Place, Olivia and Grayson arrived at the Order's townhouse and were shown into the plush drawing room.

The master of the Order sat in the wing chair, cradling a glass of brandy between his long fingers. Mr Sloane, an enquiry agent of exceptional skill, lounged on the sofa. His long hair hung loose, and he often reminded Olivia of a pirate or an explorer from the Elizabethan era.

Both men stood, though Mr Daventry studied them with keen eyes and said, "Back so soon? Did the earl not prove as welcoming as one hoped?"

"We exhausted all lines of enquiry," Olivia said, feeling like a child remiss in her studies. "But we shall explain all if you can spare the time."

Mr Daventry motioned to the vacant sofa. "I'm intrigued to learn what you discovered and have some news of my own to impart."

Mr Sloane arched a curious brow while scanning Grayson's shirtsleeves. "What happened to your coat?"

Grayson seemed reluctant to answer, and so she explained on his behalf. "We were attacked on the road. The thug shot at the carriage and shattered the windowpane. Grayson had left his coat on the seat." So he could worship her without restriction. "Despite numerous attempts, we have been unable to remove all the fragments of glass."

Mr Daventry's dark eyes widened. "Thank the Lord you both survived. Where did this happen?"

"A few miles from Mersham Hall," Grayson said.

The men waited for her to sit before settling into their seats.

"Mr Bower believes Grayson may have been the intended target." The thought sent a shiver racing down her spine. "The man fired a single shot and, despite being on horseback, was extremely precise." Had he taken aim a few minutes earlier, Grayson may not have survived.

Mr Sloane rubbed his chin thoughtfully. "So, your coat was on the seat. The lead ball hit the window, shattering the glass, but you were unharmed. Are you certain it was gunfire and not a stray stone?"

"Grayson was not sitting on the seat," she said, her cheeks turning suddenly hot at the memory of him sucking and licking her sex as if she were a delicious ice at Gunter's.

A faint groan rumbled in Grayson's throat. "I had been sitting in the seat but moved a few minutes before. Anyone who had seen us leaving Mersham Hall could have noted our positions."

Doubtless they failed to predict Grayson would spend time on his knees, though she decided not to say so aloud.

"How fortuitous," Mr Daventry said, his intense gaze flitting curiously between them. "I shall speak to Bower and see if he can describe the assailant." He paused. "If you have exhausted all lines of enquiry, perhaps you should begin by telling me everything that occurred during your visit to Mersham Hall."

Everything!

Should she mention she was a little obsessed with her husband? That their visit had been a journey of discovery in more ways than one? That every night she wore a little less to bed? That she wasn't sure how long their passionate exchanges would last?

Olivia cleared her throat. "I confronted Hamilton. He denied any involvement in my abduction and in the deaths of his friends."

"And you believed him?"

"I don't know what to believe." She relayed everything Hamilton had said last night when he caught them searching his study. Then was forced to tell both men almost every detail relating to that fateful day seven years ago. "The brutes were supposed to see me hanged. I would have died had fate not intervened."

Grayson captured her hand and held it tightly.

Mr Daventry breathed deeply and pinched the bridge of his nose. It was the first time she had seen him struggle to suppress emotion.

"You have confirmed my worst fears," he said, releasing a weary sigh. "I wish you would have spoken to me sooner. We would have done everything in our power to catch the person responsible. We would have given you back your life."

He spoke with a regret that she could not own. Had he helped her, she would not have met his female enquiry agents, and would not have made lifelong friends.

"I was afraid to face the truth. Had Lord Deville not

recognised me, we would not be sitting here now." The thought stabbed at her heart. She would not have met the wonderful man seated beside her.

Then Mr Daventry asked the one question she was dreading. "Who rescued you from the woods?" Perhaps sensing the sudden tension in the air, he added, "The villain may learn the information, may seek to silence anyone who can identify the thugs."

She glanced at Grayson, wishing she would have told him first.

He read her thoughts and whispered, "This isn't about us. It's about finding the person responsible, protecting those who helped you."

Had they been alone, she would have wrapped her arms around his neck, pressed her body close and kissed him. "Mrs Foston lives in a cottage a mile from the scene. I spent a month recuperating there before going to live with her sister in Bath. That's where I found my first position as a governess."

She had spent two years travelling with her employers until the family decided to live in Vienna permanently. Yet something had called her back to England. Perhaps her soul was already seeking answers.

"Two years later, I found myself in London where I happened upon your friend Mr Wycliff. He wished to open a women's refuge in Howland Street and hire me to manage his day-to-day affairs. Sadly, the residents objected."

Mr Daventry nodded. "Hence why he rents the house to me. The neighbours are not averse to living next door to women of gentle persuasion."

Mr Sloane laughed. "Clearly, they have never met your agents."

From London, she had gone to Chesterfield, then Egypt, before finding herself back in England again.

"During all that time, I have corresponded with Mrs Foston," she said, returning to the matter at hand. "Trimble is the name of her cook, and so no one is suspicious when she receives my letters."

Mr Daventry sat pondering the information. "Surely the local magistrate organised a search of the area. Did he not interview Mrs Foston as part of the investigation?"

"Various people from the village called at her house, but I hid in the cellar, and they never ventured from the parlour." Her heart raced as she recalled those tense minutes spent wondering if she might be found.

"Do you recall who?"

Yes. She still had the list hidden amongst her belongings. "The Reverend Walker. Mr Marston from Biddulph Grange. Mrs Annscroft. The Harkins and Mr Stowe called twice. There were others."

"I'm surprised you remember after all these years."

This was not the first time she had attempted to solve the mystery and prove her brother wanted her dead. "Mrs Foston kept a record of their names. She ensured they all had alibis and watched them better than any spymaster. She couldn't quite see my brother as a cold-hearted devil and sought another explanation."

Grayson turned to her. "Did she find any incriminating evidence?"

"No. None." Olivia's hands shook whenever a new letter arrived, yet she was always left disappointed. "Fearing someone would discover her involvement, she sent me a detailed description of the perpetrators and what she recalled of their conversation."

"But you don't know the men?" Mr Sloane said.

"No. I had never seen them before." Though their hideous faces often appeared in her nightmares. She repeated what she had told Hamilton, that they must be hired men, local labourers. "Some of the things they said make no sense. Hence why we presumed they were dull-witted farm hands."

"Perhaps I might be able to decipher their meaning," Mr Sloane said confidently. "I've dealt with more than a few miscreants in my time."

"It's hardly what one would call the King's English." No, it was pure and utter gibberish. "But one thug said, 'Hit her! This ain't like fakin' a blowen's flag in the chick'.'"

The men fell silent.

"You can see why I would be clueless." Despite her knowledge of foreign languages, she had found nothing akin to it in any literature.

Mr Daventry did not look clueless. He glanced at Mr Sloane. "Mrs Grayson will send a description of the assailants to the office. Take Cole and head to Holborn. Speak to Nathaniel in the Black Lion tavern. See if he recognises the men. I shall have Peel publish a notice in the *Police Gazette*, asking for information."

Olivia blinked in surprise. "You think the men are from London? But they knew the woods well. I'm quite certain they spoke with local accents."

Grayson squeezed her hand. "They would have checked the area before abducting you. And it's not difficult to alter one's voice. The most puzzling part is why they found a replacement when they had no proof you were dead."

Mr Daventry took his notebook from the side table and scribbled something with his pencil. "If the men work for a notorious gang, they would not want their leader to learn of their mistake. They acted on impulse, though it still took them a week to finish the job."

Mrs Gunning arrived with the tea tray and set it down on the low table. The housekeeper poured for them, gestured to her homemade Shrewsbury biscuits, and then withdrew.

Mr Daventry waited for Mrs Gunning to leave before

saying, "Faking a blowen's flag means stealing a lady's reticule. The most notorious thieves work in Holborn, namely around Chick Lane."

It took a moment for the information to penetrate her addled brain. "But Hamilton never comes to London. He has never taken his seat in the House of Lords." It was one reason why she felt relatively safe in the city. "How would he have hired the rogues?"

Mr Daventry sat forward. "If one considers that both murdered men had a drawing of Leviathan in their coat pockets, then the crimes are connected and premeditated. All roads lead to Hamilton Durrant. But I suspect that's what the villain wants everyone to believe. So, we begin by investigating his friends from the Knights of the Seven Devils."

Olivia recalled what Hamilton had said. "But they have disbanded."

Mr Daventry jerked his head in surprise. "And yet when I bribed the caretaker of the property near Seven Dials, he told me the knights are holding a meeting there six days hence."

So, her brother had lied.

Olivia sat in stupefied silence.

There were so many unanswered questions her head hurt. It was hard to imagine them ever discovering the truth. Had some devil not shot at their carriage, she would be inclined to let the matter rest.

She cast Grayson a sidelong glance. Tonight, they would make love. Then there would be no cause for an annulment. They would be bound together for a lifetime. And yet the only thing that terrified her was the villain killing him, too.

The sobering thought caused her to sit up straight. It was time to take control of her life, to safeguard her future. "Then let us make a plan of action. You said you had news to impart."

Mr Daventry motioned for Mr Sloane to speak.

"Regarding Claudette, I can find no record of a woman being found hanged in the North Wood. Not in the three years since the Earl of Sturrock died. Daventry had one of his men attempt to gain access to the brothel you mentioned in your note. But one must be recommended by a patron and attend an interview before membership is granted."

"That may work in our favour," she said. Mrs Swithin clearly kept a record of those men who used the brothel and accessed the bathhouse. "We just need to find a way to speak to the madam and persuade her to tell us who was there the night Lord Sturrock died."

Silence descended, and they sat in thoughtful contemplation.

Grayson chuckled, almost to himself. "I have a plan, though we will need the help of your agents, Daventry."

Mr Daventry arched an inquisitive brow. "You will explain your plan in detail before I agree to anything."

Grayson cleared his throat. "I suggest we break into the bathhouse, take the attendant hostage, and use it to hold one hell of a party."

Mr Sloane grinned. Which came as no surprise, as he had indulged in every entertainment before marrying. "We make such a racket, the bawdy house madam will come to investigate."

"And unless she tells us what we want to know, we shall ensure every scoundrel and rakehell in the *ton* knows how to access the bathhouse."

Olivia thought to add a caveat. "We must expect a fight. She will have men in her employ, brutes keen to thump a man before asking questions. And we might threaten to inform the Antiquarian Society, who will surely seek a writ to investigate the Roman ruins."

Grayson turned to face her. "In which case, I suggest

Daventry's gentlemen agents accompany me. I'll not risk you getting hurt, Olivia."

The comment might have roused her ire had he not looked at her so tenderly. "If Mrs Swithin enters the bath-house to find a group of men, a fight will ensue before you have a chance to ask questions. She must suspect you've paid someone to use the facilities if you're to engage her in conversation."

They all looked at Mr Daventry, seeking his opinion.

After a brief silence, he said, "The plan has merit, but I agree with Mrs Grayson. A party without female companions is no party at all. Besides, her friends have approached me, offering to assist with the case. It would be remiss of me to decline on the grounds of them being women."

The mere mention of her friends brought tears to her eyes. The fact they wished to help her left her choked with emotion.

Mr Daventry pushed to his feet. "I shall speak to Lady Roxburgh and Mrs Hunter. They both live in London and can be called upon at short notice. Along with their husbands, they will assist you with your party at the bathhouse."

Mr Sloane seemed to find something amusing. "And who will be given the most dangerous task?" When they all shot him a puzzled look, he added, "Who will tell Roxburgh he needs to wear a toga?"

CHAPTER 13

"What did Mr Daventry want to discuss with you?"
Olivia said from the confines of their carriage. "He kept you
in his study for fifteen minutes and seemed quite satisfied
when we left."

"Were you counting the seconds?" he teased, yet he had
wished the time away, longing to return home so they might
have a private moment to themselves. "Did you miss me that
much?"

"I thought it odd he wished to speak to you alone."

Daventry had asked for news from Mersham Hall.
Grayson told him about the missing maid and the stolen
painting, about Hamilton's laudanum problem and loveless
marriage. But what his friend really wanted to know was how
he found married life.

"Daventry asked if I regretted marrying you."

She inhaled sharply. "He did? What did you say?"

He'd said he had never felt so at ease with a woman. That
he had never felt the effects of a kiss so profoundly. "I told
him I don't regret it for a second. I told him every day with

you is my best day. That I'm excited to know what the future holds."

A satisfied smile played on her lips. A smile that conveyed pride in her womanly abilities to please a man. "You pleasured your wife twice in a moving carriage. If tomorrow will be better, one wonders what you have planned."

He thought to say something lascivious, but the pang of apprehension caught him off guard. She enjoyed his attentions and would seek to feed the addiction. The novelty would soon wane. He couldn't bear to think of what might happen then.

He pulled his watch from his pocket to inspect the time, knowing he must make the most of every second. "By my calculation, we still have eight hours left of today. What would you like to do, Olivia?"

She tried to blink away the languid look of desire in her eyes. "Watch you eat an ice at Gunter's, but we shall save that for tomorrow. Stroll in the park and take a picnic, but we should wait until we've caught the devil who tried to kill you, before taking unnecessary risks."

He wasn't sure he was the intended target.

Either way, someone meant to silence them.

"Then we should limit ourselves to activities at home," he said, wishing to lose himself in her body and forget their troubles for a few hours. "Do you play chess?" He thought to manoeuvre her into their chamber and take more than her queen.

"Not very well. Mrs Montague liked to play, though she took forever to consider her moves, and I found it all rather tedious."

"Playing with me won't be tedious."

"No, I don't imagine it will."

"Perhaps we might make a wager on the outcome."

That piqued her interest. "What will we stake?"

"A lady must name her price."

Excitement danced in her eyes. "Very well. If I win, you must write me a letter every day for a week. Owning something so personal will give me an incentive to beat you."

The comment reminded him of Robert Newell and his pathetic attempts at seduction. "And have you compare me to another man?"

She raised a brow. "Alexander, there's not a man alive who could hold a torch to you. But there is something powerful about the written word when the writer is honest."

He liked it when she spoke his given name. If she thought it would sway his opinion, she was right. "You may be disappointed. I would rather die than spout romantic drivel."

"Then what *would* you say?"

"You will have to wait and see." It occurred to him that he should name his prize for winning the wager. "Should I win, I want to watch you bathe while you read my first letter."

Her lips parted, and it took her a moment to gather herself and say, "What a clever strategy, sir. If you win, we both do."

He smiled. "You did not marry a fool, madam."

They looked at each other for a few intense seconds. He recalled her sweet taste, how responsive she was to his touch, how resplendent she was in her release.

"Tomorrow, we must seek out the men of the Seven Devils," he said, knowing danger lurked in the shadows. Beyond this moment, nothing was guaranteed. "Daventry confirmed Featherly and Elderton are presently in London. And we will have to interview Robert Newell."

Her shoulders slumped and she looked dejected. "I would rather avoid Mr Newell. He makes me uncomfortable. Despite his efforts to join my brother's silly club, he is not a knight."

"But he was at Mersham Hall when Mr Kane was killed,

so we cannot discount him as a suspect." Grayson's hands throbbed at the prospect of confronting Newell. He would warn the charmer to stay the hell away from his wife. "It's been seven years since you last saw him. Doubtless much has changed."

Newell could have a loving wife and a wild brood.

Grayson prayed it was the case.

She gave a resigned sigh. "Must we speak of the investigation now? We were having such a romantic conversation about letters and bathing."

He wished she would say what she meant. He sensed an urgency within her, an eagerness to forge ahead and cement their union. A hunger that mirrored his own.

"It's four in the afternoon, love. We have the whole evening ahead of us." And talk of her bathing left him aroused and impatient in equal measure.

"You surprise me, Mr Grayson." Her voice was low and seductive. "Based on your reckless behaviour this morning, I took you for a man who despised conformity. And yet you're planning to make love to your wife late at night in the dark."

The challenge in her eyes encouraged him to be bold. "Make no mistake. I would take you here, or on the study floor, or against a tree in our garden. I could be rough, slam into you so hard it might rid me of this damnable craving. But I want more than that. You deserve more than that, at least until we know each other better."

She fell silent for a moment, and he thought he had shocked her, but her mouth curled into a slow smile. "You win this game, Alexander. You have me in check-mate. There is nothing else to do but grant you your reward."

Before he could reply, the carriage jerked to a halt, and he realised they had arrived in Portland Place. A footman hurried out of the house and handed Olivia down from the carriage. Another took receipt of their luggage.

Grayson climbed down and spoke to Bower. "Tell Kendall not to replace the carriage window until next week. For now, he's to leave the board in place." There was every chance someone would shoot at them again.

"Aye, sir." Bower reached into his coat pocket, withdrew a notebook, and tore out a page. "I made a list, sir, of the servants working at Mersham Hall."

Grayson took the proffered note and scanned the information, which included the ages and birthplaces of all Hamilton's staff. "I'm certain this will prove most useful," he said, astounded at the man's thoroughness.

"You'll notice Frances Barker is from Pelham Street, Spitalfields, sir. Happen her mother still lives there. I'll keep watch to see if the maid comes to visit."

"Excellent." No wonder Daventry valued the man. "Bring her here if you find her. Regardless what time of day." Grayson turned to follow Olivia into the house, but paused to inspect the list.

Most of the servants hailed from Kent, but two of Hamilton's grooms were from London. A mere coincidence, perhaps. But if the thugs who attacked Olivia were from Holborn, they may have had an accomplice working at Mersham Hall.

Grayson made a mental note to inform Daventry, then tucked the paper into his waistcoat pocket and entered the house.

Pickins was helping Olivia out of her pelisse when he met Grayson's gaze and made a shocking revelation.

"Welcome home, sir. Mr Habberly delivered the drawings for the renovations to the property in Curzon Street." He paused for dramatic effect or to catch his breath. Who knew? "And Lady Sturrock called. After reading your marriage announcement in *The Times*, she wished to convey her felicitations."

Felicitations?

She usually gave him twenty lashes with her sharp tongue.

"Lady Sturrock!" What in blazes did she want? It wasn't to wish him well. He had a good mind to send a note informing her never to darken his door again. "No doubt her cronies are keen to learn every snippet of gossip, and she's embarrassed to admit she's clueless. I am permanently unavailable should she make another attempt."

Pickins inclined his head. "She said she would call again."

"Perhaps we should invite her to take tea," Olivia said calmly. "If only to show a united front. Should she say anything disparaging, we will tell her it's not her place to comment on family affairs."

Impossible. He would fly into a rage if she said anything hurtful to his wife. "Let us deal with the investigation before dealing with Lady Sturrock."

"As you wish." Olivia cast him a mischievous grin before turning to Pickins. "After such a tiring journey, I would like to retire to my bedchamber and bathe. And have a tray sent to my room at seven. I shall dine there tonight."

Pickins nodded and turned to Grayson. "Sir?"

"I shall attend to any correspondence," he said, attempting to suppress the ripple of excitement when he thought about joining his wife upstairs. "I have an important letter to write, but will also retire early and dine in my room."

"I shall inform the staff at once," Pickins said without a blush. Surely he knew they'd spend the next few hours writhing naked, a tangle of sweat-soaked limbs. The butler hobbled away, but not before offering an apology. "Forgive me, sir. I'm a little slow on my feet today. Terrible trouble with my bunions."

Olivia pursed her lips. "Have Cook prepare a mustard poultice. Mrs Montague suffered terribly and found strapping the feet helpful. The bandages must be pulled tight."

Pickins' gaze softened. "Thank you, ma'am. I shall be sure to heed your advice." And then he bowed and left them alone in the hall.

While it was clear Olivia longed for an amorous afternoon, she was subtle in her attempts at seduction. She touched him affectionately on the upper arm and stroked his bicep. A silent communication informing him she would be waiting upstairs should he care to join her.

He watched her climb the stairs, fixated on the gentle sway of her hips. She glanced back over her shoulder, bestowing a look that said heaven was a mere thrust away, before disappearing from view.

The house would be a hive of activity for the next hour as footmen lugged buckets back and forth. And so, despite the anticipation being almost unbearable, he settled in his study and wrote to his solicitor. After such a close call this morning, he had to act quickly and make provisions for Olivia in his will.

When writing his wife a letter, he decided to make it honest and simple. Rather than attempt to explain the host of feelings racing around inside him, he chose three words to express his permanent state of mind.

When the din in the house died, he snatched the letter and mounted the stairs two at a time. Damn it all, he was aroused before opening his bedchamber door.

Except his wife was not in his bedchamber.

There was no sign of the copper tub or the naked temptress.

The distant trickle of water and a feminine hum drew him to the adjoining door. Like a respectable gentleman, he knocked.

"Who is it?" she called in a seductive tone.

"It is your husband, madam. Come to test the temperature of the water to ensure it's not too cold."

"You may enter."

He gathered his wits. He would likely spill in his breeches when faced with her naked form.

Had his wife not been lounging in the tub, her lithe legs draped over the edge, the soft curve of her breasts bobbing above the water, he might have glanced around the candlelit room he had seen but once.

However, he did notice the curtains were closed. "As your sworn protector, I must dip my fingers in the water. The last thing I want is for you to catch a chill."

"I assure you, I am not cold in the slightest." She reached for the glass of red wine she had left on the floor and took a long sip. "I see you come bearing gifts. Is the letter for me?"

"Indeed." He stepped forward, careful not to trip over his feet while gaping at her delectable body. "It's the first of many. Remember, I am not a man who waffles."

She exchanged her wine glass for the letter and sat up, giving him an ample view of her breasts.

Mother of all saints!

He tossed back the wine, though it did little to settle his racing pulse. *Be patient!* He would soon set his mouth to those dusky pink nipples.

Olivia peeled back the folds and read the three words. "Hmm. It's rather short," she said, though he could see the glaze of passion in her eyes and knew the words had achieved the desired effect.

I want you!

"They're the most honest words I have ever penned. I could have filled the page with tedious similes, but the plain truth of the matter is, I want you. I've wanted you since you entered my study and scolded me for ignoring you."

She breathed a soft sigh. "I pray you still want me tomorrow, next week, next month, next year."

He could not imagine waking up beside anyone else.

"We married, not knowing what to expect. Yet here we are, hungry for each other, feeling like fate granted us a boon."

She glanced at the words again. "I have never read anything that resonated so deeply. I shall keep it always." She offered him the letter and nodded to the bed. "Would you place it under my pillow?"

He did as she asked, aware of the significance. She had reduced Robert Newell's letters to ash. "You *are* sleeping with me tonight?" Nothing would come between them, not even the adjoining door.

"I like this room." She gathered water in her cupped hand and washed her shoulder. "And I thought we could take it in turns sleeping in each other's beds. It may sound silly, but I've had nothing to call my own for years, and I desperately want to feel at home here."

Briefly, he scanned the pale blue furnishings before turning his attention to the beautiful woman lounging in the tub.

The strange feelings came over him again. The anger at knowing someone had hurt her. The fear that this rush of happiness might be temporary. The overwhelming surge of pride when he considered how she had forged a new life after such a horrific ordeal.

"You may do whatever pleases you," he said, wanting her to know freedom. Yet the desire to keep her prisoner in this room, keep her all to himself, proved overwhelming. "In this marriage, you have choices. You are the master of your own mind."

Her mouth curled into a smile. "Would you lock the door, then come and rub my shoulders?" Her gaze slid over him. "They ache from the long carriage ride, and your hands are much stronger than mine."

It took every effort not to race to the door and lock the

world out, but he managed the task with casual aplomb before coming to kneel behind the bathtub.

He was undone the moment he put his hands on her bare skin and she breathed a sensual hum. While his blood charged through his veins, heading in one direction, he massaged her neck and shoulders in a sensual rhythm.

"That feels so good," his temptress said. Her little moans and pants were the most erotic sounds he had ever heard. "Perhaps you *should* check if the water is warm."

It was an invitation to do more than make ripples.

His body reacted instantly, his pulse racing, the muscles in his thighs and buttocks tightening.

Thinking his hesitation was due to a miscommunication, she reached for his hand and drew it down into the water. Then she spoke the words he would remember until his dying day. "Touch me, Alexander."

"Touch me," she whispered again softly, as if the fire in her blood had not left her near mindless with need.

There was more to marriage than making love, but he had cast a spell over her, made her crave these intimate moments, made her want to crawl beneath his skin, hold him close and never let go.

He cupped her breasts, wetting his shirtsleeves, his thumbs moving over her nipples in maddening circles. God, how they ached. He pressed his lips to her neck and sucked gently.

It caused a heady mix of sensations.

She arched her back, reached up and gripped his hair, urging him to continue. "Don't stop, Alexander." She needed to be his wife in all the ways that mattered. She needed him. All of him. Every inch.

She tilted her head, her desperate mouth finding his. Their tongues tangled instantly, sliding against each other's. Wild. Rampant. The way she imagined they would writhe on top of one another in bed.

She swallowed his moan, drawing it deep into her body. Capturing something of the man who made her heart sing.

But then she stilled as his hand slipped between her thighs.

Their eyes met, and he held her there while massaging her sex.

She rocked against his hand, but he was everywhere—pushing his fingers into her entrance, stroking her nipple, breathing into her open mouth.

"Come for me, love," he whispered.

Every muscle stiffened. She was a slave to his touch, coming for him at will, shuddering at his command. The waves of pleasure ran deep, deeper than when she had climaxed in his carriage.

"Alexander!" Her body clenched around his fingers, the spasms rippling to her toes. But it wasn't enough. She needed more.

The moment he withdrew his fingers, she charged up out of the water like Leviathan, envious of every woman who had claimed a piece of him. Determined to ensure she was the only lover he needed.

She reached for him, and he was there—he was always there—taking her hand and helping her out of the bathtub.

"Is everything all right?" He sounded worried.

"Take off your clothes." She tugged at his waistcoat.

"What's the rush, love?" He stilled her wet hands.

Patience had been her greatest virtue until now. But this

restlessness consumed her. It stole her breath. It robbed her of all rhyme and reason.

"I need to feel close to you." It had pilfered the remnants of the barrier she had once placed between them. "I need you to make love to me now, Alexander, not in an hour."

Restlessness was contagious.

A groan left his lips as he quickly stripped out of his clothes. She watched as he revealed every inch of toned, bronzed skin. Giggled when he almost tripped over his breeches because he couldn't tear his gaze from her naked body.

The tension in the air was palpable.

The second he was out of his clothes, she threw herself into his arms. Sweet mercy! The feel of his hot skin against hers made her moan aloud. His mouth found hers, the kiss wild and frantic.

"Touch me," he growled. "Don't be afraid."

She could never be afraid of him. And she had been acutely aware of his erect manhood pushing against her belly.

She slipped her hand between their bodies and settled her fingers around his hard shaft. He gave her a quick lesson in how to please him, how to stroke back and forth until he was panting.

He was so thick, so hard, so long.

It was impossible to imagine taking him into her body.

He stilled her hand. "I need to be inside you, love, pushing deep, filling you. Say that's what you want."

"I want you," she breathed, every nerve tingling in anticipation of their lovemaking. "Don't make me wait a moment longer."

She gave a little squeal when he scooped her up into his arms and carried her to bed. The mattress dipped beneath them as he settled down beside her.

"Regardless of why we married, know this means something to me," he said in a voice that spoke to her heart. He trailed his fingers lightly over her abdomen. "I have never wanted anything as badly as I want you."

A strange feeling came over her, part lust, part something else. "I should be nervous, but I'm excited."

"Perhaps because you like the way I make you feel." His wandering fingers slipped down over her sex. "I like watching you come against my hand, against my tongue. Now I want to watch you come while I am deep inside you."

The seductive lilt of his voice was as arousing as his probing fingers. "Do it now. The anticipation is killing me."

He laughed as he moved between her thighs. Instinctively she wrapped her legs around him and braced herself as he pressed the broad head of his manhood to her entrance.

"I'll be as gentle as I can," he whispered before pushing inside her, his eyes rolling back in ecstasy as he edged in an inch at a time. "You feel so good, love."

Her body stretched to accommodate him, but he gave her no time to consider it further. He was everywhere at once. His mouth found hers, his tongue plunging in time with his manhood.

She traced her hands over the hard muscles in his shoulders, dared to grip his buttocks and urge him to push deeper.

He took her virginity then. Thrusting past the only obstacle that said this marriage was a sham.

He stilled and looked at her. "You're mine now, love."

"I'm the one cradling you," she teased.

"But I'm in control," he said, withdrawing then filling her again. Repeating the action until she was panting and writhing beneath him.

He moved up a little higher, angled his hips so every stroke stimulated her sex. The bed creaked in time with his thrusts.

"Alexander." Her release came in powerful waves, the

pulses thrumming deep in her core. Every part of her throbbed. Her heart pounded to the same glorious beat.

He found it equally arousing because he quickly said, "Do you want me to withdraw? Tell me now."

"No." She wanted everything he had to give.

And as she saw a look of pleasure on his face, heard his guttural groan as he flooded her with his seed, she realised she may have fallen a little in love with her husband.

CHAPTER 14

"I BELIEVE THE TIME FOR HONESTY IS NIGH," OLIVIA said, gripping Grayson's arm a little tighter as he escorted her the short distance to Lord Featherly's home on Wimpole Street. "Do you not agree?"

His heart lurched.

Had she read his mind?

They had made love again last night, and the feelings were the same. It wasn't lust alone that left him staring into her eyes as he pushed deep into her body. It wasn't lust that left him reluctant to withdraw even as they slept.

Lust was easily sated.

This constant hunger was something else.

Hence why he had penned the words 'I am besotted' this morning.

"We should tell Lord Featherly the truth," she said when he failed to respond. "Explain we are hunting a murderer in the hope it might draw the villain out."

"And leave you open to an attack?"

She brought him to an abrupt halt on the pavement. "We

are already under attack. The shooter meant to kill one of us, or at least frighten us enough so we stop asking questions."

She had a point. And he doubted Featherly would grant them an audience unless Grayson produced the letter from Peel. Then again, he might be curious to meet the woman he thought was dead.

Olivia's eyes softened. "I want this matter dealt with quickly. To know we have nothing to fear. I want to focus on our marriage, not on catching a murderous miscreant."

He cupped her cheek, the strange longing sweeping over him again. "You cannot tell him you suspect Hamilton. London will be rife with gossip. It will destroy your brother's reputation." Hamilton was like a harbinger of death. Doubtless, people avoided him on the street, hence why he rarely ventured to town.

"Then we will focus on Mr Kane's murder. Say we are trying to prove those staying at Mersham Hall were not involved, but we feel the man's death may be connected to my abduction."

He nodded and gestured for them to continue walking.

When they arrived in Wimpole Street, Featherly's butler informed them his master was not accepting visitors.

Grayson handed the man his calling card. "You mean your master is asleep?" He hoped the investigation would soon be over so he could lounge in Olivia's bed until noon. "Wake him, else we shall return with a constable."

Olivia reached into her reticule and showed the butler Peel's letter. "We are here at the Home Secretary's behest. He has instructed us to carry out an investigation."

It was a small lie. They were tasked with finding the rogue who tried to murder Lady Olivia Durrant, not question the Knights of the Seven Devils.

The butler scanned the missive, his eyes widening when

he noted the official seal. "Wait one moment," he said before closing the door.

Olivia shot him a satisfied grin. "With Lord Featherly's sin being sloth, one hopes he would rather speak to us than undergo extensive questioning at Bow Street."

"I imagine he'll leave us waiting on the doorstep for an hour. I'd wager he lies there like a babe while his valet tugs on his shirt and stockings."

Olivia smiled. "I recall he often stayed at Mersham Hall. Once, he chose to sleep in the hearth-side chair rather than lug himself upstairs."

Yes, they would have to suffer a long wait while the fool found the energy to exert himself. "I can always barge my way inside and drag the oaf out of bed."

To their surprise, the butler returned promptly and ushered them into the drawing room. "His lordship will attend you shortly. I have been instructed to offer refreshment."

Shortly? Grayson had a vision of a valet and two footmen desperately trying to get the sluggard dressed.

They agreed to take tea in the hope of extending their welcome. The maid had not long brought the tray when Featherly made an appearance.

The viscount was the same age as Hamilton, approaching thirty, though his pale complexion and shock of orange hair marked him as a much younger man. There was nothing slovenly about his appearance. Nothing to suggest he was idle. A sloth.

They stood and greeted their host.

Featherly gaped at Olivia as one would a divine apparition. "My dear, you're alive. I read the announcement and thought it was some fool's idea of a cruel joke." Featherly clasped his chest. "Why the devil did Mersham not write and inform me of the news?"

Olivia cleared her throat. "My brother only learnt of it a few days ago. When one has been presumed dead for seven years, these things must be handled delicately."

The lord nodded profusely. He looked at Grayson and hardened his gaze. "Perhaps it's a good thing Sturrock is dead. He would not have sanctioned this union. He always believed you were his father's biggest disgrace."

The comment hit like an unexpected punch to the gut. One that might have knocked the breath from his lungs had he been remotely interested in this man's opinion.

"Sturrock always was a pompous prig."

Featherly did not disagree. "Your brother's arrogance was well known amongst his friends." He gestured to the plush sofa. "Please, sit and finish your tea."

They sat, and the viscount dropped into the adjacent chair.

"I am not sure what your butler told you," Olivia said, adding a lump of sugar to her tea. "But we have been asked to investigate the murders of Lord Sturrock and Mr Kane."

"Murders!" Featherly recoiled as if he had taken a sharp slap to the cheek. "But Sturrock slipped and drowned in a bathhouse somewhere in town. And Kane was shot by Bromley. The witnesses testified to the fact."

Sturrock had not slipped and drowned.

The coroner had dealt with the matter too swiftly. No one wanted to suggest a peer of the realm had been murdered, so it was easier to deem it an accident.

Grayson wondered if that's why he had been asked to identify the body. The bastard brother wouldn't give two hoots what happened to his estranged kin.

"We know about the Seven Devils," Grayson said, trying not to sound condescending. "We know you took the name Belphegor and your sin is sloth. Nonetheless, you don't appear to be a man plagued by indolence. Yet you claimed you once stayed in bed for a week and had your servants feed you."

Featherly surprised him by laughing. "I said a great many things to gain membership to your brother's elite little club."

"You mean you lied?"

"All the other roles were taken, so I claimed the title of the most slovenly man at Cambridge. In truth, being lazy proved tiresome, and I was somewhat relieved when the members stopped meeting."

Grayson pondered the last point. Daventry was certain the meeting was next week. Since losing an agent years ago, he never made mistakes. "You stopped meeting after George Kane died?" he attempted to clarify.

"Yes."

"Why?"

The viscount looked at Olivia and shuffled uncomfortably in the chair. "We were afraid for our lives. Two of our seven members had died." He shook his head like he found the whole thing absurd. "We grew superstitious. Kipling and Elderton said the Lord wished to punish us for adopting demon names." He gave an incredulous snort. "Both men have since turned away from their sins."

Olivia sipped her tea, then returned her cup and saucer to the low table. "My brother said you used to meet at a place in London. I cannot recall where."

She did know where.

But she was trying to establish if she could trust this man.

Featherly gave a hapless shrug. "We often hired a private room at White's. A few times a year, we journeyed to Kent and spent the week hunting, gambling and talking about the old days."

He made no mention of the place near Seven Dials.

She shook her head. "Friends meet all the time. What was the point of the club? Why use the ridiculous monikers?"

"It was just a lark," Featherly confessed. "We were not plotting the destruction of the Christian church, nor was it our aim to bring down the government."

Silence ensued.

The maid returned with the coffee pot and poured her master's beverage. Grayson waited until she left before asking the question burning in his mind.

"Did you shoot George Kane?"

Featherly almost choked on his coffee. "Had I the nerve to shoot anyone, it would have been Bromley. The man was obnoxious, a stubborn fool who, in all likelihood, fired at Kane out of spite. If anything, he should have challenged Robert Newell. Both men were vying for the same position in our club."

Interesting.

Was Newell out to get rid of the competition?

"We believe the murders are connected," Olivia said in the tone of an enquiry agent. "Is there anyone outside your select group who bore you any ill will?"

"No one springs to mind."

"Has there been an attempt on your life, my lord?"

Featherly touched his neck. "No."

"Did Lord Sturrock ever mention a woman named Claudette? She may have been a kept mistress or a lover."

Featherly's cheeks turned as red as his hair. "Madam, a gentleman cannot discuss such things in the presence of a lady. Suffice to say, Sturrock's conquests covered every name from Anna to Zeraphina. Claudette would have been one of many."

Had the lord deliberately named Hamilton's wife?

The Earl of Sturrock had been a complete and utter wastrel. He had craved attention from all quarters, which is often what became of a boy who was denied affection. He had no scruples and would have bedded any man's wife.

"One wonders if you've asked Mersham these questions," Featherly said with an air of arrogance. "He argued with Kane the night before the duel. A disagreement over Lady Mersham, if memory serves."

They were going round in circles.

It was one man's word against another's.

Hopefully, the excursion to the bathhouse would prove insightful.

"Do you know where we can find Robert Newell?" Grayson vaguely knew the youngest son of Baron Aldwick. Hamilton said he had lodgings in Mayfair, though due to the effects of the laudanum couldn't precisely recall where.

Featherly glanced at Olivia, looking a little surprised she didn't know. "He has an apartment in Stratford Place, next door to Wren and Furse hatters."

Olivia rose gracefully. "Thank you, my lord. We shall inform you of our findings once we have completed our investigation."

"You're not leaving?" Featherly leapt from his chair. "But you've not mentioned what happened to you or why you disappeared. How is it you're alive when they found your body in the woods?"

Olivia cleared her throat. "I was abducted. They found someone else in the King's Wood and made the obvious assumption."

Featherly's gasp of shock sounded genuine. "Good Lord. So your captor kept you prisoner?"

"No. I ran because someone was trying to kill me."

"Ah, you thought Mersham wanted your inheritance."

They did not ask the lord how he presumed to know the details of her father's will. All members of the Seven Devils knew why Hamilton envied his sister.

"I was confused then. Things are much clearer now."

The viscount glanced at Grayson and smirked. "Newell

will probably faint when he sees you, my dear. He was extremely fond of you back in the day."

WITH STRATFORD PLACE BEING A FEW MINUTES' WALK from Lord Featherly's townhouse, and with her heart beating so hard it would likely crack a rib, Olivia decided to broach the subject of Mr Newell.

She waited until Lord Featherly's butler closed the door behind them before daring to say, "We should visit Mr Newell before returning home." If only so they could cross the man off their list and put him far from their minds.

Grayson captured her hand and placed it in the crook of his arm. "I will visit him alone." His hard tone said he would use his fists to slay the man he deemed a threat.

"It would be better if I went alone," she said, appealing to his common sense. "I might be able to trick him into telling me his secrets. He'll be friendly and free with his tongue."

Grayson growled. "Madam, do you mean to provoke me?"

A chuckle escaped her. "Forgive me. It was a poor choice of words. I merely meant he will confide in me. One look at your impressive physique and his butler will turn you away."

He looked at her, his gaze warm. "We could go home first, so you might soothe my childish fears. Your kiss is the antidote to the poison in my veins."

There was only one cure for jealousy.

"Do you trust me, Alexander?" She spoke in the soft voice she used during their lovemaking. "Do you believe I will honour my vows and give myself to no one but you?"

"Of course. I have every faith in your character."

"And I have every faith in yours. Mr Newell is a suspect in Mr Kane's murder because he was one of three people who did not attend the duel. We must rule him out if we're to make any headway with the case." Hopefully, they would do so today and have no cause to question him again. "We will visit him together."

In truth, she detested the idea of being alone with the man.

"Then let us play a game with Mr Newell so we might assess his true intentions." He explained his plan, then with purposeful strides, led her to Stratford Place.

The lavish entrance to the apartments was open. Olivia knocked on one of two doors on the ground floor. It was not Mr Newell's abode, but a maid answered and said the gentleman lived on the third floor, to the right of the staircase. She added that the man often joked the climb helped improve his stamina.

Grayson muttered something derogatory beneath his breath, but gestured for Olivia to continue upstairs.

"Let him think you're alone." He moved past Mr Newell's door to stand out of sight. "You have two minutes, then I am coming in."

She tapped her finger to her lips, urging him to be quiet, as she had already seized the brass knocker and hammered twice.

A thin man dressed in black answered and inclined his head politely. "May I help you, madam?"

Olivia coughed to banish her nerves. "Yes, please inform Mr Newell an old acquaintance is here to see him. One who did not perish seven years ago in the King's Wood."

The servant's brows twitched. Maybe he thought it was a veiled way of saying she'd come for an assignation. But he maintained an impassive expression before asking her to wait a moment.

"Well?" Grayson whispered.

She shrugged. "He has gone to speak to Mr Newell."

The servant returned and welcomed her into the narrow hall. He escorted her to the sitting room, where a maid was quickly tidying the cushions and clearing the empty glasses from the side table.

Seconds later, Mr Newell burst into the room, dressed in nothing but a blue silk robe. His mussed hair suggested he had just leapt out of bed. The dark shadows beneath his eyes said he was recovering from a night of dissipation.

He approached her with outstretched arms. "Olivia! Good God! I heard you were alive but thought it a prank. An imposter trying to gain funds from Mersham. Maybe a case of mistaken identity. But here you are, as beautiful as when I last saw you."

Olivia stepped back and raised her hands to prevent the man from sweeping her into an embrace. "You should get dressed, Mr Newell."

Heaven forbid Grayson should stride in now.

"Mr Newell?" The man brushed a lock of dark hair from his brow. His gaze slipped snake-like over her body, slithering all the way to her toes. "We were on much friendlier terms when last we met. We might have wed had you not feared your brother's wrath."

She caught a whiff of stale brandy on his breath. "That was not why I refused your offer."

"Had you married me, Olivia, you would have had no reason to stage your own death. I would have taken care of you, loved you."

Olivia glanced around his untidy apartment. This would be her life had she been foolish enough to believe in his romantic protestations. Then again, she would have inherited half of her father's wealth. Doubtless that's what Mr Newell had found so appealing.

"I did not love you, sir, and saw you as nothing more than a friend. And I did not stage my own death." Why

NO LIFE FOR A LADY

would she hurt an innocent woman just to gain her freedom?

Mr Newell smiled. "And yet here you are, visiting me in my private apartment days after your wedding. A man might jump to the obvious conclusion."

A loud knock on the door sent her heart skittering.

Panic and relief vied for prominence.

Grayson would surely punch Mr Newell when he witnessed him in a state of dishabille. And yet she longed to have her husband beside her, a strong figure of support.

"You have jumped to the wrong conclusion," she said, hearing angry voices in the hall. "Ask yourself why I have not sought you out before. Ask yourself why Mr Grayson accompanied me today."

Mr Newell barely had a second to gather his thoughts before Grayson burst into the room. The harried servant followed behind, pleading with Grayson to wait at the door.

Grayson's stern expression turned thunderous as he scanned Mr Newell's loosely tied robe. He raised a hand to silence the servant, stabbed his finger at the far wall and growled, "Get bloody dressed. Get dressed before I wrap that silk belt around your throat and turn your face the same shade of blue."

Among other spirits, Mr Newell must have downed a decanter of courage last night. "You cannot tell me what to do in my own damn house. Sturrock was right about you. You're an ill-bred beast."

Grayson stepped forward, and Mr Newell stepped back. They continued the dance until their host found himself pressed to the wall.

Olivia quickly reached into her reticule and removed Peel's letter. "We have the Home Secretary's permission to question you about the deaths of Mr Kane and Lord Sturrock. That is why we are here."

"Get dressed and answer our questions," Grayson said through gritted teeth, "or I shall drag you to Bow Street in your birthday suit."

"This is an outrage," the man said before storming out of the room.

Grayson turned to face her. "Tell me he never laid a hand on you."

"Of course not."

There was little time for a private conversation because the maid entered as though she had been tasked with keeping an eye on them. The young woman fixed Olivia with a curious gaze. It was a look one expected to see from the aristocrats who had heard the news of her resurrection.

"Is something the matter?" Olivia said, confused by the woman's scrutiny. "You look like you have seen a ghost."

The maid jumped out of her skin and bobbed too many times to count. "I beg your pardon, ma'am. I don't mean to stare." She lowered her voice. "Mr Newell never much speaks of his talent with a brush, but I have to say the likeness has near stole me breath."

The explanation offered no clarity. "Likeness to whom?"

"To the painting, ma'am." Olivia must have frowned because the woman added, "The painting of you hanging in Mr Newell's chamber. He told me he painted it before you died, and—"

Grayson whipped around and darted from the room.

His destination was evident, and Olivia scurried behind him, trying to grab hold of his coat before he throttled Mr Newell.

"Grayson, wait!"

But he charged ahead, kicking open two doors before bursting into the gentleman's bedchamber.

"What the devil? Get the hell out!" Mr Newell stood in nothing but his breeches. His room was in utter disarray. If anything, he deserved the moniker sloth. "Give me a moment to dress, and I will answer your damn questions!"

Grayson glanced at the picture hanging opposite Newell's bed. He cursed to high heaven while she stood looking at Monsieur De la Cour's artwork, hardly recognising the woman in the painting.

Her own innocent smile broke Olivia's heart. It was the smile of a woman who knew nothing of the horrors awaiting her. Her wide eyes were bright and full of hope, not dark and shadowed by one wicked event.

Her throat tightened at the memory.

She wished she could travel back in time and leave a clue to fate's wicked plans. She would warn her younger self to pay closer attention. To look for evidence, to note the odd nuances of a traitor.

Then the tears fell. Silent tears. A quiet kind of grief for someone who had lost their life but hadn't died.

The arguing in the room grated. Where was the respect for the woman who had lived such a happy but brief life?

"Stop it," she said, in the timid voice of the girl from long ago. "Stop it!" she cried when they failed to listen.

She stormed past them and tried to unhook the gilt frame from the picture rail. The gold chains rattled like a prisoner's shackles.

"What are you doing?" Mr Newell demanded.

"Taking back what is mine." She would be damned if she would leave the poor woman hanging so this letch could ogle her.

"The painting is mine. I bought it and have the receipt."

She stopped abruptly, her knuckles white from gripping the frame so tightly. "Hamilton sold it to you?"

"Yes! He said he couldn't bear to look at it a moment longer." Mr Newell reached for his shirt and dragged it over his head. "He said it reminded him of the unholy thing you had done. That you had abandoned him on a selfish whim."

Her breath caught in her throat. She could imagine her brother saying precisely that. "Was he drunk?"

"Drunk?"

"Drunk when he told you?"

Mr Newell frowned. "He didn't tell me himself. He banned everyone in the house from speaking your name. He had his father-in-law get rid of it on his behalf."

"Mr Stowe?" She released her grip on the frame.

"Yes."

But Mr Stowe was the one who mentioned the painting. He was the one who drew attention to the theft. It made no sense unless he wished to taunt Hamilton.

She looked at Grayson. His green eyes flashed with a blend of intrigue and rage, but he read her mind. "Why would Stowe sell you the painting?"

Mr Newell had the decency to look embarrassed. "Because he knew I held the lady in high regard, and Hamilton wanted the painting to go to someone who thought fondly of his sister."

And yet Hamilton had been genuinely shocked when she had mentioned Robert Newell's letters. Therefore, she would wager her brother knew nothing of the transaction.

"What did you pay for it?" Grayson snapped.

"Two hundred pounds."

"I shall give you two thousand, providing you have a genuine receipt. If not, I shall take it without giving you a damn penny."

"It's not for sale," Mr Newell countered.

To prevent an inevitable fistfight, she said, "We've spoken to Lord Featherly. He said you were missing from the house the morning Mr Kane was shot." She did not regret the lie. When one fell into a nest of vipers, it was better to hiss along

176

with them. "There's a witness who places a man in the King's Wood. It's now evident someone from the house shot Mr Kane."

Mr Newell's cheeks flamed. "But he's lying. Ask Mersham. When Elderton raced back to the house to raise the alarm, Featherly was the only person who failed to answer his bedchamber door. It was locked. When the housekeeper arrived with a spare key, we found him asleep on top of the coverlet. Except he was dressed and had mud on his boots."

Was this an elaborate story?

A tale to blame someone else?

Grayson snorted. "You wanted to take my brother's position in the club and were at Mersham Hall to partake in an initiation. Kane was also vying to take on the role of Satan."

"Kane? Who in heaven's name told you that?"

"Lord Featherly."

Mr Newell laughed. "Kane was there to continue his liaison with Lady Mersham. He didn't give a damn about the club. She's had her claws into all of us at one time or other. Last year, it was Kane's turn to humiliate his host."

Hamilton knew of Anna's indiscretions.

That's why he sought solace in his drawer of brown bottles.

"Keep the painting," she said with an air of contempt. She glanced up at the angelic image. "That woman died seven years ago. I shall not waste another day mourning her loss." She turned to Grayson. "I would like to leave now."

Being the only person she could truly depend upon, her husband obliged her.

CHAPTER 15

GRAYSON'S MOUTH WAS HOT ON HERS. A SENSUAL FIRE OF desperate kisses conveying the three words scribed in the letter he had given her this morning.

I need you!

This was more than a fleeting desire. This was a hunger that ravaged the mind and body. A hunger sated briefly by the climax of their lovemaking, only to growl again when the ripples of pleasure subsided.

Thank heavens they were in a parked carriage late at night and their breath had fogged the glass. Though they could not partake in anything more daring than kissing. Not when they planned to lure the madam of the bathhouse into a trap.

The last thought proved sobering.

"Alexander," Olivia panted against the mouth that offered every distraction. "Should we not keep watch for the attendant?"

He looked at her beneath heavy lids. "Bower will inform us the moment the man arrives." He moved to kiss her again, and she let him.

Seeing her portrait hanging opposite Mr Newell's bed

yesterday had caused a sudden epiphany. She had spent years languishing for a life she no longer wanted. In a matter of days, she had come to love her new life so much more.

"Alexander." She pushed at his chest, fought the urge to splay her hands and caress the hard muscles. "What if the attendant doesn't come? What if Mr Daventry's information is wrong? It's getting late, and Lord Roxburgh will use any excuse to cancel our plans."

He laughed. "I cannot wait to see Roxburgh dressed in a toga. Daventry wagered ten pounds he'd be the first to curse the Romans' flimsy attire."

Olivia found herself smiling. Lord Roxburgh despised costume parties and never dressed for a masquerade. Mr Hunter shared the same distinct views, and so it would be a most eventful evening. Besides, she would rather focus on the amusing aspects of their plan than worry about the outcome.

A sudden knock on the carriage door revealed Mr Hunter. The handsome gentleman wore his greatcoat buttoned to the throat, his mouth in a thin, disgruntled line.

"The Romans wore sandals, Mr Hunter, not boots," she said, hoping the quip about his footwear would improve his countenance.

Though he seemed tense, the gentleman managed a smile. "You should be grateful I'm here at all. Had my wife not insisted we help you, I'd have told Daventry what he could do with his toga."

Despite needing his support, Olivia thought to give Mr Hunter a chance to renege on their agreement. "I understand if you would rather return home. We may find ourselves outnumbered. I don't want you to get hurt fighting for our cause."

Mr Hunter muttered under his breath. He might have voiced his concern aloud had Rachel not appeared beside him.

"I have a strange suspicion the attendant isn't coming." Rachel raised the collar on her pelisse and leant closer. "We should force our way inside. Mr Bower is skilled at picking locks."

Olivia thought to mention her training, but that would lead to an inquisition, and she wished to avoid speaking about the past.

"You don't have to help us." Olivia cast a covert glance at Mr Hunter. "Mrs Swithin's men are sure to make trouble."

Being an insightful woman, Rachel looked at Mr Hunter, too. "Did my husband give you cause to think we wouldn't help you?" Before Olivia answered, her friend added, "There's a chance I am with child. He is a little concerned about my welfare, that is all."

Olivia could not contain her excitement. "But that's wonderful news." Mild panic surfaced. The stairs leading to the underground chamber were rickety, the stone floor slippy underfoot. The thought of Rachel suffering an injury had Olivia singing a different tune. "Please, I must insist you return home, Rachel. It's not safe."

Rachel tutted and reminded everyone she had survived a gunshot wound and would survive an argument in a Roman bathhouse. And so, after a brief consultation with the Roxburghs, they agreed to have Mr Bower pick the lock.

The man pulled odd implements from his pocket and had the shabby green door open in twenty-six seconds.

Grayson lit the lantern the attendant had left on the table in the hall, while Mr Daventry's man set to work on the cellar door.

A clicking noise preceded Mr Bower yanking it open and peering into the gloom. "Happen, I'll come down into the baths with you, sir. I'll hide in the shadows should you need an extra pair of hands."

Grayson agreed. Having Mr Bower's help was equivalent to three pairs of hands.

"It will be easier if we leave our outdoor clothes in the cellar," Olivia said as they descended the stairs. "The steps into the bathhouse are narrow and easier to navigate when one is unencumbered."

Lord Roxburgh groaned as he shrugged out of his greatcoat to reveal a purple toga trimmed with gold brocade. "If it takes an eternity, I shall make Daventry pay for this."

"Why? Your wife persuaded you to come," Eliza said with a grin as she hung her pelisse on the newel post. "But you may think of a suitable punishment if it pleases you. Three laps around the garden maze?"

The lord noticed how the white garment flattered his wife's figure. He was practically drooling when he said, "I see there are some benefits to dressing like buffoons."

Grayson was more interested in the glaring disparity between their costumes. "Why are you wearing purple when we are in white?"

The lord offered a playful grin. "Because I would rather not dress like a commoner."

Mr Hunter scoffed. "When a man is concerned with his own self-importance, it usually means he is lacking."

No doubt Lord Roxburgh would have offered a witticism had Grayson not drawn attention to the real reason they stood in a cold, damp cellar. "Has anyone managed to conceal a weapon?"

Rachel gestured to the leather pouch attached to her thin belt. "I have a shagreen case containing two vials of lemon juice, pins and scissors."

The lord sighed. "Lemon juice may help fade your freckles, but—"

"Don't mock her," Mr Hunter countered. "She disabled an intruder with her unconventional methods. But fear not. She has a Skean Dhu strapped to her thigh. It's the blade of a Highland warrior."

Rachel pushed a golden lock of hair behind her ear and offered an angelic grin. "One should never enter the fray unless prepared."

From a shadowed corner, Mr Bower cleared his throat. "I have a homemade garrotte in one pocket, a pistol in the other, and a knife in each boot. And I can put a man to sleep with one click of his neck."

He demonstrated the action, which might have made a woman gasp had she not been beaten in the woods.

"Then we're glad you've joined us," Olivia said, equally glad the thugs she'd encountered were no match for Mr Daventry's man. "We should make haste before the attendant arrives." Before he alerted Mrs Swithin and gave her time to gather more men.

"I shall enter the chamber first and light the candles," Grayson said, taking the lantern. He touched her gently on the arm and lowered his voice. "Should we find ourselves under attack, you're to leave and get help. I swore no man would hurt you again, and I mean to keep my vow."

Fear gripped her heart when she pictured him brawling in the basement. "I will be fine, but please promise me you will have a care."

He offered a confident grin. "I have mallets for fists and would fight to the death to protect you."

Their breath mingled in the air between them.

They would have kissed had they been alone.

He had meant to reassure her, but she knew life was precarious. It only reminded her of how quickly fate rode roughshod over one's plans.

Grayson climbed down into the subterranean chamber, and one by one, the others followed. Rachel and Mr Hunter hung back and exchanged whispers.

Olivia recalled Rachel's fear of enclosed spaces. "It's a vast chamber with more than one exit." And yet the only other door led to the brothel. "It is perfectly safe, Rachel."

Rachel nodded and gestured for her husband to descend first. While her fears were genuine, she wanted a private moment to ask, "Are you happy, Olivia?"

The question came as a shock. "As happy as one can be in my situation." Not wanting anyone to think ill of Grayson, she added, "The case is taxing, but I do not regret marrying my husband."

She felt it then ...

A rush of euphoria. A flood of happiness. Warm feelings that easily turned to despair when she considered what she could lose tonight.

It was love.

What else left one ecstatic and terrified in equal measure?

"Mr Grayson seems to care for you." Rachel paused to peer through the hatch in the floor and inform her husband she would be down in a moment. "It's evident you like him, too. Ours was not the only carriage window misted."

Olivia captured Rachel's hand and squeezed it affectionately. She wanted to sing the praises of the wonderful man she had married, but now was not the time for excessive displays of sentiment.

"I have never been happier." She released her friend's hand and gestured for her to enter the chamber. "Fear not. There's more than enough headroom below ground."

Rachel nodded and navigated the steps with ease.

Olivia entered the bathhouse to find the sconces and standing candelabra lit. Candlelight cast a golden glow over the room. Tonight, the water in the pool looked like a shimmering black mirror, a portal to a distant time and place.

"I am not surprised Mrs Swithin wants to keep this a secret." Rachel ran her hand over the crumbling statue of

Neptune in the alcove. "How did she discover it lay buried beneath the row of terraced houses?"

"Perhaps she found some old plans," Mr Hunter replied. "Over the centuries, the land has been raised to combat flooding. It would have been covered long ago. Still, one wonders why the Antiquarian Society has not staked a claim. Or why the King has not seized ownership. The coroner must have mentioned it in his report."

"The coroner died of consumption two years ago." The man was in his late sixties and had been ill for some time, so his replacement had said. "The file relating to the case is missing, although we were assured such things occur frequently."

Eliza hummed. "Perhaps the coroner neglected to mention the exact location of the bathhouse."

"It can hardly be a complete secret. All Mrs Swithin's clients must know it exists." Olivia glanced around the room, looking for Grayson and Lord Roxburgh. "I presume my husband is searching for the other entrance."

Eliza nodded and pointed to the arched corridor leading from the main chamber. "That seems to be the only way out of here. In typical bathhouses, this pool would have been heated. The Romans were all about balancing the humors. Mr Grayson believes the door to Mrs Swithin's brothel can be found where the bathers would have stored their clothes."

The men returned.

"We've found a door and assume it leads to the brothel." Grayson held his lantern aloft and jerked his head towards the passageway. "It's near a smaller pool with a fountain."

"We should move there immediately and make a loud racket." Lord Roxburgh was keen to deal with Mrs Swithin so he could change out of his fancy toga.

They all agreed, and Mr Bower appeared like a wraith out of the darkness and followed them through the corridor.

The door was made of iron, not oak, and reached by a set of worn stone steps. Grayson thumped it hard with his fist while the other men cheered and sang an uproarious song about a sailor's last voyage on the high seas.

"What shall *we* do?" Eliza cried above the din.

Olivia smiled. "Watch our husbands make fools of themselves and remind them of it later?"

"The men have excelled themselves." Rachel laughed and shook her head. "How are we ever to compete?"

They did not need to champion the cause.

Grayson stopped banging. He cupped his ear and listened, then waved for them all to take their positions.

The scraping of a bolt against metal sent Olivia's heart racing. They were expecting to come face-to-face with a man of Goliath's proportions. Yet the fellow who appeared at the door was no taller than five feet. He wore a red doublet and hose and an oversized codpiece that looked obscene.

Unperturbed, Lord Roxburgh beckoned the man forward. "Ah, you're just in time for the party. I was told you were bringing the cigars and brandy."

"You ain't allowed down here," the man said in a surprisingly deep voice. He pointed to the staircase behind him, though Olivia could look at nothing but his huge impediment. "Who let you in? Was it Leech?"

Reluctant to name anyone, Olivia offered the man a beaming smile. "We're here for the themed event ... the Roman orgy."

Grayson looked at her and arched a brow. She suspected there would be a blood bath should another man lay his hands on her.

The man snarled, baring a mouth full of rotten teeth. "Orgy? There's only one orgy here, and that's on All Hallow's Eve. Now, move your arses. Upstairs before I fetch Mrs Swithin."

With that being the desired response, Grayson gestured to the corridor. "But there's a man selling tickets through there. This place will be teeming with eager fornicators unless someone threatens him with the madam."

The air turned blue with the imp's curses. He made the mistake of stepping down into the bathhouse, whereby Grayson grabbed him by his red doublet and lifted him three feet off the ground.

"What! Get your hands off me!"

"Call for your mistress, and we shall let you live."

Lord Roxburgh balled his hands into fists. "Might we take it in turns to punch him? I'm desperate to practise my right hook. Let us make a wager. The first one to break his jaw wins a hundred pounds."

"Mrs Swithin!" the imp cried.

"Form a line," Olivia said, suppressing a giggle when the man tried to wriggle free. "I'm sure Rachel wishes to use her case of pins."

"Mrs Swithin!"

Rachel rooted around in her leather pouch. She removed the shagreen case, retrieved a pin, and pricked the man in the buttock.

"Ow!" He kicked his legs frantically in the hope Grayson would lower him down. "Mrs Swithin! Come quickly!"

Another fellow appeared—a hulk of a henchman with no neck and a pumpkin-sized head. He came bounding down the stairs and launched himself at Grayson, but Mr Bower lunged from behind the door, wrapped his arm around the beast's neck and did his odd clicking manoeuvre.

The henchman dropped to the floor like a sack of potatoes.

"Mrs Swithin!" the little man sobbed.

The men joined in, calling the madam's name until she appeared at the top of the stairs with two liveried footmen.

"Why the hullabaloo?" the middle-aged madam said in the voice of a society matron. She descended the stairs with a duchess' grace, her white nest of a wig wobbling as if a family of birds fluttered inside. "Put Willy down before you do the poor man an injury."

Grayson obliged.

Willy tugged on his doublet and grumbled to himself. "They're here for the orgy. There's a rogue selling tickets at the Bishopsgate entrance."

Mrs Swithin lifted her chin and studied them with a knowing eye. She looked at Grayson, and a mischievous smile formed on her painted lips.

"They're not here for an orgy," she said, sounding amused as she observed their Roman costumes. "More's the pity. It's been a while since we've had the pleasure of receiving such a handsome group of gentlemen."

She sent both footmen to inspect the adjoining chamber.

"Lord Roxburgh," she said as if she were greeting him at an elegant soiree. "I heard you recently married. A love match, so the gossips say. And yet here you are, trying to convince me you seek a dalliance."

"Do we know each other, madam?" the lord said with just a hint of curiosity. "You look vaguely familiar."

Mrs Swithin tapped the side of her nose, then changed the subject. "There is a more pressing question, of course. What is the punishment for trespassing these days?"

The madam seemed to find the situation amusing, yet a peer had been murdered in her bathhouse, and she had helped to conceal the evidence.

Olivia stepped forward. "We have a letter from Peel, granting us permission to search these premises. Perhaps we should send for him. Let him decide if we have grounds to be here."

Mrs Swithin's bottom lip quivered ever so slightly, but it

was enough to know she did not want the Home Secretary snooping into her affairs.

Indeed, she raised her chin. "What do you want?"

"We want you to tell the truth about what happened the night the Earl of Sturrock died." Grayson folded his arms across his broad chest. "We know Claudette was with him. We know she met an untimely end. I'm sure those at Bow Street might be keen to learn why the earl's companion is dead, too."

Silence descended, broken only by the annoying drip-drip of water and the odd peal of laughter upstairs.

Olivia thought to strengthen their argument. "Once news of these ruins becomes public, the King will be keen to stake his claim. After all, it's a matter of national heritage."

Mrs Swithin found that comical. "The King has already staked his claim. I have agreed to leave the properties to the Crown and to provide privileges if called upon. I doubt His Majesty will accept Peel's interference in the matter. Not when he hires the bathhouse for his own private use."

Well, that explained the secrecy surrounding the bathhouse and brothel. Though Olivia doubted the King knew Lord Sturrock was murdered.

"Perhaps the King will not look upon you so favourably when he discovers you've lied to him," Lord Roxburgh said with his usual aplomb.

"We are closing in on the suspects," Olivia lied, for they were utterly clueless. "Once the culprit is arrested, the story will be in every broadsheet. Help us, and we shall explain that you knew nothing other than what your attendant told you."

Mrs Swithin's cheeks ballooned, and she bemoaned her less than faithful servant. "So, you have spoken to Leech. I knew the devil was guilty of something when he failed to arrive for work this evening. One suspects he is on the stage to Dover."

Or Mrs Swithin had silenced the attendant.

Grayson thought so, too. "You must admit his absence is suspicious. First, someone murders my brother, then Claudette is found hanged in the—"

"Claudette isn't dead. I told that buffoon a tale to stop him from babbling to all and sundry."

"So you do know what happened that evening," Olivia stated, still processing the revelation about Claudette. Finding the harlot was a priority. "Am I to understand Claudette no longer works for you?"

Before the madam could answer, the footmen returned to confirm the bathhouse was not overrun with randy patrons. At the same time, the henchman woke from his forced slumber, and Willy took to waving a piece of lead pipe he had found from somewhere amid the ruin.

Tension mounted.

Grayson stood tall. "We've come prepared to fight."

Mrs Swithin's sharp gaze swept over them. After a few uncertain seconds, she banished her men back to the brothel.

The sense of relief was palpable.

The madam closed the door and came to stand with them in the small stone chamber. "This house caters to man's many appetites. And my clients expect anonymity. Should it become known I have revealed a patron's secrets, I shall have a house full of empty beds."

"We merely seek the truth so we can punish the villain," Grayson said darkly. "If possible, we will gain a confession. Then there should be no need to mention your part in the affair."

No need to mention it?

Olivia tried to suppress the rising panic. The only way to keep Mrs Swithin's secret was for Grayson to silence the villain permanently. Had that always been his intention? Kill the devil who killed his brother, and to hell with the conse-quences?

Was that why he'd been willing to marry a stranger?

Only this morning, he had mentioned making provisions for her in his will. Why the rush? He was in his prime. The strongest man she had ever known.

Mrs Swithin patted her white wig and gave a weary sigh. "Claudette does not work here. She never has. The earl paid for private use of the pool so he could meet his mistress."

"Do you know where we might find her?" Olivia implored. "She is the only person who knows what happened that night."

Mrs Swithin raised the quizzing glass hanging on a gold chain around her neck and stared at Olivia. "So it is true. Lady Olivia Durrant has risen from the grave only to shock the *ton* by marrying Sturrock's by-blow."

Olivia disliked the madam's mocking tone. "If you recog-nised Lord Roxburgh, why do you need the quizzing glass? I am beginning to believe you were once of the *ton*, Mrs Swithin. Hence why you are so preoccupied with society's tittle-tattle."

The madam smiled, and her mouth didn't look so wrin-kled. "Well, aren't you the clever little lady?"

"Tell me where I can find Claudette," Olivia countered, for she was tired of this woman's waffling.

"You know where to find Claudette. You must have spoken to her since making your miraculous return."

Olivia frowned, but then a vision of Anna formed in her mind, and she felt like an utter fool. "Lady Mersham refuses to shop anywhere other than London." She pictured the pile of bills found in Hamilton's drawer, many for a modiste in town. "And regularly makes the trip from Kent. You permitted her to use the baths, knowing she was being unfaithful to her husband."

Mrs Swithin laughed. "This house is built on adultery."

"Did Lady Mersham kill my brother?" Grayson demanded to know. "Or did her husband discover them together down here?"

Please don't let it be Hamilton!

"To my knowledge, no one else came down here. She had argued with Lord Sturrock. I saw her storm through the house and climb into a hackney paid to wait outside. There wasn't a speck of blood staining her pretty white gown."

Olivia was struggling to deal with the shocking revelation, while Grayson looked ready to rain down the devil's fury.

Understanding the importance of asking questions, Mr Hunter cleared his throat. "Lord Sturrock was a member of a select club. Did he happen to mention it to you?"

Mrs Swithin gave an indolent wave. "Yes, that silly devils and knights thing they often harped on about. It was all rather tedious. They had my girls call them by those ridiculous names."

"They?" Eliza asked, noticing the woman's blunder. "Someone other than Lord Sturrock was a patron here?"

Realising her mistake, Mrs Swithin pursed her lips and exhaled through her nose. "You know that is privileged information."

"Is Lord Mersham a patron of your establishment?" Olivia thought to grab the woman's hand and beg to be put out of her misery. "Please. I must know." If she learnt nothing else, she had to know if she could trust Hamilton.

The madam's gaze softened. "No, dear. He is not."

Olivia breathed a sigh of relief. "Your attendant saw a man down here, rifling through Lord Sturrock's clothes. He must have been upstairs that night." Then a thought struck her. Perhaps Mrs Swithin might refer to the men by their demon names instead. "Lord Sturrock was known as Satan. Wrath was his sin."

"Yes, though I often thought lust was his wickedness."

"Do you know the names of any other knights?" Olivia locked gazes with the woman and tried to convey desperation. A silent plea from one damaged woman to another, for they had surely both suffered at the hands of disloyal men.

The madam shook her head, and her wig wobbled. "You're a determined woman. One has to admire that." She paused and offered a grin that said to hell with the consequences. "If you are asking me which devils I would want to warm my beds, I would have to say Belphegor and Asmodeus."

CHAPTER 16

GRAYSON SAT AT THE DINING TABLE, STARING AT A PLATE OF ham and eggs. He should be thinking about Mrs Swithin's revelation. Featherly and Elderton were patrons. But three years had passed, and the madam could not confirm they were at the brothel the night Blake died.

Instead, thoughts of Olivia filled his head.

She hadn't stirred or opened her eyes when he climbed out of bed this morning, though he had watched her sleep for ten minutes or more—counting his blessings.

Perhaps Daventry was an angel, sent to rescue lost souls from the wilderness and place them on the right path. An ordinary man did not weave miracles. An ordinary man couldn't see into a person's soul and find their perfect mate.

The pad of footsteps on the stairs drew his attention to the door. He stood, expecting Olivia, and wondering how she had dressed so quickly.

She wasn't dressed. She burst into the room in her night-gown, her hair wild and loose around her shoulders, her sparkling blue eyes wide. In her hand, she clutched the velvet box and the letter he had left on her nightstand.

He drank her in and repeated the three words he had written on the note. "Happy Birthday, Olivia."

Her gaze raced hungrily over him like she might eat him for breakfast. "How did you know? We've been so preoccupied with the case, neither of us thought to ask the most obvious questions."

"Daventry mentioned it when we spoke in his study." And he had decided she deserved something special. "I didn't forget the way home from Stratford Place yesterday. I meant for you to browse in Rolland's window. I wanted to know what you liked."

She flicked open the box and showed him the pretty topaz necklace, though the gems lacked lustre next to eyes of breathtaking blue.

"It's beautiful." Her excitement thrummed in the air.

It proved intoxicating. "Not as beautiful as you."

A coy smile played on her lips. "Had you stayed in bed, I would have thanked you properly."

From the gentle sway of her hips and the pert nipples pushing against her nightgown, she wanted more than a helping of eggs.

His body reacted instantly, urging him to race upstairs, strip off his clothes and pretend the last hour hadn't happened. "Now I am kicking myself for being a considerate husband and letting you sleep. Perhaps you would rather have married a rake."

"Do you not boast of being a scoundrel?" She bit down on her lip and scanned the room.

"What are you thinking, love?" It had nothing to do with the breakfast menu. He knew that. But she had an urge to feel full.

"I remember what you said in the carriage the other day and wonder how it might work here."

"What did I say?" He wanted to hear the words from her

lips.

"That you would take me on the study floor." A faint blush touched her cheeks. "That you might pound hard to banish the craving."

He could ram into her until Michaelmas and still be ravenous.

He glanced at the table, set for their morning meal. When it came to sating his hunger, he doubted Cook had anticipated his needs or catered to his appetite.

Olivia read his meaning yet came up with a surprising suggestion of her own. "You agreed to treat me as your equal. I want to be the one doing the taking."

He opened his arms wide. "Where do you want me?"

She thought for a moment. "Sit on the chair."

"Lock the door." He drew the chair from the table, shrugged out of his coat, and then did her bidding.

She turned the key in the lock and padded slowly towards him. "Should I press my mouth to your body? Arouse you the way you did me in the carriage?"

He almost choked at the thought of her taking his cock in her mouth. "There's no need. I've been hard for the last five minutes." And they would save that for when they were not so rushed. "I'm desperate to have you."

"You want it quick, then?" She seemed pleased, not disappointed.

"I want you. Any way you please."

She looked at the fall of his breeches. "Let me see you."

Confident she'd be pleased, he undid the buttons and pulled his cock free. He palmed his erection just to tease her. Yet he was the one panting at the prospect of making love.

"Perhaps I should touch you first," he said.

"There's no need." She slipped her nightdress up to her waist, revealing the dark triangle of silky curls he would bury his face in tonight. "My body craves yours almost every minute of the day."

That's what worried him.

They needed more than this.

Yet he would rather die than deny himself the pleasure.

"Straddle me," he growled.

She closed the gap between them. He could tell by the way she walked, her sex was swollen in anticipation of their joining.

She mounted him.

"I like your letters," she breathed as he took himself in hand and nudged at her entrance. "I like the way you make simple words convey such feeling."

"The truth can be a potent aphrodisiac." He groaned and his head fell back as he pushed into her heat. Hell, he could happily spend the rest of his days like this.

She gripped his shoulders and took him deeper. "Alexander."

"Yes, love." While buried to the hilt, he wrapped his arm around her waist, set his mouth to her nightgown, and sucked her nipple.

She arched her back, raising herself up only to sink slowly back down. Repeating the rhythm over and over again.

"Sweet heaven," she breathed.

"Yes," he echoed, for his wife was undoubtedly divine.

"Might we spend every morning like this?"

Was it a trick question?

He could certainly rise to the challenge.

"I'm yours when ... when ... whenever you want me," he gasped, losing all train of thought as she rode him faster, harder. Hell, his balls were so tight he'd likely spend any second.

He reached under her nightgown and gripped her bare buttocks.

Mother of all saints!

He clenched his jaw and exploded inside her, spilling everything of himself, flooding her with his devotion. Had he been a selfish man, he might have sagged back in the chair and caught his breath. But he would be damned before he left his wife unsatisfied.

Slipping his hand down between them, he massaged her sex.

Unabashed, and with the same unbridled passion she showed him every time they made love, she writhed against his hand.

"Alexander, don't stop." She closed her eyes.

A noise in the hall caught his attention, although Olivia was oblivious to anything other than his teasing fingers. He heard Bower's deep, rumbling voice and his butler's muffled reply.

Damnation!

Pickins was about to knock on the door.

Needing his wife to find her release quickly, he whispered, "Tonight, in the privacy of our chamber, I'm going to suck this little bud until you're shouting my name." Though he was nowhere near as hard as he'd been moments ago, he pushed inside her enough so she might feel some sensation. "Tomorrow, I'm going to lift up your skirts in the garden, push you back against the tree and fuck you senseless."

Pickins knocked on the door, but Grayson couldn't stop now.

"Would you like that, Olivia? Me pounding hard? The wind breezing over your bare buttocks? Me, making you come so many times you'll lose count?"

Her body stiffened, and he closed his mouth over hers and swallowed her sweet cry. She shuddered in his arms, and he dragged his mouth away in time to watch her release ripple through her.

"Sir!" called Pickins.

Olivia's dazed smile died when Pickins tried the door-knob. "Good heavens. What will we do? We can't let him in."

"No, not while I'm still inside you, love. I will fix my clothes and meet him in the hall. Bower is here, and I shall attend him in the study while you wash and dress."

"Mr Bower! Good Lord! What will you say?"

"That we were having a private moment and did not wish to be disturbed." He looked at the velvet box on the table. "That it's your birthday, and I wished to give you a special present."

A coy smile touched her lips. "I like your presents."

"Being a generous man, I shall shower you with gifts as often as you'll let me."

"Sir?" Pickins sounded weary as he shouted through the door. "You might want to receive Mr Bower. He has brought the maid from Mersham Hall."

"The maid?" Olivia was off his lap in seconds.

"Have him wait in the study. I shall be there shortly." Grayson stood, handed her his handkerchief, and quickly tucked himself away. "Wait at the door while I distract Pickins."

He found himself smiling as he kissed her on the mouth. Not because their illicit encounter had left him invigorated, but because he was pretty damn sure he was in love with his wife.

He strode into the hall and took Pickins to one side so Olivia could slip out of the dining room and take to the stairs.

"Be prepared, sir. The maid is in a dreadful state." Of course, he made no mention of the locked door or asked why Grayson had appeared without his coat. "Sorry for disturbing you, but I couldn't turn them away."

Having so recently pleasured his wife, Grayson refrained from giving his butler a reassuring pat on the arm. "Pay it no mind. I instructed Bower to bring the maid here." And it was exactly the development they needed if they hoped to solve the case. "Have Sally bring the tea tray."

Pickins inclined his head and hobbled away towards the kitchen.

Grayson entered the study to find the maid sobbing in Bower's arms. He moved to sit behind the desk and they both jumped when he cleared his throat.

"Forgive the disturbance, sir." Bower released the petite maid, who quickly dashed tears from her eyes. "But I happened past Spitalfields this morning and found Miss Barker knocking on her mother's front door."

"What remarkable timing." Did the man not sleep?

"Not so remarkable, sir. The stage from Ashford arrives at The Golden Cross at eight. A maid at Mersham Hall gave a description of Miss Barker, and the porter at the inn said she came into Charing Cross this morning."

"I see." He should have known Bower left nothing to chance. "And I presume Miss Barker is upset because she didn't expect we'd find her."

"She's upset because her mother was taken ill, sir, and has gone to stay with her sister in Hanbury." Bower's gaze softened when he glanced at the pretty maid. "When Miss Barker left Mersham Hall, she worked at a tavern in Ashford for a few days to gain the money for the stage. She's nothing left for lodgings or the fare to Worcestershire and is at a loss what to do."

He doubted Olivia would see the maid destitute, but it would depend on what part Frances had played in her abduction. Bower certainly seemed taken with the woman, and he did not suffer fools gladly.

"Please, sit down." Grayson gestured to the two chairs opposite his desk. His gaze drifted to the wing chair near the fireplace. It seemed like months ago when he had sat quietly listening to Olivia's harrowing story. "My wife will join us shortly." This time, his mind wandered to their passionate encounter in the dining room.

Was this to be his life now?

Would everything remind him of her?

Would he be forever besotted?

He sat behind the desk and waited for Frances to blow her nose. "You left Mersham Hall in a hurry. You're the reason my wife was left alone on the lane. Someone took her journal and copied her handwriting."

"It wasn't me, sir," she blurted. "I swear it. Give me a quill and paper, and I'll prove it." She looked at the man beside her. "Ask Mr Bower. I couldn't read the street names when I sat with him atop the box."

Bower nodded. "It appears Miss Barker cannot read or write."

"That doesn't mean you were not complicit in the act of writing the forged letter now, does it?"

She looked at Bower and frowned.

"Mr Grayson means you assisted the person responsible."

The maid's cheeks coloured.

"Tell him what you told me," came Bower's encouraging response. "Tell him everything. Mrs Grayson has suffered terribly, and he won't rest until he catches the devil."

The maid took a moment to gather herself and was about to speak when Olivia came bursting into the study. She was breathless, her hair still loose, and she was definitely not wearing stays.

"I pray you haven't started without me."

The maid sobbed again. She jumped to her feet and crossed the room. "My lady, you have to believe me. I would never have left you alone had I known what would happen."

Olivia blinked and straightened her shoulders. "Like me, I am sure you have cried a thousand tears since then. Tears of guilt, no doubt. I might believe in your innocence if you'd not copied the words straight from my journal."

Grayson cleared his throat. "Apparently, Frances cannot read or write. Perhaps you might confirm whether it's the case."

Olivia frowned. "I—I just assumed she could."

"No, my lady, and I was too ashamed to say."

Grayson had Bower move to the wing chair and motioned for Frances and Olivia to sit. "Perhaps we should start from the beginning."

Olivia nodded. Hands clasped tightly in her lap, she turned to face the maid. "On our walk to the village, you complained of stomach cramps and I sent you home. Were you sick? Or was it a ploy to abandon me?"

The maid brought a blue handkerchief to her nose and sniffed. "No, my lady." She looked at Bower for reassurance. "I pretended to be sick because that's what your brother told me to do."

Olivia jolted in the seat. "Hamilton told you to feign illness? Hamilton told you to let me walk to the village alone?"

"Not because he wanted to see you hurt, my lady."

"It's Mrs Grayson," she snapped, though his heart softened whenever she claimed his name. "And you had better explain yourself. Else I shall have the magistrate charge you as an accessory to murder."

Frances gasped. "When I left you in the lane, I met his lordship. We'd fallen in love, and he persuaded me to meet him in the orchard. It's the only place we could be alone together."

Olivia looked horrified. "The orchard? One can only imagine what he wanted. He has abused his position in the most despicable way. No wonder my father feared him taking the helm."

Hamilton was nothing like the powerful monster whose name he had taken. He was a weak man who had made foolish mistakes.

Frances was keen to set the record straight. "We couldn't help ourselves. Love is like that."

"Indeed," she said with a little more sympathy.

"And his lordship was in such a terrible state, what with your father being ill. He needed someone to confide in."

"How long were you lovers?"

"Since your father was bedridden, ma'am, and until his lordship was forced to marry Miss Stowe." The maid paled. "I should have sought another position, but I couldn't bear to leave him. Not when he was so unhappy."

Olivia fell silent.

Grayson considered her story. Just because she was Hamilton's alibi didn't mean he hadn't arranged the abduction. "It can't have been easy being maid to his wife."

Frances looked at Olivia. "It was penance for me leaving you to walk the lane alone, ma'am." She averted her gaze to her lap. "And for giving his lordship your journal to read."

Olivia's eyes widened. "You did what!"

"He was worried about you and asked me to read it. I said it would be better if he looked through it himself. And so I left it on his desk like he asked. He gave it back to me the next day."

The life seemed to drain from his wife's body. She sagged in the chair and released a weary sigh. "You have given me every reason to believe my brother orchestrated the whole affair."

The maid sat forward. "I'm sure you're wrong."

"Might anyone else have seen the journal?"

Frances shook her head. "I don't know."

After an uncomfortable silence, Grayson explained the

maid's predicament. "One might suspect she ran because she couldn't bear to face you."

The woman confirmed his theory. "When I heard talk below stairs about what happened to you in the woods, I knew you'd have questions. Lady Mersham would likely learn the truth about me and his lordship. The woman's wickedness is of the devil's own making."

Grayson inwardly groaned. "Is she wicked because she made her husband a cuckold? Because she throws herself at any man, whether or not he's willing?"

"Because she trapped his lordship into marriage, knowing someone else had fathered the boy."

So it was true!

Poor Tobias was probably Blake's bastard son. Oddly, Grayson's chest felt warm upon realising the boy might be his kin. That said, Hamilton would never admit the child wasn't his.

He was about to ask if Hamilton knew about his wife's many lovers, but a loud knock on the front door stole his attention.

He firmed his jaw, ready to tell Lady Sturrock to bugger off back to Grosvenor Square. But the choir of voices echoing in the hall confirmed he had more than one visitor.

He listened carefully. So did Olivia, because her expression turned from curiosity to horror. "Grayson, I believe Lady Mersham has come for a visit. Hamilton must have given her our direction."

Frances whimpered. "Oh, you can't tell her I'm here." With wild eyes, she looked at Bower. "Please, sir. You must help me."

Bower stood ready to take on the world for a woman he hardly knew. "Miss Barker can stay in Hart Street while you're investigating the case. We may need her testimony."

A knock on the study door brought a flustered Pickins, who offered a salver and presented a calling card. "The Countess of Mersham is here, sir, with her son, Viscount Allcroft."

Yet it was Stowe's card Grayson plucked from the tray.

"Is she here with her parents?" he asked, his mind a whirl of suspicion. Why the hell had they all travelled to London? Did the lady fear they were getting close to learning the truth? Was Stowe worried they'd discover he had sold Olivia's portrait?

Pickins inclined his head. "Shall I show them to the drawing room, sir? Arrange for refreshment?"

"What of Lord Mersham?" Olivia asked.

"From what I gather, he remained in Kent, ma'am."

Her shoulders sagged with relief and disappointment.

Grayson gathered his thoughts and quickly decided on a plan. "You will remain here and meet our guests, Frances." He ignored her whispered complaint. He wanted to witness Lady Mersham's reaction when she looked at her maid. "Mr Bower will be your protector and make arrangements to keep you safe."

The maid accepted her fate but not before quickly whispering, "She was carrying Mr Kane's child last year but lost the babe early."

There was no time to discuss the revelation because a boy with a mop of dark hair came charging into the study.

Evidently, Tobias wasn't sick.

Mrs Stowe chased after him, only to come to an abrupt halt. "Forgive me, Mr Grayson. Tobias gets restless when he's stood for too long." She scowled at the boy and muttered, "Come here."

Pickins tried and failed to usher them out.

Olivia rose and greeted the woman. "Good morning, Mrs Stowe. Would you mind introducing me to my nephew?"

But the young viscount had the manners of a street

urchin. He picked up the brass paperweight and dropped it on the floor. He began ruffling the papers until Grayson clasped his hand and said firmly, "Do as you're told and greet your aunt."

Defiance flashed in the boy's brown eyes. Grayson had been hit with that look before. Every time he'd locked horns with Blake. If someone didn't get to the root of the problem soon, the next Earl of Mersham would be an arrogant wastrel.

Tobias raced out into the hall, and Pickins hobbled after him.

"Mother, have I not told you to keep him under control?" Lady Mersham flounced into the room wearing a fashionable red pelisse and poke bonnet. Her irate gaze slipped from Mrs Stowe to Grayson, where it softened and lingered before darting to the maid. "Frances?" Confusion marred her brow. "What on earth are you doing here?"

Olivia explained the morning's events, omitting to mention their rampant lovemaking and the maid's shocking disclosures.

"What possessed you to run away?"

"Fear," Olivia said when the maid couldn't find her voice. "She felt responsible for what happened to me and thought I would see her dismissed offhand."

Lady Mersham batted her lashes. "Mrs Grayson doesn't blame you at all. And I am willing to forgive this little mishap. You'll come with us to Mivart's. We're here for a few days so Mrs Grayson can meet her nephew, and then you will return to Kent."

Frances stared blankly.

"We cannot let her leave." Olivia must have thought honesty was the best policy, or she hoped to force Lady Mersham's hand. "She is a witness to a crime and must remain here."

"A crime?" Lady Mersham seemed to find the thought

amusing. "Surely you're not referring to what happened to you in the King's Wood?"

"I'm afraid we cannot discuss the details."

A sudden crash in the drawing room brought all conversation to an end.

Upon inspection, Grayson found Mr Stowe chasing Tobias around the sofa. "Come here, you little rascal." Stowe puffed and panted and had to stop and grab hold of the gilt arm. "I swear you'll be the death of me, boy."

Tobias grinned and laughed as if possessed by Satan.

Indeed. There was no doubt the boy was Blake's child.

CHAPTER 17

Hart Street, London
Office of the Order

"I THINK WE KNOW FROM OUR OWN EXPERIENCE," MR Daventry said from his seat behind the desk, "that the boy is in want of his father's attention."

Olivia silently agreed. With a stern look and a firm word, it had taken Grayson a minute to settle Tobias. The child had sat quietly, hands folded in his lap, watching Grayson like an obedient pup, following his every word.

She had stared at Grayson, too.

She craved his attention. Like the laudanum in Hamilton's little brown bottles, one taste of her husband's lips banished her woes. But this deep stirring in her chest amounted to more than infatuation.

She was in love with him.

Deeply in love.

Should she tell him?

Should she wait?

"I recognised his cry for help only too well," Grayson said, unaware it took every effort for her not to touch him, not to beg they go home and spend the afternoon in bed.

"The Stowes cannot control him," she said, though she wasn't sure Hamilton could do a better job. "They indulge his every whim." And like a cardsharp, Tobias read the game and won every hand.

Mr Daventry straightened. "Do you think Tobias is Sturrock's child? Do you think the maid told the truth about Kane?"

Grayson snorted. "Being a victim of Lady Mersham's unwelcome attentions, I can see how a weaker man would fall for her charms. And having heard Frances Barker's testimony, I see no reason for her to lie."

Olivia decided to say what both men were thinking. "Hamilton surely knows of his wife's infidelity. It means he is still the prime suspect in both murders."

Mr Daventry pulled a letter from the drawer and offered it to her. "You'll see Lord Mersham was in debt before he inherited. It gives him a motive to get rid of you and have your father change his will."

With a shaky hand, she took the letter and scanned it with only mild surprise. Hamilton had owed numerous gambling debts, which amounted to an astonishing thirty thousand pounds.

"His inheritance would have covered the debts." Her brother didn't need her share of the wealth to keep him from the Marshalsea. "He often squandered his allowance and sought pleasurable pursuits to ease his grief."

Losing their mother had hit them both hard.

There were many ways of coping.

Not all were moral.

"Do you still believe he tried to kill you?"

She searched her heart but found it was no longer filled with hatred. "No." She took a giant leap of faith. "Despite what Frances said, I think Hamilton is innocent of the crime against me. I cannot say the same when it comes to the deaths of Lord Sturrock and Mr Kane."

Mr Daventry rubbed his jaw thoughtfully. "When a man is addicted to laudanum, he may act in a way that appears out of character. He may hallucinate, or at the very least, act without conscience."

Grayson nodded. "Hamilton may have followed his wife to the brothel and killed my brother. Equally, Featherly and Elderton were patrons of Mrs Swithin's establishment."

They sat contemplating the evidence.

"Despite wearing a disguise, why would a lady visit a brothel?" Mr Daventry said with some suspicion. "Sturrock could have met her anywhere. It screams of disrespect."

Was that why they argued that night? "Mrs Swithin confirmed it was the first time Anna had visited."

"And where is your sister-in-law now?"

"Staying at Mivart's Hotel."

While taking tea with them yesterday, Anna had revealed she often came to town with her parents and son. Hamilton always stayed in Kent, preferring the quiet air of the country to the hustle and bustle of city life.

"I shall post a man at Mivart's." Mr Daventry dipped his quill in the inkpot and wrote a brief note. "Call me cautious, but I find it odd she followed you to London yet did not mention the visit while you were at Mersham Hall."

"She said her father insisted they come. Mr Stowe felt I should meet my nephew. It had been rude of them to ignore the request to bring Tobias to Mersham Hall. That their issue was with Hamilton, not me." Clearly, the Stowes knew about his laudanum habit.

Mr Daventry frowned. "I wonder if that's why he sold the

painting to Newell. Perhaps he knew Hamilton wanted rid of you and hoped to arouse suspicion." But then he waved it away as a weak suggestion.

Olivia's mind was a jumbled mess of possibilities.

Their theories were like pieces of string tangled in knots.

"I know I lack an enquiry agent's skill for deduction," she said to her once employer, "but I cannot see a way to gain the evidence we need."

"Yes, it's one devil's word against another's," Grayson agreed.

"Which is why we must visit the place in Seven Dials two days hence and see who attends the meeting. Maybe your brother *has* come to town, just not with his wife."

Doubtless, Mr Daventry was used to confronting villains and risking his life. Did he not fear death? Was he not worried about leaving his family to cope without him?

She placed her hand on her abdomen. Based on the number of times she had made love to Grayson, she could already be with child. Was that not reason enough to abandon the case?

"What if seven men attend the meeting?" she said with some apprehension. Had Lucifer and Satan been replaced? "They may outnumber us."

Mr Daventry seemed unperturbed. "I will ask Sloane and D'Angelo to accompany us. That should suffice." He paused before adding, "But I do have good news. There has been a development in your case, Mrs Grayson."

A development!

The words filled her with dread.

Why had he waited until now to speak?

She swallowed and tried to focus. "We're like family. Please call me Olivia." She paused to catch her breath. "Am I to understand you have identified the men who attacked me?"

The thought left her trembling to her toes. On many a

sleepless night, she had told herself they were dead. Cruel men always received their comeuppance. Perhaps their next victim hadn't been so easily bested.

His eyes shone with sympathy. "Yes. As expected, they worked out of Chick Lane. A notorious place that has housed the criminal fraternity for more than a century. The landlord of the tavern recognised Hawkins based on your description."

To calm her racing pulse, she reached for Grayson's hand. "Is Hawkins the one with red hair and a face full of freckles? Or the man with a squashed nose and an inking on his middle finger?"

"The latter. Cole followed him out of the Black Lion and into the alley, where he thrashed him until he confessed. We know it's him because he identified your mother's ring."

We know it's him!

For years, she had been clueless.

She blinked against the sudden flash of light in her eyes. Mr Daventry's face grew hazy. Her world swayed. She was about to swoon like a chit in a hot ballroom. She was about to let the devil beat her again.

But Grayson was there, kneeling beside her, cupping her cheek and reassuring her all was well. "He won't hurt you."

"He can't hurt you," Mr Daventry said. "He's dead."

"Dead?" The word was more an incredulous gasp.

"He managed to yank himself free from Cole but ran into the road and was hit by the mail coach. Ironically, the impact snapped his neck."

After a few seconds of stunned silence, Olivia asked the only question that mattered. "Did he say who hired him?"

Mr Daventry shook his head. "No. But we know Hawkins was once a member of the Blue Crown Boys who used to operate from the King's Head tavern. Their leader was stabbed to death by a rival gang five years ago."

The news brought no comfort.

There were always rogues for hire.

"What of the man with the freckled face?" Where was the thug who took pleasure stripping off her clothes and fondling her breasts? He might have done the horrid things her brother feared were it not for Mrs Foston's timely arrival.

"That's where it gets interesting." Mr Daventry took his notebook from the desk and flicked to a page. "Quinn returned to London to explain they had lost you. According to Hawkins, he journeyed by private coach, paid for by the person who hired them. The resurrectionists found a replacement body. Hence why it was a week before they discovered you."

Olivia breathed a relieved sigh. "Then the woman was already dead." Praise be! She had lived with the guilt for seven years, suspecting an innocent woman had been murdered.

"Yes, though we have no way of knowing where she came from."

Grayson sat forward. "If you gained that much information, why did Hawkins not say who hired him?"

"Because he didn't know." Mr Daventry faced her. "Hawkins claimed he didn't know who you were until after the event. He ran because he thought Cole would kill him, not because he wished to withhold information."

"The gang leader must have feared his men would turn traitor," Grayson said. "A poor man will sell his soul for a sovereign."

"Indeed."

"What of Quinn?" she asked while dealing with the odd wave of disappointment. She had often imagined seeing the men standing before judge and jury, where they would look her in the eye and plead for forgiveness. The reality was, neither man was sorry.

"When he returned to London, his colleagues put weights

in his pockets and threw him in the Thames. Punishment for letting you escape and for not doing a thorough job."

A calm sort of silence followed.

Like a gentle breeze after a storm.

A moment to catch their breath.

The rumble of Mr Bower's voice in the hall caught her attention. "Has Frances said anything more since yesterday?"

Mr Daventry glanced at the door. "Only that she is sorry. Bower seems rather taken with her, but he likes being a man one can depend upon."

Rather like Grayson, she thought.

The only time he showed a glimpse of vulnerability was in bed, when he gave himself over to his passions. When he let her take control.

"I'm intrigued by your description of Mrs Swithin," Mr Daventry said, "and mean to make enquiries into her establishment."

"We plan to interview Elderton this afternoon." Grayson cast her a side-long glance because he knew she was tired of going round in circles. "After we have visited Featherly and questioned him about the discrepancy in his story."

Mr Daventry nodded. "I shall have a man watch Lady Mersham, but what about her father? What do you know of Mr Stowe's background?"

It suddenly occurred to her that she didn't know much at all. "He moved to Godmersham to escape city life after inheriting a substantial sum from his uncle. That was twenty years ago."

Mr Daventry tapped his finger on his lips. "We're missing something, yet I cannot make the connection. Perhaps Newell lied about the painting. I suggest you return to Stratford Place and ask to see the receipt. Let him prove he bought the portrait."

The thought of seeing Mr Newell again made her shudder. She would ask Grayson to go alone, but then he would probably punch the fellow and face a dawn appointment.

"About the case," she began, deciding to inform Mr Daventry that, after today, she no longer wished to pursue the matter.

"Yes, we'll follow the leads until we meet in Seven Dials," he said before informing them he had much to do, ushering them out of the study, and closing the door.

"You must be relieved." Grayson relaxed back in the carriage seat, trying to establish why his wife nibbled her bottom lip, why she stared absently out of the window. "The thugs are dead."

"Yes, but the culprit is still at large."

He wished she had not met his gaze, for he saw fear and torment there. "The villain is unlikely to strike again. He will flee once we close in on him."

She was quick to challenge his theory. "What if it's Mr Stowe? He was brazen enough to follow me to town."

"What would the man hope to gain?"

She shrugged. "Nothing other than it made it easier for him to manipulate my brother."

"It's hardly a motive to murder an earl's daughter."

"No. Sadly, Hamilton is the only one with a motive for all three crimes." Her shoulders sagged. "But I just don't think he is capable of such brutality."

She touched her abdomen again, and he knew she was thinking about the many times he had spilled his seed inside her. That, in all likelihood, she could be carrying his child.

The prospect roused the need to play protector.

To gather his wife close and never let her go.

"My brother was no match for Lord Sturrock," she continued. "How did he manage to drown a man much stronger than him?"

"I agree. It makes little sense." When they visited the meeting place in Seven Dials, he hoped they didn't find Hamilton behind the rostrum, preaching to his followers.

"Let's pray we discover a damning piece of evidence today." She sounded weary. "This is the last time I shall visit Hamilton's friends, though I have the strange suspicion we'll not get past their front doors."

Their carriage slowed to a stop outside their home in Portland Place.

Grayson alighted and handed Olivia down. "It's a short walk to Wimpole Street. Let's deal with Featherly one last time, then return home for an hour before tackling Elderton."

He meant to spend an hour taking luncheon, but he read the desire in her gaze and knew she had another activity in mind.

For the first time since hearing Daventry's revelation, Olivia smiled. "I have a better idea. Let's deal with both men first and return to spend the rest of the day in bed."

He pasted a rakish grin, agreed it was an excellent plan and offered his arm. He didn't want to feel the pang of alarm pounding like a drum in his chest. Her addiction had reached its peak. Would it come crashing to the ground?

They walked in companionable silence.

But he felt compelled to broach his concerns.

"How are you finding married life?" He had never felt so close to a woman, so connected on every level. One thing was certain; love was not overrated.

She glanced up at him. "Much better than I expected."

"What is it you like about living with me?"

She hugged his arm. "Everything."

"Can you not be specific?"

"What do you like about living with me?"

Was she avoiding the question so as not to hurt him?

"I love watching you sleep." It calmed his spirit, left him at peace. "The merest touch of your hand ignites a fire in my soul. The mornings are bright and full of hope. The nights dark and long and sensual."

She looked at him, wide-eyed. "You're so strong and dependable. You know exactly what to say at any given moment."

Yet he was terrified to mention the word *love*.

"I love watching you parade naked about our bedchamber. I like the smell of your skin when I wake in the morning. I like that I can feel your gaze caressing me from the other side of the room."

Her comments restored his faith in the future.

And yet neither of them had spoken those important three words, the words he had penned in the letter he hadn't given her today.

"Then it's fair to say we get along well."

She rested her head on his arm. "Extremely well."

He watched her for a moment and was so engrossed he didn't see the man who barged into his shoulder and almost knocked him off his feet. "What the devil?"

Pain seared through him, but he swung around to see the fellow marching away at too fast a pace.

"Are you all right?"

"Yes," he said, though he was a little dazed.

"What is wrong with people? He walked straight into you despite there being plenty of room on the pavement." She touched his shoulder, concern marring her brow. "It may be bruised in the morning."

"Oddly, it's my s-side that took the brunt of the blow." It felt like he'd taken a punch to the gut because he couldn't quite catch his breath. He touched his abdomen only to find his waistcoat wet and sticky. He looked at his hand and saw it glistening with blood.

His blood.

Too much blood.

Olivia gasped.

Pain shot through him.

She screamed as he dropped to his knees.

And then his world went black.

CHAPTER 18

OLIVIA FELL TO HER KNEES ON THE PAVEMENT NEXT TO Grayson, panic roaring in her ears. She reached out with shaky hands but didn't know where to touch him, didn't know what to do.

"Help!" she cried, choking on the word. "Please help us!"

Blood seeped through his waistcoat.

Fear seeped into her heart.

She touched his neck and felt for a pulse. He was alive.

"Grayson?" No response. "Alexander?"

Do something.

Stem the bleeding.

Check his head.

Gathering her wits, she dashed tears from her eyes and began unbuttoning his waistcoat. "Help! For the love of God, please help us!"

She tugged his shirt from his breeches and saw blood bubbling from the puncture wound two inches wide. Nausea sought to cripple her, but she pushed to her feet, banged on doors, hammered on windows, and screamed for somebody to do something.

"Don't die. Don't die. Please don't die," she whispered, leaning over him, her palm pressed to the wound.

People on the opposite side of the street stared, keeping their distance as if he had an infectious disease, not a terrible gash across his abdomen.

Two men appeared, one carrying a black leather bag. Speaking quickly, they asked many questions. When did it happen? Was it a knife? Had she seen the length of the blade?

And then they took over, shrugging out of their coats, deciding not to move him, insisting she step back so they could treat the injury.

She stood, cold to her bones, her hands red with Grayson's blood, watching them pour liquid over his midriff. Waiting in purgatory, not knowing if she would spend the rest of her life in heaven or hell.

Life was precarious. Like that dreadful day on the lane, happiness had been snatched from her in a heartbeat.

And she had not told him she loved him.

Tears fell.

One man asked her a question, but it took her a few seconds to reply. "We live in Portland Place. I'm his wife."

I'm his wife!

She wanted to shout it from the rooftops. Never had anything left her feeling so proud. She belonged to him. He belonged to her. Their lives were entwined, but she needed more time.

Please don't die!

"I have stitched the wound." The deep voice dragged her from her reverie. "But he has lost a fair amount of blood. There may be an infection, a fever."

She blinked and focused on the middle-aged man whose blood-stained hands bore the evidence of his efforts. "But he will live?"

He winced, uncertainty clouding his eyes. "That I cannot

say. But he looks strong and healthy, and I am sure he has every reason to recover. We will summon help to bring him home. Let him rest for a few days. And give him plenty of fluids."

She nodded. "What do we owe you, sir?"

He patted her arm, his smile full of pity. "Nothing, but take my card in case you need further assistance. I've given him laudanum for the pain. He may not wake for a few hours."

She glanced at the card, then offered the man a smile she hoped conveyed the depth of her gratitude. "Thank you, Dr Pearce."

Feeling more afraid than she had in the last seven years, she stood and waited as another man appeared with a horse and cart. It took four strapping fellows to lift him. Seeing Grayson laid out like a cadaver, so still and unresponsive, his coat draped over his chest, put everything into perspective.

She would find the person responsible.

Then, there'd be the devil to pay.

"I shall escort you home," Dr Pearce said, returning the gloves she'd thrown to the pavement.

"Thank you. I shall need help to carry him upstairs."

It was three or maybe four hours later when Mr Daventry entered Grayson's bedchamber, barely able to catch his breath.

"Forgive me. I was at Bronygarth and have only just received your note." He stared at Grayson, who looked so terribly pale as he slept in the large tester bed. "What happened?"

She offered a brief recount of the event. "Doctor Pearce confirmed Grayson was stabbed with a blade. Thankfully, the wound is not too deep. It happened so quickly. The black-guard barged shoulders with him and—"

"Did you see his face?"

"No. We were talking." They'd only had eyes for each other.

When Mr Daventry approached the bed and touched Grayson's forehead, he struggled to keep his emotions at bay. "He's hot. Let's pray it's not the start of a fever."

She recognised her own fear and frustration. "I'm hoping he will wake soon and can drink something."

"It's my fault. We're closing in on the devil, and I should have warned you. I should not have let you wander the streets alone."

She wanted to blame someone, but Mr Daventry was not at fault. "This has to be related to his brother's murder. It's the second time someone has attempted to kill him." Her voice broke. "The culprit is the only person responsible."

"And as God is my witness, he will pay." Mr Daventry gathered himself and closed the gap between them. "I can only imagine how you must feel. It must have been distressing." He reached for her hand and jerked back when he saw it was stained with Grayson's dry blood.

"I cannot bear to wash them." She showed him both palms. "It's all I have of him." Though she prayed their child was growing inside her. "I didn't tell him I loved him. I was scared, and now he will die not knowing, die believing he wasn't worthy of love."

A weak smile touched his lips. "Do you think he would leave you to tackle this problem alone? The man I know would fight to the death to protect the woman he loves."

Tears slipped down her cheeks. "I have sat at his bedside and whispered the words so many times. I pray he has heard me."

"You can tell him again when he wakes."

Grayson didn't wake. He slept soundly through the night.

Mr Daventry kept watch while she lay on her bed in the adjoining room and closed her eyes briefly. She returned to find him telling Grayson stories about their time at school. When they'd had no one but each other to depend upon.

She didn't waste her breath telling him to go home. "Shall I send for coffee, maybe eggs and toast? I asked Dr Pearce to call later this morning. He will inspect the stitches and check for signs of infection."

"I'll have coffee but have no appetite for food." He glanced at her hands. "I see you took my advice and washed away the evidence."

"As you said, the mind is a powerful thing. I must proceed with a hopeful heart, not wallow in misery." She bent and kissed Grayson on the lips. "Good morning, my love."

Please wake!

Mr Daventry watched her. "It is God's greatest gift, is it not? To love someone unconditionally? To feel a deep, abiding love in return?"

She briefly contemplated her life up to this point. "I would suffer seventy years of misery to spend one more day with him." Emotion bubbled in her throat. "I have never known such pain."

She had loved her parents dearly.

But Grayson was her present, her future, her everything.

"It is a testament to how much he means to you." Mr Daventry dragged his gaze from his friend and looked at her. "I knew you would suit. I knew you could both be happy once you'd dealt with past demons."

Most mortals lacked Mr Daventry's foresight. "Then use your remarkable ability to make miracles and tell me he is going to survive this."

He should have woken by now.

"This isn't how it ends for you both. I am certain of that."

She hugged his comment tightly to her chest as she straightened the bedclothes. She repeated it silently as she filled the washbowl and sat wiping Grayson's face and wetting his lips. Then she curled up beside his warm body and slept for a few hours.

The mumble of voices drew her from slumber, and she opened her eyes to find Mr Daventry and Dr Pearce discussing Grayson's condition.

"It is not uncommon to sleep for days after suffering blood loss and trauma. The body has various ways of coping with pain."

"Can we not attempt to wake him?" Mr Daventry said.

"If we see no improvement tomorrow."

Olivia climbed off the bed and joined the men. "You said he needs fluids, but he's unable to drink."

"Take a pipette and moisten his lips as often as you can. It will suffice for now." The doctor's expression revealed a flicker of concern. "If there is no change tomorrow, there's a possibility he may have sustained other injuries."

She jerked in response. "Other injuries?"

"He may have hurt his head in the fall."

"But you examined him and found no cuts or bruises."

The doctor seemed uneasy. "Let us wait until tomorrow. We will assess the situation then. I see no point worrying unnecessarily."

No point worrying? Now he had planted the seed in her mind it would grow like ivy, choking all hope.

A light knock on the door brought Pickins. "I beg your pardon, ma'am, but Lady Sturrock is here. She asks for an audience with Mr Grayson. Shall I tell her he is indisposed?"

The mention of the woman's name fired her blood. Pickins could send her straight back to hell. Grayson would not want his stepmother taking tea in his drawing room. Yet Olivia needed a means of releasing the pent-up anger and frustration. Who better to feel the sharp edge of her tongue than the lady who had made her husband's life a misery?

"No. Show her into the drawing room, and I shall join her shortly."

Pickins blinked rapidly and cupped his ear. When she repeated her intention, he asked, "Am I to offer her refreshment?"

"By all means." With renewed confidence, she turned to Mr Daventry. "I'm sure you have important matters to attend to. Should there be a change in his condition, I will send word to Hart Street."

"I would like to stay. Ashwood will deal with all enquiries in my absence, and I would be of no use to anyone in my present state of mind." He looked at Grayson and sighed. "Would you mind if Sybil came to visit for a few hours?"

"Not at all." She understood his need to console himself by spending time with the woman he loved. "And please, make yourself at home. Ring for anything you need."

After quickly tidying her hair and changing into a dress that wasn't creased, she descended to the drawing room.

She steeled herself before entering, remembering she was an earl's daughter and would have been extremely wealthy had it not been for a traitorous devil.

Lady Sturrock looked disappointed when she entered the room. She took a moment to examine the woman who had refused to show her stepson the slightest affection.

The lady's pinched face made her appear stern, not ill. Her mustard bonnet sported too many feathers and was surely a means to distract from her forbidding countenance.

"Lady Sturrock. Good morning." She did not waste a smile on the woman. "To what do we owe the pleasure?"

Her hawk-like gaze journeyed over Olivia, and she turned up her nose. "Lady Olivia. How is it you're alive when the world thought you were dead?"

Tired of answering the same question, she merely said, "It

is Mrs Grayson, and I'm sure you have been party to recent gossip."

As someone who looked permanently offended, the lady's expression did not falter. "As family, I would have expected to receive news of your nuptials before the announcement appeared in *The Times*."

"And yet my husband assured me he had no family." Olivia sat in the chair opposite the matron. "I'm told you are estranged."

Lady Sturrock scowled. "Where is Grayson? No doubt he is too busy to see me. It's usually the case."

A sharp stab of emotion threatened to ruin Olivia's calm exterior. "My husband is in bed. He will not be joining us today." But she prayed he would be well enough tomorrow.

The comment was met with an irate huff. "His blatant disregard for family affairs is a testament to his lack of breeding. He has ignored my efforts to bring him into the fold. Indeed, now he has married you—though I dare say your choices were limited—we might pull him up to the mark, so to speak."

Olivia bit her tongue. Insults cut deeply when delivered with cool aplomb. "Your comment leaves me curious about your background, my lady. Grayson is the most honourable man I have ever met. Many men of the *ton* are wastrels who whore about town and squander their inheritance. If you judge my husband by your son's standards, I can see why you're confused."

The lady's eyes blazed. "Clearly, you have been fed on a diet of lies, wicked lies. Jealousy forms the basis of Grayson's feelings towards his brother."

Olivia resisted the urge to laugh. "Then permit me to reveal certain facts that have been documented as part of an ongoing investigation."

"Investigation?" The furrows on her brow were as deep as trenches. "An investigation into what, exactly?"

"Grayson hired an enquiry agent because he believes someone murdered his brother." She didn't mention that she was the agent or that Grayson had married her, not hired her. "He is determined in his cause to see justice served."

"Murdered Blake? He slipped and fell in a bathhouse."

"It's a brothel, not a bathhouse. Forgive me for being the bearer of bad news, but we have evidence to suggest he was unlawfully killed. Grayson won't rest until he has caught the culprit and in the process has almost died twice."

Lady Sturrock snorted loudly. "What utter poppycock!"

Olivia jumped to her feet and tugged the bell pull. When Pickins entered, she asked him to fetch her emerald green reticule. "And would you kindly tell Lady Sturrock why Mr Grayson cannot attend her today?"

Pickins hesitated.

"You may speak honestly."

The butler nodded. "The master was stabbed yesterday. He has not opened his eyes nor spoke a word since the men carried him into the house."

Olivia's heart clenched, but she continued, "And who is upstairs with my husband?"

"Mr Daventry, ma'am. And the good doctor."

"Thank you, Pickins. You may leave us." She turned to see Lady Sturrock clutching her throat, her eyes wide with alarm. "Everyone in London knows about Mr Daventry's enquiry agents. And when Pickins returns, I shall let you read the letter from the Home Secretary."

The matron looked like she might swoon. "But if Grayson dies, who will I turn to for support? I shall be thrown to the wolves." She wasn't interested in the investigation. She didn't attempt to dispute the claims about her son. "Merciful Lord! This cannot be happening. Not again. Not to me."

"What troubles you, madam? I am assured you care nothing for my husband's welfare." No, she had not wanted another woman's son in her house. She had left Grayson in that wretched school, alone and unloved.

"I—I cannot afford to live on my stipend," she confessed, though did not shed a single tear. "I'm forced to come and ask my stepson to supplement my income."

Olivia's eyes widened in astonishment.

"You want the man you have treated cruelly to come to your aid? What about the money from your dowry or property as part of your jointure?"

Lady Sturrock looked mildly ashamed. "We eloped. There was no dowry or marriage settlement, and that selfish oaf left me to live on a pittance."

Olivia resumed her seat. "I assume your son supported you until his untimely death three years ago."

"Indeed. I had a small windfall but have been struggling ever since. Whoever heard of a man in his prime dying in a bathhouse?"

"It's a brothel, and your son had many adulterous affairs. Doubtless many men were out for his blood."

She shook her head in dismissal. "Yes, well, what can one do when one's father is as cold as a mortuary slab? Being the beloved son, Grayson inherited everything not entailed. Hence why I am in this unfortunate predicament."

Olivia thought to enlighten the lady and so explained what she knew of the relationship. "If a man loved a woman so deeply, one would assume he would love the child in much the same manner. But Godwin Gray had no love for Grayson. Do not pretend it was any different."

Lady Sturrock's mouth twisted into a bitter line. "Godwin said the boy was so like his mother, he couldn't bear to look upon him. We all suffered because that woman died. Some of us are suffering still."

Anger flared.

How dare she play the victim!

"My husband suffered for your indifference. He almost died in a bid to prove he is worthy." That had to be why he risked his life for a brother who despised him. "Do not dare sit here and ask for my pity. Not when Grayson lies gravely ill upstairs."

The lady had the sense to remain silent.

"Had you been kind to him, had you shown an ounce of compassion instead of resenting a woman who was dead, I might have offered assurances." She stood and swallowed past the lump of emotion. "You lost your right of entitlement when you left a small boy alone in the wilds of North Yorkshire."

"But I was powerless to act."

"Your behaviour since, tells me you're lying." Olivia marched to the door and yanked it open. Pickins and John Footman almost fell into the room. "Now, I would like you to leave so I might tend to my husband."

Lady Sturrock lifted her chin and rose gracefully. "Thank you for seeing me, Mrs Grayson. I pray you will remind my stepson of his obligations."

The moment the woman crossed the threshold, Olivia slammed the drawing room door shut. Oh, the bare-faced cheek of the woman.

Needing a moment to calm her temper before heading back upstairs, she went to the drinks tray and poured a swift sherry.

A light knock on the door brought Pickins. "I thought you should know her ladyship has left, ma'am. I presume you're no longer in need of your reticule."

"No. Thank you, Pickins."

She downed the sherry in one gulp.

"We stand in awe of your ability to tackle that woman."

Olivia turned to meet the butler's amused gaze. She managed a weak smile but then noticed the letter in his hand.

"Tell me that is not Lady Sturrock's modiste's bill."

"No, ma'am. I found it in Mr Grayson's coat pocket." He tried to keep his expression impassive but had to dab a tear from his eye. "The one he wore when he was injured. It is addressed to you."

"To me!" Olivia raced across the room, knowing it must be the letter he had failed to give her yesterday. She practically snatched it out of Pickins' hand. "You may leave me. Thank you."

Once alone, she sat on the settee and hugged it to her chest. She could picture Grayson sitting at his desk. She could hear him repeating her name in a voice as rich as fine wine.

Eyes heavy with tears and her hands shaking, she broke the seal and read the three words he had intended to convey.

I love you!

CHAPTER 19

THE DREAM WAS VIVID. SHE WAS RUNNING IN A VERDANT field, chasing a rainbow, her loose hair caught in the breeze. Laughing, she glanced back over her shoulder to see Grayson racing behind, looking handsome and healthy.

It was idyllic, so peaceful it had to be heaven.

That's when fear choked her, when she woke with a start to find herself slumped in the chair in Grayson's candlelit bedchamber.

"Olivia. He's awake." Mr Daventry loomed over her, pointing to the bed where her husband lay sleeping. "He opened his eyes a moment ago and whispered your name."

Dr Pearce was at the bedside, taking Grayson's pulse.

She jumped from the chair, almost sending Mr Daventry flying, and darted to the bed. Capturing Grayson's warm hand, she spoke to him in the intimate way she did when they were alone and feeling amorous.

"Alexander, my love. I need you to wake up now." She brought his palm to her lips and kissed him tenderly. "I need to hear your voice. I need to know you're still here with me."

Tell me you love me!

Don't leave me!

He opened his mouth, but no sound left his lips.

How she wanted to set her mouth to his and breathe life into him, give him all of her strength, the will to survive.

Dr Pearce moved to speak to Mr Daventry, and so she leaned closer and said, "I love you. Marrying you was my best day. The days since only get better."

He squeezed her hand, and his eyelids flickered.

"I am here, Alexander. I will always be here."

Dr Pearce hurried back to the bed. "While he is stirring, let me give him a tincture. And he might take another sip of honey tea."

Pickins knocked on the door and entered the room. He addressed Mr Daventry. "Sir, Mr Sloane is waiting for you downstairs. He said you must leave now if you mean to make the meeting in Seven Dials."

"Tell him I'll be a few minutes. Thank you, Pickins."

"You're going to Seven Dials?" She left Grayson's bedside and crossed the room. "But I thought the meeting was tomorrow."

Mr Daventry gave a sympathetic smile. "It's tonight at midnight. We discussed it yesterday after you met with Lady Sturrock."

She frowned. "Sorry. The last few days have been a blur."

Yes, the Stowes had called with Tobias this morning and were shocked to hear the terrible news.

Being so distraught, she hadn't given a damn about upsetting Mr Stowe. After her barrage of questions, he confirmed he had sold the painting to Mr Newell at Hamilton's behest. When questioned about Hamilton's intention, he admitted Anna had played mediator and confirmed her husband wanted rid of the portrait.

They hadn't stayed long.

She had wanted rid of them, rid of everything that reminded her of why Grayson lay injured in bed.

"You were asleep, and I haven't had a chance to tell you," Mr Daventry said, "but I have sent a note to Mivart's asking Lady Mersham to meet me at the Hart Street office at ten o'clock. I said I would send my carriage to collect her. Said I had important information about Lord Sturrock's death she may be keen to hear."

"But why?"

"Because any information she gives will help us prepare for the meeting in Seven Dials. We need to know why she instructed her father to sell the painting. And she may know who killed Sturrock." He glanced at Grayson. "I have decided to hurl accusations and hope they hit the target."

"But she knows how to manipulate men."

"I love my wife. The lady's charms won't work on me."

Whatever transpired tonight, Olivia would keep searching until she found the man who stabbed Grayson. If it took a week, a month, a year, so be it. How could they walk the streets knowing the blackguard roamed free?

"I'm coming with you." She glanced at her husband and pushed her fears aside. "When he wakes, I want him to know our troubles are over, that we can live our lives in peace."

Mr Daventry shook his head. "Grayson would call me out for putting you in danger. Stay with him, and I shall return with news."

"No. You'll take me with you, or I shall wander Seven Dials alone until I stumble upon Featherly or Elderton or whichever devil is the villain."

Mr Daventry considered her through narrowed eyes. "I'm certain everything is connected to the attack on you in the woods. Someone wanted you dead, and I cannot risk putting you in harm's way."

"But you agreed I could go with Grayson." She didn't wait

for his reply. "I must admit to being disappointed. I thought you were one of the few men who empowered women. Yet here you are, the same as the others, considering me weak because I am female."

"You know that's not true."

"And you know I may be of some help tonight."

He sighed. "Let's hear what Lady Mersham has to say first."

Olivia tried not to grin at the minor victory. "Agreed."

Mr D'Angelo stood at the drawing room window, his arms folded across his chest, watching the dim street. "She is ten minutes late."

Mr Sloane glanced at his colleague from his fireside chair. "It's a woman's prerogative to keep a man waiting."

Olivia turned to Mr Daventry, seated next to her on the damask sofa. He studied a note Mrs Gunning had delivered moments earlier. "I doubt Anna will come. We're wasting time. Should we not head to St Giles and find a means of accessing the building?"

"I have a key," came his confident reply.

"From the caretaker?"

"Yes. He said the Blue Crown Boys once used the old wine shop to store their contraband. They used numerous premises around St Giles and Covent Garden. The building belonged to Jim Jenkins, the man who led the gang seven years ago. No one knows who owns it now."

Olivia's heart missed a beat. Her brother held meetings in a place used by the thugs who'd tried to kill her? "Then there is a connection between the Seven Devils and my abduction."

"So it would seem."

"And you did not think to tell me this earlier?"

He handed her the note. "This confirms Jenkins owns the property. You should know I never rely on hearsay."

She recalled the information they had found in Blake's book. The men had met at White's for a few years before moving to their secret location near Seven Dials.

What was their connection to Mr Jenkins? And if the men had not met this past year, who was meeting there tonight?

Mr D'Angelo pushed away from the window. "Lady Mersham is here. Bower is handing her down from the carriage."

"Remember what I said. Appeal to her vanity if you must. But we need answers, and we need them quickly."

Olivia snorted. "You're in luck. Anna cannot hold her own water. She will tell a handsome man anything."

Mrs Gunning appeared and introduced the lady. All the men stood as Anna swept into the room. Her eyes widened like a child's in a confectioner's shop as she scanned the three strapping men.

Mr Daventry stepped forward. "Permit me to introduce myself. I am Lucius Daventry, the baseborn son of the Duke of Melverley and head of a group of enquiry agents skilled in solving murders."

Anna batted her lashes. "Clearly, you know who I am. Else you would not have invited me to your little soiree."

"Mr Sloane and Mr D'Angelo are amongst the best agents in London." Mr Daventry gestured to Olivia and mentioned the connection, but the lady couldn't tear her gaze from Mr D'Angelo.

"Are you of Italian heritage, sir?"

"Yes, on my father's side."

"Do you visit Italy often? I should very much like to go."

"Not of late." Mr D'Angelo struggled to feign interest in

the golden-haired goddess. "My wife is with child, and the journey can be taxing."

Anna was undeterred in her effort to capture his attention. "Her confinement must be equally taxing for you. Nine months seems like an awfully long time, does it not?" It was obvious what she was insinuating.

Mr D'Angelo gave an arrogant sneer. "On the contrary, I find myself in awe of her ability to please me while having every consideration for our unborn child."

Anna shrugged. "Still, the lack of spontaneity must grate." Bored, she moved on to Mr Sloane. "Has anyone ever said you look like a pirate, sir? A swashbuckler from the high seas?"

"Practically everyone."

Tired of this nonsense, Olivia jumped to her feet. "Good evening, Anna. We're glad you could tear yourself away from Mivart's to join us."

Anna blinked many times. "Olivia? What are you doing here?"

Was the woman really that dense?

Had she not recognised Mr Bower?

"I worked for Mr Daventry before I married Grayson. I am investigating the murders of Lord Sturrock and Mr Kane."

Anna's light laugh breezed through the room. "I understand your experiences have been quite disturbing, but not every death speaks of sinister motives."

Mr Daventry stared through dark, menacing eyes. "Perhaps you imagine life is one amusing fairytale, my lady. Perhaps you do not see that your not so innocent flirtations have left a sea of destruction in their wake. Men have died because of you."

"I haven't the first clue what you mean."

"Tobias is Lord Sturrock's son," Olivia snapped, though

she wished it wasn't true. "You were carrying Mr Kane's child last spring. Now both men are dead."

"Don't be ridiculous," she countered, but her flushed cheeks betrayed her. "I came here because I received a cryptic note asking if I would like to learn Blake's secrets."

"Why would you care?" Why would she venture across town late at night if Blake was merely her husband's friend? "I shall tell you why. Because you were in love with him."

When Anna laughed again, Olivia glimpsed the pain hidden behind her airy facade. "I didn't come here to listen to your baseless accusations. I would like to leave now. Might your coachman return me to Mivart's, sir?"

Mr Daventry shook his head. "Refuse to co-operate, and I shall arrest you for both murders. My coachman will ferry you to the Queen Street office and then to Newgate."

Panic flashed in her pretty eyes. "Look at me." She gestured to her large breasts and slender figure. "Do I look like a woman capable of murder? Where is your evidence?"

Mr Daventry glanced at Olivia, prompting her to reply. "We have Mrs Swithin's statement. You wore a disguise and went by the name Claudette. You were at the bathhouse on Bishopsgate less than an hour before the attendant found Lord Sturrock's body. Mrs Swithin swears no one else was there that night."

The life seemed to drain from Anna's face.

"Perhaps we should all sit down," Olivia said, "before I reveal the other incidents that tie you to this case."

Anna froze but eventually found her confidence. She crossed the room and laid her hand on Mr Daventry's arm. "I am the Countess of Mersham," she began in her teasing voice. "No court in the land would accuse me of a crime based on the word of a bawdy house madam."

"You're an adulteress. The men of the jury will presume

you're guilty before you speak." He shirked away. "Sit down. I will not tell you again."

Anna huffed and found a seat. She was used to men fawning over her, blinded by her beauty, not indifferent to her charms.

"This is your one opportunity to explain yourself." Mr Daventry instructed Mr Sloane to take a statement which he expected Anna to sign. "If we're to catch the person responsible for the deaths of your lovers, you need to be honest about your involvement."

Stripped of her feminine wiles, Anna sat like a timid girl in the chair. "Isn't it obvious? Blake seduced me one summer while visiting Godmersham. I was a naive girl of eighteen and thought he would marry me, thought he loved me, but I was wrong." She spoke quickly, as if desperate to get the business over with.

"What about Hamilton?" Olivia said, her heart aching for her foolish brother. How had he not known of this woman's schemes? "How did you persuade him to marry you?"

"I—I seduced him after your funeral, then later told him I was with child." She had the decency to look ashamed. "We're not at all suited, and I regret it deeply, but what else could I do?"

Rage twisted in Olivia's gut. "Do your parents know Tobias is Lord Sturrock's son? Do they know their daughter is a devious harlot?"

Olivia caught Mr D'Angelo's smirk.

Anna brought her handkerchief to her nose and sniffed away her fake tears. "Mama knows. I had no choice but to confide in her. Papa thinks Hamilton is Tobias' father."

"And you send the boy to Crundale because you're worried people might notice he looks like Blake." Olivia tried to breathe through the sudden urge to slap the woman. "You told your parents about Hamilton's laudanum problem, and now they pander to your every whim. And because you're a selfish hussy, you continued your affair with Blake after you were wed."

"You make it sound sordid." Anna glanced at the men, confused by their obvious disapproval. "Blake used me, manipulated me. What sort of man asks a lady to meet him in a brothel?"

"The sort who beds married women," Mr Sloane said.

"Blake kept me dangling on a string. He promised we would take our son abroad, but he had me meet him at the brothel." She gritted her teeth. "And do you know what he wanted to tell me? That he was in want of a wealthy wife and would look to marry an heiress next season."

"And so you killed him," Daventry growled.

"No! I told him to go to hell and left." She swallowed against an evident wave of emotion. "Had I stayed, he might still be alive. He might have changed his mind. And so why would I do such a dreadful thing? I loved him."

Olivia couldn't muster an ounce of sympathy. Because of this woman, two men were dead, and Hamilton had to live with the fact his heir wasn't his son. Anna was somehow to blame for the attack on Grayson, to blame for the whole sorry mess.

"Did Hamilton tell you to sell my portrait to Mr Newell?"

Her mouth twisted in disdain upon hearing his name. "No, but that scoundrel hounded me night and day until I agreed to give him the painting. He said he knew about Blake and would tell Hamilton if I did not oblige him."

And yet Robert Newell said Hamilton wanted rid of it. "You told your father Hamilton couldn't bear to look at my picture. You had him sell it to Mr Newell on your behalf."

"I had to say something. Part of it is true. Looking at your likeness made him ill. And I would rather spend a year in a nunnery than visit Mr Newell at his home."

Despite following the conversation closely, Mr Daventry randomly said, "Do you know a man named Jim Jenkins?"

Anna thought for a moment. "No, I don't know anyone by that name. Although my mother's maiden name was Jenkins."

It could not be a coincidence.

"And she hails from London?" he said.

"Yes, though she had quite a tragic childhood. Her parents died, and she was left in the care of her older brother. But I don't know his name. I believe he paid for her to stay at a boarding school for girls though my mother never talks about her past."

"Olivia." Her name left his lips in a soft whisper. He needed her, needed to hear her voice, feel her touch. Desperate, he called a little louder. Why didn't she come? "Olivia!"

He'd inhaled her jasmine perfume, felt the gentle press of her lips on his palm, experienced the profound sense of calm he always did in her presence. Yet she was not close now.

Had he died?

His head throbbed, and his side hurt like the devil. There was no pain in heaven, so he couldn't be dead.

"Olivia?"

"Hush now," came a man's voice he did not recognise. "Might you take something more to drink, sir? You must have something if you mean to build your strength. And a drop more laudanum, too, I think."

Grayson forced his eyes open, only to see a middle-aged man peering down at him through crooked spectacles.

"Who are you?"

Was this purgatory?

"Dr Pearce. I attended you in the street and stitched the

wound." The man pressed his fingers to Grayson's wrist and mumbled to himself. "Your heartbeat is steady, your temperature normal."

Gratitude surfaced despite having no recollection of this man saving his life. "I owe you a debt money cannot repay." He clasped the doctor's wrist, keen to make the man understand the depth of his appreciation. "Should you ever need assistance, in any regard, you may depend on my help."

The doctor shook his head. "Do not fret over that now. Save your energy, my friend. When your wife returns, you will want to take her in your arms and settle her fears."

Grayson glanced around the candlelit room. It must be late, for the embers in the hearth had almost died. "Is my wife sleeping?"

He wanted to climb into bed next to her, relish the heat of her body, the smoothness of her skin, the sweet smell of her hair.

"She has gone out but will return shortly." The doctor removed a brown bottle from his bag and read the label beneath the lamplight. "I can summon your butler, and he can explain."

Gone out?

But the long case clock in the hall had struck eleven.

His heart thumped faster. "Where the hell did she go?" He tried to sit up but was forced to clutch his bandaged side.

"Please! Do not alarm yourself. She left with your friend. The man who has spent every hour at your bedside."

"Lucius Daventry?"

"Yes, Mr Daventry. I recall Pickins saying they needed to leave for a meeting near Seven Dials." Dr Pearce pulled the cork from the bottle. "Just a small drop of laudanum should suffice."

Grayson pulled back the bedsheets and sat upright,

though it took immense effort. "Would you mind tugging the bell pull? I need help to get dressed."

"Dressed! But you must stay in bed, sir!"

The room whirled before his eyes. "Not when my wife risks her life to catch a murderer." What the hell was Lucius Daventry thinking? "I mean to leave this house in five minutes. Now tug the damn bell pull."

Dr Pearce shook his head profusely. "But the wound will bleed if you exert yourself. If you must go out, let me bandage it tightly."

"Very well. Just make sure I can breathe." He didn't want to think of Olivia in the rookeries at night, stalking a murderer. He prayed there was no meeting, and that for once in his life Lucius Daventry had made a mistake.

CHAPTER 20

OLIVIA HELD THE LANTERN ALOFT AND STAYED CLOSE TO
Mr Daventry. It was so dark in the warrens around Seven
Dials that one noticed nothing but the figures of men lurking
in the shadows.

Dark did not mean peaceful.

The piercing cry of hungry babes rent the air. Dogs
howled. The songs of drunken men mingled with violent
shouts and curses. Children still roamed the streets despite
the late hour. Families huddled around lit brasiers, desperate
to feel some warmth in their miserable lives.

One glimpse of the filth and the abject poverty, and she
would never consider herself a victim again.

A woman approached them, clutching a crying babe to
her chest, begging for a penny. Olivia reached into her pelisse
pocket, but Mr Daventry stopped her.

"Take this." He handed the woman a card, and she looked
at it with confused eyes, wondering how she might feed it to
her child. "Visit the address in the morning and speak to Mrs
Granger. She will assess your needs."

And with that, he led Olivia away.

"What good is a penny?" he said, his tone tinged with anger. "We need to find ways to feed the poor permanently, not just for one night."

And yet she had been desperate to ease the woman's woes. Or was it just a means to soothe her conscience. "Who is Mrs Granger?"

"She manages the house I own in Tower Street. She will hear the woman's story, assess her situation, and see if she can find her work and lodgings."

"Might I assist in any way?" This man's efforts to help humankind amazed her more each day.

He cast her a sidelong glance and smiled. "Certainly. We shall discuss it once we have solved this case and seen the devils hang."

They entered the dark, cobblestoned alley. Mr Sloane and Mr D'Angelo were waiting beside a set of iron railings, near a flight of stone steps leading down into a dingy doorway.

"Two people approached from different directions," Mr D'Angelo informed them. "One, a woman in a dark cloak. She knew her way around the tangle of streets. She lowered her hood to a man who tried to accost her in an alley, but he moved past and went on his way."

"Was it Mrs Stowe?" Her heart thumped so fast she could barely form the words. "It has to be her." Mrs Stowe needed Anna to marry Hamilton and must have thought Olivia would get in the way.

"She looked plain and rather nondescript."

"Robert Newell descended the steps ten minutes ago."

Olivia gasped. Shock rendered her mute.

Why would Mr Newell collude with Mrs Stowe? What did he hope to gain? Was asking her to elope part of a wicked plan?

She wondered how they had come this far in their investigation yet had only just learnt of Mrs Stowe's involvement.

"When you questioned the caretaker, did he not give you the name of his employer?"

Mr Daventry shook his head. "His employer corresponds by letter and never signs the missive. For obvious reasons, Mrs Stowe wished to keep her ownership secret."

The hairs on Olivia's nape prickled to attention. Wickedness hung in the air like thick fog from the Thames. "What is the plan?"

"We enter the building, find them together and force them to confess." Mr Daventry's voice carried a dangerous undertone. He looked at his agents, who both nodded in agreement. "You're certain no one else joined the party?"

But neither man had a chance to answer because the sudden clip of booted footsteps echoed in the alley behind them.

Mr Daventry listened. "Two men are approaching."

Mr Sloane, being renowned for his skill with a blade, pulled a knife from his boot, ready to take aim.

A man broke through the darkness, carrying a leather bag.

"It's Dr Pearce," she said, her heart plunging to the pit of her stomach. What had brought this man to the bowels of hell? How did he know where to find them?

She hurried forward. "Dr Pearce?"

Tell me it's not bad news.

Tell me he is alive.

But then Grayson appeared behind him, clutching his side as he moved slowly through the alley. Tears burst from her eyes. He looked so tall and handsome and so dreadfully ill.

She covered the gap between them in seconds. "You should be in bed, not out on a cold, damp night." She touched his arm but wanted to run her hands over every inch of his body.

"I don't want to be in bed without you." He bent his head

and kissed her deeply, but she tasted every painful grimace. "I never want to be without you."

"Forgive me, Mrs Grayson," Dr Pearce interrupted. "But your husband is a stubborn mule who would not see sense."

Grayson smiled. "Dr Pearce insisted on accompanying me. He climbed into my carriage and refused to leave."

Mr Daventry stepped forward. "It's good to see you have not lost that steely determination." His dark eyes softened. "It's so damn good to see you on your feet."

"I hear you've been playing nursemaid," Grayson teased.

"Someone needed to put your life in order." Always suspicious, Mr Daventry glanced at the doctor. "How did you find us? I don't recall mentioning the address."

"We saw Bower atop his box, cradling a brace of pistols."

"Then, I advise you take Pearce and return to the carriage. Wait for us there." He paused and grinned. "But I know you won't abandon your wife, so the doctor will have to join us."

"We may need his services."

The poor doctor looked terrified but nodded.

"Then, let's enter the building and see what Mrs Stowe has to say."

Grayson gasped. "Mrs Stowe?"

Olivia took hold of his arm, hugged it tightly, and said a silent prayer of thanks. "Come, while Mr Daventry gains access to the old wine shop, I shall quickly tell you what we learnt from Anna."

They crept down the flight of stone steps. Mr Daventry opened the door, muttering his relief that Newell hadn't drawn the bolts. He had told her to blow out the lantern so as not to alert the villains, and so they stood in the dark room amid empty shelves, scattered crates and discarded bottles.

Mr Daventry pointed to a door behind the long counter, and they moved into a narrow hallway.

Voices echoed from the basement.

Two voices.

"Wait here," Mr Daventry whispered to the men before turning to her. "Olivia, you should enter the room alone. Just for a few minutes." He raised a hand before Grayson could object. "Try to gain a confession. They'll speak openly if they feel they have the advantage."

The voices below stairs sounded irate, but she nodded.

Grayson tapped her on the shoulder and pressed his mouth to her ear. "I won't be far behind you."

She steeled herself and then crept down the stone staircase into a basement that was as cold as a crypt. She peered around the open door to see Mrs Stowe and Mr Newell seated at a large round table.

Candlelight cast shadows over their devious faces.

"But you said she was dead." Mr Newell pushed his hand through his dark hair and growled, "You made me believe Mersham had done away with her for the inheritance."

"She disappeared from the woods and never returned home," came the woman's cold reply. "What else was I to think? I presumed he had learnt of our plan and sought to seize an opportunity."

If she had gone home, would they have tried to kill her again?

"What the devil shall we do now?" Mr Newell said.

"You're panicking unnecessarily."

"But Featherly said she's investigating Sturrock's murder."

Mrs Stowe snorted. "The man drowned in a bathhouse. There is no evidence to suggest otherwise."

Heavens! Grayson would likely drown this unscrupulous pair when he learned the truth. Indeed, he was liable to storm into the room any minute, and so she swallowed down her nerves and made herself known.

"On the contrary, we have amassed a great deal of evidence." She stepped into the room, and both blackguards shot to their feet. "Mrs Swithin gave a sworn statement saying she saw you in the bathhouse, Mr Newell."

The man quickly overcame his shock and pasted an arrogant grin. "She is mistaken. I would never set foot in such an establishment."

"You have never been to a brothel?"

"No!"

"So, by your own admission, you know it's a brothel, not a bathhouse." She thought quickly. Mrs Swithin hadn't seen him, so he might have bribed the attendant. It would surely explain why Mr Leech had disappeared. "Of course, Mr Leech said you forced him to let you into the bathhouse through the Bishopsgate entrance. That way, Mrs Swithin could claim she never saw you. Indeed, we have Mr Leech in custody."

Mr Newell rounded the table. "Someone had to make that bastard pay."

"Robert! That's enough!" Mrs Stowe demanded.

"Pay for what?" she said in a softer tone.

Mr Newell sighed. "For killing you, my love."

Olivia froze. Why had he used an endearment? Why would Lord Sturrock want to see her hanged in the King's Wood? And why in heaven's name had he committed these vile crimes in her name?

It made no sense.

"You wanted vengeance?" she said, sensing movement near the door, knowing it was Grayson. "Because you thought Lord Sturrock had hurt me?"

"Not Sturrock, that evil toad you call a brother."

"Robert!" came Mrs Stowe's warning. She shuffled out from the table and took sly steps towards the door.

Mr Newell reached for Olivia's hand before she could step away. "Mersham had to pay for killing you. And so I devised an excellent plan, where he would take the blame for killing Anna's lovers."

Olivia gripped his clammy hand in the hope of dragging every wicked morsel from this murderer's lips. "Except the coroner recorded a verdict of accidental death for Lord Sturrock. And Mr Bromley was presumed guilty of shooting Mr Kane."

He pulled away—thank goodness—but grew suddenly restless. "I couldn't let him escape punishment. I planned to kill the next man Anna bedded, except the trollop hasn't taken another lover since losing Kane's child."

Olivia breathed deeply to settle her racing heart. To avenge her, Mr Newell must be more than a little besotted. It was why he had forced Anna to sell him the portrait.

Then another thought struck her.

One that chilled her blood.

Had Mr Newell stalked them and stabbed Grayson?

"You tried to kill my husband!"

"Tried?" he mocked. "I rather hoped I had succeeded."

GRAYSON HEARD THE FOP'S ADMISSION AND COULD NO longer remain silent. Despite the damn ache in his side, he held himself upright and stepped out from the shadows.

"Next time you want to kill a man, aim for his heart."

Newell's eyes widened. "You're supposed to be dead."

"You underestimated the power of love." He placed a reassuring hand on Olivia's back before stepping forward to shield her from this lunatic. "Do you think I would leave my wife to suffer your unwanted attentions?"

"Unwanted? She loves me and would have married me had she not been terrified of that bastard Mersham."

Grayson wondered how anyone could be so blind to reality. "And yet in the throes of passion, it's my name she calls."

Newell cursed and gritted his teeth. From his stance, Grayson knew he was about to throw a punch. As soon as the fool lunged, Grayson delivered a swift uppercut to his jaw.

The impact sent Newell reeling, and he landed with a thud on his arse. "You killed my brother," Grayson growled. "You killed him out of some misguided notion of vengeance. Make no mistake. I shall see you hang for it."

Mrs Stowe shuffled closer to the door. "Praise be. I am so glad you came when you did. For seven years, this rogue has made my life a misery." She clasped her hands to her chest. "When trying to console him on the day of your funeral, I mistakingly said I thought Hamilton had killed you. He's been like a dog with a bone ever since."

Oh, this woman was a monument to deceit.

"If you thought my brother was a murderer, why let your daughter marry him?" Olivia said, blocking the woman's path.

According to Anna, Mr Stowe had raised an objection.

Perhaps he did have doubts about Hamilton's character.

Mrs Stowe glanced at the door. "The foolish girl was with child and had no choice. But I know the earl is hiding something. He can't sleep without downing an unhealthy dose of laudanum. And my poor grandson must suffer his frightful moods."

"Earlier, you said my brother learnt of your plan and seized an opportunity. What plan was that?"

She shook her head. "I meant *he* had a plan. He stole your journal and wrote a note to make us think you had taken your own life."

Olivia gasped in shock, but Grayson knew it was feigned. "You saw him with my journal in his study? Why did you not say so before?"

"Brothers can be quite protective of their sisters." Mrs

Stowe sounded as if she spoke from experience. Had Jim Jenkins taken good care of her? "At first, I assumed you had given it to him, but then he quickly hid it in a drawer when I came to invite him to Crundale for dinner."

So, that was how she had gained access to Olivia's private musings. Did she expect them to believe she had identified the journal in seconds? Doubtless, Bickford left her waiting alone in the room.

"But I am confused," Olivia said, frowning. "We suspected Mr Newell was involved in Lord Sturrock's murder and followed him here. But the caretaker said this meeting was arranged weeks ago, before my return to Mersham Hall. Why would you meet with Mr Newell?"

Mrs Stowe opened her mouth but snapped it shut.

"Surely you know why you're here?" Olivia pressed.

"B-because there's a rumour about town. Someone saw you two months ago in Covent Garden." She gestured to Mr Newell, who scrambled to his feet, then rubbed his jaw. "I asked Mr Newell to come here so we might try to prove the story was true. Obviously now, I came to reassure him you were alive and that his lordship was innocent of your murder."

"Could you not have met him in Mayfair?"

Grayson watched Newell intently, fearing the fellow might lunge with his knife again. "Why would she meet him in Mayfair? Criminals tend to flock together, and she is the owner of this old shop."

Mrs Stowe's eyes bulged, and she started shaking. "Well, there is little point in me remaining here. You want to question Mr Newell, so I shall leave you to your business."

"Oh, there is every point you being here." Olivia firmed her jaw and glared at the woman. "Jim Jenkins left you the shop when he died. He left you all the proceeds of his ill-gotten gains. We have proof."

It was another lie, but a lie that prompted the woman to say, "I was his only living relative. We had been estranged for thirty years. How should I know how he came by his money?"

"What the hell has this got to do with anything?" Newell scoffed.

"Nothing." Mrs Stowe straightened. "Nothing at all."

Olivia turned her attention to Newell. "Mrs Stowe is the sister of the man whose thugs beat me half to death in the woods. They would have hanged me had I not escaped. Instead, we know the resurrectionists found another body, and Hamilton presumed it was me."

Realising his shirt was damp, Grayson touched his abdomen. Blood coated his fingertips, but he quickly wiped it on his coat.

Newell finally worked out that he had been duped. He was little more than irate when he said, "They beat you? But they were meant to keep you for a night. We were meant to find you in a hovel with those men so I could—"

"Be quiet!" Mrs Stowe might have darted for the door had Daventry and his men not stepped into the room.

"So you could do what, Robert?" Olivia said.

Newell frowned. "So I could offer to marry you, and you would have no choice but to accept."

A heavy silence descended.

Grayson's heartbeat thumped in his ears. He was trying not to show any outward signs of panic, but throwing the punch had torn his stitches and reopened the wound. Damn. He'd hoped to batter Robert Newell once they'd heard the truth.

"Mrs Stowe saw it as an opportunity to get rid of me." Olivia dabbed a tear from her eye. "She needed Anna to marry Hamilton. Else her daughter would have been ruined."

"We shouldn't forget about the money." Grayson clutched his abdomen and winced. "Tobias is the heir to an earldom.

When the boy is a little older, one suspects Hamilton will suffer an accident, leaving the Stowes free to manipulate him without his father's interference."

He used the term *father* loosely.

Her voice filled with anger, Olivia said, "I have lived in fear for years. Plagued by nightmares of what happened on that fateful day." She balled her hands into fists. "There's no escaping now. Have the courage of your convictions, and be honest. Admit you wanted rid of me. Admit you're the mastermind behind this whole affair."

Newell seemed to feed off her distress. He swung around to face Mrs Stowe. "Tell me they have made a mistake. Tell me you haven't tricked me into killing two men."

Mrs Stowe sneered. "You were easy to manipulate. And I needed to get rid of that devil Sturrock before people learned the truth about Tobias." She glared at Grayson. "If only my nephew had a better aim. We wouldn't be standing here now."

Was she referring to the shooting?

Wickedness was in the blood. Mrs Stowe may have raised herself up the ranks by marrying a gentleman with money, but she was a criminal from the rookeries at heart. While her daughter carried a title, she was no different from the harlots selling their wares in Covent Garden.

"You've damn well ruined my life," Newell cried.

"Your stupid obsession was your downfall."

In a fit of fury, Newell whipped a blade from his boot and stabbed the air in a threatening manner. "There is nothing stupid about love."

Grayson had to agree.

Daventry came to stand beside them. He cocked his pistol and took aim. "Put the weapon down, Newell. You don't want another death on your conscience."

"I'll not die by the damn noose." He snarled at Mrs Stowe

like a rabid dog. "I'll not die until I have seen you rot in hell, witch!"

Chaos erupted.

Releasing a feral growl, Newell flew at Mrs Stowe. Amid a violent scuffle, he thrust the blade deep into her black heart just as Daventry fired the fatal shot.

Both villains fell to the floor in a heap.

The acrid smell of sulphur and Olivia's scream filled the air.

She started shaking from the shock. "Are they dead?"

He was already shaking and would hit the floor, too, if he didn't sit down. Blood seeped through his waistcoat. His shirt clung to the wound. "Pearce!" he called amid Daventry's shouts for his men to fetch the magistrate and coroner.

But it was too late.

He glanced at Olivia, his eyesight failing him, and then the desperate need to sleep dragged him down into a dark, dark abyss.

CHAPTER 21

SHE FELT HIS HAND ON HER CHEEK, THE TOUCH SO GENTLE she closed her eyes and snuggled closer to his warm body. Being so tired, it didn't occur to her that he might be awake. Indeed, she had slept next to him for two days, not moving to wash or dress, only holding him and willing him to live. Praying he would not leave her to face life alone again.

"This is my idea of heaven," he whispered against her hair before pressing a lingering kiss to her head.

His rich voice was sweet music for the soul. She stopped herself from shooting up and raining kisses over his face. Instead, she spoke softly. "In each other's arms, we have found peace—paradise here on earth."

"I thought the same last night when I woke to find your naked body curled around mine. Though my chest was damp with your tears."

She sat up, not bothering to preserve her modesty. "When you appeared outside the old wine shop, my heart burst with joy. But when you collapsed ... well ... I thought I had lost you forever."

He reached up and caressed her bare arm, his thumb

skimming the outer curve of her breast. "Forgive me. I couldn't stay here knowing you were about to face the black-guards. Dr Pearce was right to offer caution, though I could think of nothing but seeing you."

"The poor man made me promise you would remain in bed for a week." When his smile turned sinful, she added, "I vowed to care for you, assured him you would refrain from all vigorous activities."

His gaze wandered languidly to her breasts. "I can lie here, injured and helpless, and let you take the lead."

With hunger in her belly, she scanned the breadth of his chest. The need to make love to him banished all rhyme and reason. "Let's see how you fare tomorrow. Today, I shall feed you broth and wash every inch of your glorious body."

"Some parts may need extra attention," he drawled.

She laughed for the first time in days. "I shall be thorough."

He captured her hand. "Straddle me."

"Maybe tomorrow." She would not risk opening the wound again, and didn't have the heart to tell him he would have to wait a week. "Besides, Mr Daventry told me to inform him the moment you woke. He means to visit if you have the strength. And Dr Pearce will call again this morning to check the stitches and change the bandage."

Talk of the men left Grayson briefly lost in thought. "The last thing I recall is Daventry sending D'Angelo to fetch the coroner. What of Newell and Mrs Stowe?"

The image of their lifeless bodies flashed into her mind. "They're dead," she said, relieved, not sorry. Without them, the world was a safer place. "Dr Pearce treated you at the scene while we were waiting for the coroner. Then Mr Sloane stole a handcart as it was the only way to get you through the web of streets and alleys."

"I vaguely recall Bower dragging me into the carriage."

She owed all men concerned a debt of gratitude.

"Mr Bower and Mr Sloane have gone to Mersham Hall to tell Hamilton what we've discovered." And to arrest the groom who had shot at Grayson. Mrs Stowe's nephew had to be the spy at Mersham Hall. If Hamilton had any sense, he would come to town and deal with his wayward wife.

"They should confiscate his bottles of laudanum while there."

"I imagine he will need a means of dealing with his troubles. Mr Daventry sent a note to say Anna has given a statement. She's still at Mivart's and refuses to go home. Truth be told, I think she's in shock."

It was Anna who'd suggested Blake use the old wine shop for their meetings. Of course, it had been Mrs Stowe's idea. She had given Anna the key explaining it was an empty property she owned, and Blake thought the dangerous location was a means to test the princes of hell. And the caretaker was paid to listen in on the meetings and report to Mrs Stowe's coachman.

"Hamilton should send his wife to live in the Outer Hebrides."

"He has a dilemma. Does he divorce Anna for adultery and make Tobias illegitimate? Or does he continue to accept the boy as his son?"

"For the child's sake, I pray it's the latter," he said, knowing life was more challenging for illegitimate offspring. "Besides, I doubt one would find an unblemished bloodline in the whole of the *ton*."

Upon hearing a sudden knock on the door, Olivia grabbed her nightgown from the end of the bed and dragged it over her head.

"Enter."

Pickins appeared, looking like he had lost his last penny.

He saw Grayson was awake and his countenance improved dramatically.

"Bless the Lord, sir. It's good to see you with your eyes open. Shall I fetch a tea tray? Or perhaps you'd like something stronger to drink? Dr Pearce won't object to you having brandy. It's good for the constitution."

"Coffee will suffice. Have Cook prepare a light repast."

"I shall see to it at once." Pickins bowed. He was about to leave the room when he remembered why he had come. "Lady Sturrock is downstairs. She seeks another audience."

"Not again," Olivia groaned. As Grayson had slept through his stepmother's last visit, she explained the nature of the lady's dilemma. "And so she appeals to you, her only family, to help save her from a desperate fate and provide her with an allowance."

Grayson laughed. "I should go downstairs and remind her of the time she made me enter the house through the servants' quarters. Or when she banished me to dine in my room because I looked too much like my mother. Or the fact I spent three hundred and fifty days a year at boarding school."

"I have already reminded her of her failings." She had been nowhere near harsh enough. "But I am more than happy to speak to her and relay a message."

"No, you'll not suffer her again. Pickins, fetch my portable writing desk from the study."

Pickins nodded and withdrew.

"What do you mean to do?" she asked.

His smile looked devilish. "Tell her I will provide her with a house and a reasonable allowance."

Olivia jerked her head. "You will?"

"Yes, on the condition she relocates to the wet wilds of North Yorkshire. I shall permit her fifteen days a year in town."

She laughed at his ingenious plan. "I cannot wait to hear what the gossips make of it." If anyone deserved to be the subject of tittle-tattle, it was Lady Sturrock. "Oh, Mr Daventry called on Mrs Swithin yesterday. You'll never guess who she is."

He cupped his hands behind his head and relaxed back against the pillow. "Erm, a society matron who fell on hard times?"

"How did you know?"

"It's obvious."

"She's not of high society, more on the outskirts though she parades like a duchess. Her husband died in debtor's prison and left her penniless. She had only one means of making a living. Mr Daventry is still digging into her past."

"She certainly keeps abreast of the gossip."

Olivia watched her husband for a moment. It felt good to have a normal conversation without worrying about chasing criminals. It was so good to see him smile when she had spent days imagining she might never witness it again.

"I love you." The words left her lips with ease.

His gaze turned hot, intense, and his sigh spoke of utter relief. "I love you. I wrote you a letter to that effect, but it must have been lost amid the laundry."

She chuckled to herself and reached under her pillow. "I have a confession to make."

"Have you been fondling me while I'm sleeping?"

"No." She gave a half-shrug. "Well, sometimes."

"Touch me as often as you please."

She showed him the letter. "Pickins gave it to me. It was addressed to me, so I read it." It was the best letter she had ever received.

He sat up, cupped her upper arm and drew her close. "Then let me repeat it, lest you be in any doubt. I'm in love with you. I'm madly in love with you." He claimed her mouth in a long, lingering kiss. "There's another letter for you in my study, but I shall save you the trip and tell you that it says."

A shiver of excitement ran through her. "What?"

"Marry me, Olivia."

She laughed. "We are already married."

"Say you'll marry me because you want to, not because Daventry thought it would be a good idea." He pushed a lock of hair behind her ear and stroked her cheek. "We'll invite our friends to dinner and have them witness us exchanging vows again."

"You mean without the vicar?"

"Daventry will attend. He's an angel sent here to play matchmaker. I doubt there's another man closer to God."

She smiled as she recalled how Mr Daventry had orchestrated their first meeting. "We owe him everything. I would never have found you had it not been for him." She would have spent her life alone and afraid.

"Well?" he prompted.

She kissed him tenderly on the lips. "Yes. I will marry you, Alexander. This time my vows will be filled with nothing but love. It will be the best day of my life."

His mouth curled into a tempting smile. "Let's work on making today a good day. Your husband may be incapacitated, but he still has full use of his hands."

EPILOGUE

Bronygarth - Five years later

OLIVIA RELAXED ON THE BALCONY OF LUCIUS AND SYBIL Daventry's home, rocking her daughter to sleep in her arms and laughing at the scene of pure chaos on the lawn. It was a warm summer's day, and it was Roxburgh's turn to wear the blindfold while the children ran up to him and tugged his coattails.

She turned to Sybil, who sat sipping lemonade. "For a man with no family, Lucius has done a remarkable job creating one."

Love softened Sybil's gaze as she looked at her husband, who held their youngest son's hand and encouraged him to prod the lord. "Yes, by my last count, he is godfather to eighteen children."

"And a brother to nine men," she said, knowing of Grayson's abiding affection for his friend. A loud cheer drew her attention to the women playing croquet. "We ladies think of him as kin, too."

Sybil smiled. "I think he prefers matchmaking to solving crimes. He is content now all his agents have found love, but nothing gives him greater pleasure than seeing Grayson happy."

She looked at Grayson, holding their young son against his broad shoulder. He caught her gaze, and her heart swelled. Their love had lasted longer than a month or year. She believed it would last a lifetime.

"I often think of them alone at that school. If they could have glimpsed the future, the time may have been more bearable."

Sybil shrugged. "Sometimes hardships make people stronger."

"Yes," she mused, moving her parasol to shade Amelia from the sun. "We have a family motto. 'The Graysons do not run from their troubles'." So far, they had faced nothing taxing. "We appreciate what we have and will fight to keep it."

"Marriage is about more than love. It's about finding someone who shares your ideals and has the strength to weather the storm." Sybil raised her glass in a toast and then sipped her lemonade.

Olivia thought about Hamilton and his dreadful marriage. Anna had left England to live in France, where she continued to add to her list of conquests. Tobias had remained at Mersham Hall, and Hamilton doted on the boy. He had tried to persuade Frances to return, but she had married Mr Bower.

Lucius left the fun and games on the lawn and came to sit next to Sybil on the bench. He didn't need to say anything, but it was clear he looked upon the scene in the garden with evident satisfaction.

"Sybil tells me Mr Ashwood is to take a more senior role in the Order." There had even been talk of hiring more agents.

He reached for the pitcher on the low table and poured himself a glass of lemonade. "I need help at the helm." He glanced at Sybil as if he missed her. "I want to spend more time at home, and Ashwood is extremely capable."

"Sir Robert asked Lucius to train a few men for his Metropolitan Police Force," Sybil said proudly. "They may join the Order for a few months and work on cases."

"Your agents have years of experience, so it makes perfect sense. And what of your matchmaking, Lucius?" She often teased him about his ability to find a woman's ideal mate. "Perhaps Sir Robert's men are in need of companions, too."

He tried to suppress a chuckle but failed.

"What have I said?"

Sybil gave Olivia's knee a reassuring pat. "My husband has reached new heights in his bid to find every lost soul a partner."

Intrigued, she said, "But all your agents are married."

Lucius laughed again, so much so, he had to dab tears from his eyes. "You should have seen their faces when they came out of the tent. It was a perfect blend of excitement and confusion."

"The tent?"

"Roxburgh won't mind if you tell Olivia," Sybil said. "She understands the value of bringing two like-minded people together."

Olivia was desperate to know of his new scheme.

It took a moment for Lucius to stop laughing. "Roxburgh asked me to help chaperone his sister and her friends to the Bartholomew Fair last week. Miss Ware had spoken about visiting the fortune-teller's tent and so—" He stopped to laugh again. "I paid the woman to tell a tale."

"But that's not the funny part," Sybil added, and was forced to continue the story because her husband struggled to speak. "Roxburgh wants his sister to marry the Duke of Dounreay, but she is being rather stubborn. They are a perfect match. The fortune-teller told Miss Ware that she would marry a man who bares his knees in public."

While amusing, the story wasn't as funny as expected.

"But when the woman asked what she should say to Miss Ware's friends, Lucius told her to tell Miss Langley that she would find her prospective husband sitting in a cowpat."

Lucius composed himself. "Miss Langley believes she is destined to marry a farmer when she is secretly in love with St. Clair—though her brother would never permit a match with his closest friend. And Miss Stanford was told she would see her husband's buttocks before seeing his face."

Olivia found that funny but was a little disappointed. "Why would London's best matchmaker trick them into believing a lie?"

He gave a confident grin. "Who said I was lying? I made a prediction based on what I know of their situations."

He might have said more but was called back to the lawn because it was his turn to wear the blindfold.

Olivia took a moment to consider the amusing story and to stare at the wonderful man she had married. Only a fool would have shackled herself to a stranger. Yet from the beginning, she had felt an instant spark and couldn't imagine life without Grayson now.

She smiled to herself.

Based on her faith in Lucius Daventry, she knew Miss Langley was about to find the sophisticated Mr St Clair covered in cow dung.

THANK YOU!

I hope you enjoyed reading ***No Life for a Lady***.

Sadly, that's the end of this series for now.

Will the impeccable Mr St. Clair slip on a cowpat?
Will Miss Langley's secret love for her brother's best friend
ever be more than an obsession?

Find out in ...

More than Tempted
Scandal Sheet Survivors - Book 1

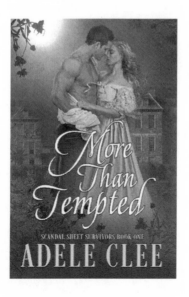